PLAYING DEAD

THE BLACK PAGES BOOK THREE

BY AUTHOR

DANNY BELL

Publisher's Note: This is a work of fiction. Names, characters, places, and
incidents are a product of the author's imagination. Locales and public names are sometimes used for atmospheric purposes. Any resemblance to actual people, living or dead, or to businesses, companies, events, institutions, or locales is completely coincidental.

Ordering Information:
Quantity sales. Special discounts are available on quantity purchases by corporations, associations, and others. For details, contact the "Special Sales Department" at the email address above.

Playing Dead (The Black Pages Book Three) / Danny Bell – 1st ed.

For Whitton, Kate, Misti, and Lauren

Four people who inspire in their own way

May I always be so lucky to call you my friend

And most of all, for my grandma, Estelle.
I think this one might be her favorite.

FOREWORD

W riting this book was scary because there was so much that could go wrong with it. For one thing, I let Elana sit out for an entire book in her own series. Already that might not sit well with some readers, and I like my readers. I don't want them to be upset, that thought makes me quite nervous.

But the harder part of writing this book, what was really scary, was how personal the subtext in this story was to me. This is the third book in the series and—if you read book two, *Warning Call*—it would be easy to see Chalsarda, the hyper-competent warrior elf, as someone who is self-assured, rock solid, and not defined by what a bad person had done to her. This book might make you feel differently about her.

It is not much of a secret that I have had a lot of bad days and a lot of bad people in the formative years of my life, and I'm not complaining. I'm an adult now, I've learned to deal with it and I know that it's all subjective. We've all had our bad days and bad people and some of us don't make it out as quickly as others, if at all. But what I think isn't talked about enough when it comes to people who have survived trauma, is the raw portions of our lives. The parts where we know we're relatively safe from the external threats, but we don't know how to live on the other side. At least not yet.

I've known good people who have been in that transitional space, and the common thread is that if you listen to them, look past their words and hear who they are, you find good people who are not all of the actions you see from them in that moment. They may be withdrawn, or they lash out, or they're reckless, or any number of things. And that's what writing this character and her story allowed me to do, it allowed me to process a lot of that experience in comforting confines of a book.

Chalsarda is obviously strong in every way that counts. After all, this is a fantasy and if I or anyone I know had experienced what she had, I couldn't promise that we'd take things as well as she did. But she's just strong, not perfect or infallible, and that's why this story is important to me. Because I have been in the place where being strong carried with it the false idea that I had to be perfect, and anything less was failure. And I've seen it in too many people the same way. I want people reading this to be able to maybe understand the difference.

This is a book that would not be possible without far too many people to mention individually, but it's further proof that if you're hurting, you don't need to heal alone. The people who love you want to hear from you. Therapists want to help you. And everyone has gone through something and no one is perfect and none of us are ever alone.

I hope you like this book. Like I said, this was a scary thing for me to write and share, but I did, and it belongs to you now.

PLAYING DEAD

THE BLACK PAGES BOOK THREE

As the arrow soared skyward, I knew I'd never see it again; I just hoped it didn't hit anything important.

"Excellent work, my young pupil. You're improving," I offered, trying to remember just what exactly was off in that direction.

"How is that possibly an improvement? The target is that way," Ann sighed, pointing straight ahead. "I just tried to shoot a cloud. And not on purpose."

"Well, for one thing, at the least arrows are firing up into the air and not down into the dirt," I began thoughtfully. "And for another, you're managing to release the bowstring without hurting yourself. These are both vast improvements."

"If this is elvish sarcasm, you have to tell me. I think it's a rule," Ann deadpanned, adjusting her glasses.

I wasn't sure how elvish sarcasm would differ from regular sarcasm, but I smiled and said, "You have been training now for a month, yes?"

"Five weeks," Ann muttered.

"Yes, five weeks, and in that time, you have made improvements. No matter how small, any improvement is still a step forward."

Ann scoffed at that but didn't respond immediately, and I knew her frustration. She was comparing herself to me, rather than herself. As long as Ann did that, she would never be pleased with her progress, and for now, I wasn't going to tell her she should do otherwise. As long as she wasn't satisfied, she wouldn't give up, which could be occasionally useful, but she would need to learn her own lessons in time. Ann would gain nothing by my spelling out those lessons for her.

"Did you ever suck at this?" she asked after a moment.

"Of course," I remarked. "You cannot be proficient without first failing."

Ann looked as though she wanted to respond to that but lacked the words to do so. Without another word of protest, her shoulders slumped with resignation, and she sighed and said, "Dude, whatever you say. Should I go try to find that arrow, or…?"

"I believe the arrow can wait," I said with a smile, quite sure the arrow was now a permanent fixture on the hillside. "You've earned a break."

"Works for me. Can we get out of the sun though?" she asked as she wiped her fingers across her hairline. "I think the heat is getting to me."

I nodded in agreement. It didn't feel unusually warm, but Ann didn't share my constitution, and her complexion was starting to look a bit pallid now that I thought about it. "Perhaps some cold tea will do us good," I suggested.

Ann offered me a look that suggested I said something foolish. "Do you mean iced tea?" she asked. "I don't think anyone says cold tea."

"Oh my friend, you are in for a treat," I said. "There is quite the difference between the two!"

With our gear put away, we rounded the path back towards the side of the house, past the swimming pool and other outdoor entertainment that I'd never use. If I never hosted another party in my life, it would be too soon. I thought of the debauched events I'd played host to for Abarta and shuddered for a moment, thankful to be free of those obligations.

Until just a few months ago, I'd been bound to serve a Celtic deity, a trickster god named Abarta, until a moment of weakness caused him to transfer ownership of me to a friend, Elana Black. Elana was, as it turned out, an obligation of his born from his perverse idea of love. Abarta had sworn to protect her, even as her demise would be vital to his other sworn duty, that of returning his family to our plane of existence. I was merely a pawn in his greater schemes, though a useful pawn nonetheless, and in charging me with training and protecting Elana from physical harm, he had unwittingly set the two of us down the path of true friendship. But over the course of nearly two hundred years, I'd been made to do so much more than that, most of which I was not proud of. Elana hadn't owned me for more than a moment before restoring my freedom and breaking the magical bonds that held me, and the rest is history.

"I still don't know how or why you got a place this big," Ann asked as we stepped inside. "I feel like this is where like, Brad Pitt would live or something."

The size of the house was still something of an embarrassment for me, given that I was its sole occupant. Nestled in an intentionally remote stretch of Thousand Oaks, along with a host of very wealthy individuals who valued their privacy, stood about ten-million dollars' worth of house. It wouldn't have been my first choice, which I was sure would surprise Ann, but it had everything I needed in the short term. Distance enough from Los Angeles that I could lay low without so much distance that I couldn't be available if I were needed. More than enough land that I could keep my skills sharp, and most important of all was the full-time security detail to keep out anyone who might "accidentally" happen to find me. The reach of my former master was far and wide, and I didn't trust him to consider our business truly concluded.

"Well, I wouldn't get used to it," I sighed. "I have accumulated more than a couple of favors in my time, and this happens to be one of the bigger ones."

Ann looked around with an inspecting eye and asked, "So this is what? Fae Airbnb?"

I chuckled in spite of myself, all things considered. "You could say that," I replied, opening the refrigerator to retrieve the pitcher of cold tea I'd prepared earlier, suspending the tea pouch above the brew and allowing a portion of the liquid to drip before discarding it.

"You mind if I just lay down for a minute?" Ann asked, mildly out of breath. "I guess it was... are you seriously not hot right now?"

"Please, of course," I responded as I poured our glasses. By the time I had made it to the living room, Ann was sprawled out on a couch looking as if she had just run a marathon.

"Ooh, gimme," she replied greedily as she eyed the cool glasses in my hands.

"This will do you good," I said, handing the tea to her. Half the glass had been emptied by the time I sat down.

A sound of satisfaction involuntarily left my friend as she rested the glass on her forehead. "You were right, that was magic."

"I'm glad you approve."

Ann seemed to steady her breathing in relative silence for a moment, resting her eyes as she did. "Is it cool if I ask you something?"

"Of course," I responded, moderately curious. "What would you like to talk about?"

"Your like, origin story?" Ann asked. "Or childhood or whatever? Sorry, I know it's weird, and we're cool but like, I don't really know anything about you prior to, you know, that thing last year."

That thing she referred to was our troubles with monsters, gods, and sorcerers. I could understand how she had difficulty pinning down which thing to reference. I could also understand her curiosity. Our friendship had always developed in the present, and over the couple of months we'd gotten to know each other the subject of my past never really seemed to come up.

I took another sip of my tea before replying. "I'd be happy to answer your questions, but perhaps you could be more specific?"

"I don't know." Ann hesitated. "Maybe just... your story?"

"Very well, my young friend," I began. "This is a story that I have told myself many times. When I am alone, before I rest, and even in less convenient times. It is the story of my life. But this time will be different, because for the first time, I will be able to share that story with someone else, and I am pleased to know that you will be my first."

"Okay, that sounds kind of like the start of a fairy tale," Ann said cautiously.

"Perhaps," I acknowledged. "I come from a faraway land, unknown to the people of this world, in a city called Verisia. I was born to the kindest and most supportive woman I have ever known, my mother, Aeleth. She was a hero, a healer, and my friend."

"Moms are pretty great," Ann agreed sleepily.

"My mother was responsible for everything I had become, with one key difference. She was determined to stay in Verisia for the remainder of her days, and I was tempted to follow in the footsteps of my father and seek adventure."

Ann perked up at that. "Your parents split up?"

"They are… together," I said carefully. "But they are apart as well. Verisia is a thriving, welcoming community. Our city is a hub, travelers pass through coming from all over, and our elven knowledge and craftsmanship is highly sought after. However, our people are connected to the land under the city in an extraordinary way. We can be happy there for all our days, sharing a bond with the land. But if we leave, the land rejects us, and we are not allowed to return."

"So then why did your Dad leave?" Ann asked, then quickly added. "I'm sorry if that's too personal."

I shook my head from side to side. "Not at all. I do not know specifically what he sought, but I've always believed that his was a gamble that my mother would follow him eventually and they would seek their fortunes together. It was a wager he lost. My mother was dedicated to helping her people and to raising me. And she excelled at both, I might add."

"But the call to adventure was too great?"

"Ha!" I laughed in spite of myself. "Not hardly. Of course, I'd always been curious, certainly, but leaving for riches and glory never held enough interest for me on their own to convince me to leave. And seeing the good my mother did for our neighbors and those who passed through was more than reason enough to suppress that remaining curiosity. Until of course, he came along."

Ann sat up at that, nearly spilling her tea. "A fella? An evil warlord intent on razing the city? Oh! A distant prince who required the help of a champion to save his kingdom?" Then, becoming aware of exuberance and looking ashamed she slumped back down into the couch. "Sorry, didn't mean to interrupt."

"Quite all right, it's nice to know that someone is invested in my story," I assured her. "And you were right the first time, it was a fella, as you said. Alistair Wright. He was an odd man, very funny and very earnest. He'd come from no land that I'd ever heard of, though I'm certain you are familiar with England." Ann nodded vigorously at that as I continued. "For better or worse, I'll always remember how we met. He was lost in Verisia and slammed into me as he was staring at what I could only assume was the sun. He fell to the ground, I helped him up, and it seemed as if we'd always known each other somehow. He spent months in town pining for me—and forgive me—I grew accustomed to his company. Until the day he told me his secret."

I didn't say anything more for a moment, unsure if my friend was prepared to hear what came next, but the silence, as uncomfortable as it was, told me that I'd already come too far to stop now.

"Alistair told me one day that he needed to return home and that he'd reached my fair city by way of entering into a book authored by a man named Charles Godfrey Leland. That my world, for as real as it seemed, was not real to him. Not until he met me, and I had made it real for him."

"He was like me!" Ann exclaimed. "And Elana and Olivia! He was a traveler!"

"He was a traveler," I confirmed. "But nothing like you. He invited me to come with him, told me that he knew of a very powerful individual who could grant me the ability to move between worlds as he did. And I was... I was young, roughly the age you are now. And I was stupid; I hadn't thought about what I'd be giving up. And the thought of never seeing him again was unbearable. And so I—"

The sound of the glass thumping against the floor as it fell snapped me back to reality and I saw my friend was now shivering and sweating, her eyes closed and her head tilted in a way that no one could fall asleep to. Her breaths were suddenly shallow and audible. "Ann!" I shouted, moving to her aid.

No!

This wasn't just exhaustion; this was something else entirely. She'd begun to sweat everywhere, and her skin was hot to the touch. Ann was running a fever. Her pulse had quickened and—

"Please don't stop the story on my account, you were just getting to my favorite bit. Unless, of course, you think, perhaps, your story was just so exciting that she slipped into a coma."

I recognized the voice before I turned around. I'd never wanted to hear that voice again, but somehow I wasn't surprised that out of all the enemies I'd made, he would be the first to find to me. Nor was I surprised that he'd be the one stupid enough to test me when I was no longer chained.

"Boy, she sure went out like a light, didn't she? Really hung in there. Poor little trooper, though to be fair, I was getting a bit bored waiting like this," the man continued.

I turned back to see him with my own eyes, and there he was with his white slacks and pink button-down shirt, dressed for all the world like he'd just stepped off a yacht and wanted people to know it. The fool wasn't even wearing shoes. There was one exception to the ensemble, and that was the wizard staff that he clutched with his left hand, and I was sure I wouldn't find it in the latest J Crew catalog.

My skin became hot and my vision narrowed at the sight of him, all smug and smiles as he stood just outside the opened sliding glass door, and he seemed to notice. "Oh, there she—"

I didn't give him the chance to finish as I hurled Ann's glass at his face. He responded with the flash of a blister shield, sending shards of the mug exploding to his left and right, but he didn't anticipate how badly I wanted my hands around his neck, and before he could respond to my frontal assault, I had cleared the length of the room and tackled him through an unfortunately placed patio table.

His grip on the staff loosened and he parted from it as we rolled wildly through the yard. In one fluid motion I managed to grip his throat with one hand and pick up a broken chair leg with the other and brought him up with me as I pinned him to the side of the home with a painful-sounding thud. His eyes rolled hard, and he winced, gripping my wrist with both of his hands.

"I swore I would kill you!" I seethed, menacing him with the improvised weapon.

"Don't think... Ann would appreciate that," he gasped, his eyes looking back into the house.

Ann. Of course. His timing wasn't a coincidence; he must have done something. But if the goal was simply to hurt me, he wouldn't have stood around to gloat. He wanted something.

"How did you get in here?" I pressed. "How did you even find me?"

"Magic," he choked out through a pained smile, as if that answer was explanation enough for anything.

Not being content with that answer and lacking any faith in him whatsoever, I jammed the jagged edge of the chair leg into his thigh as I released my grip on his neck. "This is your femoral artery. Try anything, and I let it out for a little sunshine. Now talk."

"Oh relax, I'm a wizard, yeah? Did you miss that bit? If I were trying to kill you, I wouldn't have had to say hello first," he said, tenderly rubbing the sides of his neck. "Besides, it's not as if I'm here looking for a Valentine; I'm here with business."

"I would never do business with you!"

"No, I don't imagine you would." Annoyance laced his voice at that. "Hence, your friend."

Jabbing my weapon about half an inch further into his leg, I snarled, "What did you do?"

"Poison, obviously. I would have thought that was obvious at least; please try to keep up. Very exotic, very mystical, and very rare. It just so happens that I am the only one who can help."

"Then help as if your life depends on it," I threatened. "Because it does."

He smiled at that and calmly put a hand down on the chair leg, gently pushing it away from his thigh. "No one is hurting anyone today. You have too much to lose, and I have use of you." He reached into a pocket on the front of his pants and retrieved a necklace, holding it up for me to see in the sun. It was a thin, gold rope attached to what looked to be a ceramic flower about the size of a half dollar, six lavender colored petals attached to a yellow pistil. "This right here will not only help stave off the poison coursing through your friend's veins; it will act as a countdown of sorts. As the amulet absorbs the poison, the petals will wither. Unfortunately for poor Ann, I've loaded her up with enough poison to kill, well, you."

"So this is what then? A finger in the dam?"

"Consider it incentive. You can save her, assuming you do as I say. If you accept, I will give you a location and a name. There will be a task waiting for you. Complete the task, get the antidote. Simple as that. Refuse, and I suppose you could consider this a farewell gift of sorts. You'll get to watch slowly, moment by moment, as the petals fall from her neck until she expires." He craned his neck into the room to look at Ann and continued, "Though if you have questions, I'd make them fast, I'm not sure how much longer she has."

"Of course I have questions! Why would you do this? Why me of all people?" I yelled. "What could be so important to you that you'd risk death by attacking me like this?"

"Let's get one thing clear to start with: you're not going to kill me because if you want any part of this, you're going to swear otherwise. Now if we're good on that, the matter of your task is just going to have to be one of those wait and see scenarios that I know you're oh so fond of. But the important bit, the really good part…" He paused and smiled at me, taking a bold step in my direction, his eye contact unblinking. When he spoke again, it was to mock me. "I know that Chalsarda is a free elf. And with no master, you're little more than a stray. Now do you want to help your friend or not?"

More than anything in that moment I wanted just to run him through right then and there and be done with him, but if I allowed myself that satisfaction there was no guarantee that I could find an antidote in time for Ann, even with the amulet. I doubt he would have come here if there was any chance of my discovering a cure on my own. Like it or not, I was going to have to play along. For her sake.

"What is the deal specifically?" I asked, trying to maintain any semblance of control in this situation.

"You perform the task given to you tomorrow, and I will see it to it that you are given the means to make your friend, Ann Bancroft, well again. And for such time as we are working together, you will bring no harm to me. Do we have a deal?"

My grip on the chair leg tightened as I tried to fight back the creeping sense that this was a terrible idea. It was no good though; he had me here. There was no other way. I dropped the chair leg and snatched the amulet from his hand. "Fine, we have a deal."

"Let me hear you say it," he said, looking quite satisfied with himself. "Let me hear you say my name."

I made an agreement with myself—no, a promise to myself, that when this was finished, he would never hurt me or anyone ever again. I stared at him hard enough for him to know exactly that and didn't stop until I could see in his eyes that he knew I would be coming for him. Right when I felt he was ready to flinch, I did as he asked.

"We have a deal," I said slowly. "Alistair."

2

listair left shortly after our agreement, handing me a cell phone and instructing me to keep it on at all times. He had no reason to stick around after that, and I certainly didn't want to be around him for any longer than I had to be. Besides, there was an urgent matter that required my immediate attention. No sooner had he left, and I'd made sure that he was gone, than I was by Ann's side and placing the necklace on her. The thought had occurred to me, albeit briefly, that I didn't really know that much about it other than what Alistair had told me, and he wasn't the most reliable source of information. Still, he'd done something to Ann, and I couldn't come up with a reason why he'd choose poison as his preferred lie. And if he genuinely needed something from me, keeping her alive was in his best interest. So a new piece of jewelry it was, then.

The effects were immediate. The moment the two ends of the gold rope touched behind her neck,.they magically fused

PLAYING DEAD

into a single solid hoop. Then the amulet, now resting on her chest, lost one of its petals as the color drained from it before it crumbled into dust. Something about that caused Ann to bolt upright, wide-eyed and gasping for air violently.

Okay, well at least it does *something*.

All in all, it was likely the best possible reaction I could have hoped for. I did my best to calm Ann down, but she was disoriented and profusely sweating. My best guess was that the amulet instantly broke her fever and magically stalled out the effects of the poison. There was little I could do for Ann other than making the sort of soft shushing noises I would make to calm down a startled horse. Our eyes met, and I offered her water, anticipating her needs. Ann hurriedly nodded her head in agreement, and by the time I returned with a fresh glass she already appeared to regain her senses.

"It... it happened again!" she stammered, her breaths still too rapid for my liking.

It was an astonishing claim, and one I wasn't expecting. "You've been poisoned before?" I asked, trying to clear some of the shattered glass around the room.

My response visibly upset her, and she grabbed a fistful of the couch as she cried out, "I've been poisoned?"

I turned to face her at that. "Yes, but if that's not what you're referring to, then what exactly happened again?"

Ann was insistent. "That's going to have to wait until you explain what the hell you mean about this poisoning business!"

"Well, precisely that," I began. "You've been poisoned. Oh, and don't remove that necklace; it's keeping you alive at the moment."

Her tiny fist clenched to her chest, and she raised the flower to about nose level, as far as the rope would allow. "Did you poison me?"

"Of course not!" I snapped. "I'm sorry about that, but no, it wasn't me. I would never."

13

"Yeah, I know, sorry."

"Please, don't apologize." I nearly blushed at that. I just yelled at a dying friend, and she was apologizing to me. "Remember Alistair from my story? He was my—"

"Ex," Ann finished for me.

I had planned to use the word lover, but I liked her word better. "Exactly. And he has poisoned you as a means of getting to me. Did I not get to the part where I mentioned that he was a manipulative sociopath willing to hurt whoever he has to in order to get what he wants?"

"You might have been working up to it before I almost died." Her admission came with its share of grim sarcasm.

"There's nothing to be done about it at the moment, I'm afraid," I began. "I never expected him to… that's not right; I always expect something from Alistair. He is vile. But I hadn't anticipated him to find me so soon. It was stupid of me to think he would just leave me alone, that he wouldn't do anything he could to hurt me."

Ann's look softened as she rose from the couch and crossed the length of the room to face me. "I know what this is, so I'm going to put a stop it before you let this eat you up even a second longer." She spoke softly. "Knowing that I've been poisoned sucks, but you didn't do this to me. You didn't put me in danger or whatever other reason you're going to convince yourself somehow makes this your fault. You're not responsible for the actions of an abusive ex. Terrible people do terrible things, and one of the worst things they all invariably do is make their victims feel like it's their fault for what they do. He did this to me, not you. I don't know the full story, but I think I know enough. We'll figure this out together, okay?"

I was stunned by her words. Not that I should have been. I'd seen flashes of greatness from Ann; it was just that her wisdom was precisely what I would tell someone else in a similar situation, and it was precisely the sort of thing I'd never be able to say to myself. She was right, of course, but I knew I wouldn't simply stop feeling guilty on the strength of those words alone.

I met her expectant gaze, and by way of reply I opened up a palm to her. "Would you like to know?" I asked her. "The full story?"

Ann blinked at that, staring at my hand. "Are you sure?" she managed to ask.

Part of the power specific to Ann and those like her is that if a hand is offered freely to them, they can accept it, and with that comes the permission to know their story in an instant. Not all of it, but the important parts or the parts they're willing to share. And it could work both ways: Ann could have shared her story with me in the same way if she so chose. Of course, I've learned the hard way that unknowingly offering your hand to someone with her power means nothing. A freely given hand means a freely given story, whether you know it or not.

"Yes," I replied, withdrawing the hand, remembering the gravity of the situation. "When you are well, and this business is behind us, if you still want to know, I will share it with you. Completely."

Ann understood and forced herself to look away. "Right, of course. I don't know what it would do to me right now."

I rested a hand on her shoulder, and she looked up into my eyes. "Thank you, my friend," I told her with a smile. "You are right, of course. But for whatever Alistair is responsible for, you have my promise that I will make it right. Not because this is my fault, but because I want to see you alive. Now, what was it you were trying to say before? What was it that happened again?"

Ann began to look unwell again, though it had nothing to do with the poison in her veins. She fidgeted a moment, a look on her face suggesting that she was contemplating whether it was too late to take it back. "It's going to sound crazy." It came out as a half-hearted attempt to get out of saying what she had to say. I crossed my arms and waited. If Ann wanted to avoid the topic, she would have to do so without my help.

"Fine!" she exclaimed. "I saw the future, okay?"

That wasn't what I was expecting, and I didn't know that she understood how dangerous that statement was.

"You what?" I asked incredulously.

"I mean, probably. I think so. It's weird, all right?"

Ann was visibly nervous, and I knew that reaction wasn't going to make this any easier. I took a second to compose myself, and in a more measured tone, I tried to start over with her. "Why don't we start from the beginning. You said this happened before?"

Ann sat back down on the couch and sighed heavily. "Yeah, a couple of times. One of them was before Christmas. With Elana."

"What did you see?" I asked, sitting beside her.

"It's not that easy to explain," Ann began. "It's sort of like watching three separate movies all at the same time. I think what I'm seeing are possibilities. They only happen while I'm asleep, so I just thought they were bad dreams, until..."

Ann trailed off at that, and in spite of myself, I prompted her to continue. "Until what?"

"Until Logan didn't come back." There was a sickness in Ann's voice as she said it. "I had a vision, or I guess visions, and in each of them, one of them didn't come back. I saw Elana, Olivia, and Logan go through that weird portal each time. I saw the goblins come at us. All of it was clear in my mind, but then it changed suddenly. There was a future where any one of them didn't come back. And it happened exactly as I saw it in my dream."

"I see." My poor friend. This would be distressing enough for anyone to deal with, and with recent events as they were, I briefly considered not immediately telling her what I knew.

That was a foolish thought, of course. Upsetting or no, she had to hear it, and now.

"Ann, who else have you told about this?" I asked.

She shook her head at the question. "No one. It's crazy enough as it is, but I couldn't tell Olivia that I saw a vision of her in tears, with Logan gone. I don't think that she'd forgive me. I don't think she should. If I'd told her, then maybe he would've—"

"No, stop that." I chided her, not wanting her to finish that thought. "You didn't know what you were then—what you are—and saying something might have only made things worse. You don't know that you could have changed anything. Besides, you said it yourself. You thought it was a bad dream, yes?"

"I did," she confirmed.

I put my hands on her shoulders, gentle as I could, so as not to upset her, but I turned her to face me as I met her uncertain gaze. "Ann, my friend, it is of the utmost importance that you don't repeat any of this to anyone, do you understand? Not to Elana, not even to me unless you are certain we are alone. I need you to promise me."

"I can do that," Ann began shakily. "But why?"

"Because you are a Sibyl," I said after taking a deep breath. "Amongst those who travel, every so often an extra gift is bestowed. Call it a secondary ability. The rarest of them all is what you possess. And that rarity will make you a target for the worst sorts. And there's worse news, I'm afraid. This is only the beginning. Eventually, you will see more and more, and you will be burdened with sight and knowledge that is not for you. It could very well be that it will never be worse than this, just the occasional glimpse of the near future. But I've seen it go so much further than this. I knew a woman once who saw entire lifetimes, including her own."

"What happened to her?" Ann asked.

"I'd rather not talk about her," I admitted, realizing a moment too late how dangerously close I'd gotten to revealing something terrible.

"Is there anything I can do?" I was unsure if Ann meant for me or if the question was about her condition. I chose to believe it was the latter.

"There are those who might be able to help, people with direct knowledge of your ability," I confirmed. "But going to them exposes your secret, and I'd rather not risk it. I will try to find you reading materials, but it may take some time. This is one of those topics that is closely watched and from unexpected angles. The good news is that I know early enough that I might be able to actually help."

"That's something, at least," Ann replied. "Thank you."

"Of course," I said, hopeful that I could do as I said. "So, tell me. What did you see this time?"

"You, for starters. But it was vague, not like with Logan. In one vision, I saw you soaked in blood. Literally, head to toe. It was drying and sticky, and none of it was yours. It was unsettling. And in another, you were crying. You were distraught, inconsolable. Alone. I don't know what you'd lost, but it looked like it had broken you. But there was one more outcome."

My first options didn't sound particularly appealing. "I hope the third involves kittens and birthday cake."

"You were content," Ann said hopefully. "I don't know if that's the right word, but something close to it. You were peaceful and bright. Victorious would be the wrong word, I think. You didn't look like a conquering hero, just someone who was okay. Bruised and tired, sure, but you were okay. I think no matter what, you're about to go through hell. I'm sorry."

"No apologies necessary," I assured her. "These are only possibilities. The future is not written in stone. We can determine our own fate."

"Well, that's great to hear, because I saw something else," Ann remarked worriedly.

"Someone else?" I asked. "Alistair, perhaps? Someone we know?"

She shook her head at that and struggled to find her words. "In my dream," she started slowly. "I saw my future. It... it was..." Ann trembled slightly, her eyes pressed shut. I rubbed her shoulder comfortingly, letting her get there in her own time. She looked at me, tears forming behind her glasses. "There was nothing in it. No paths, no mistaking it. There was nothing."

The next day I set off towards Los Angeles. I'd received the call from Alistair earlier in the morning then was appropriate, but he offered a name, a place, a time, and little else. Which I considered a small wonder. I would take my bright spots where I could see them, and the less I had to hear from that smug bastard the better. Ann had wanted to go home and rest, but I insisted she stay put. Between the active security system, the protective charms, as rudimentary as they were, and the increased patrols, I couldn't think of any place better suited. I didn't leave her in a house; I'd left her in a fortress. Besides, I didn't think Alistair would do anything to Ann, not while he still needed me. He'd already played that card and well. But in case there was something bigger at play, I didn't want to risk not knowing exactly where she was until this whole affair was sorted.

There was a ridesharing app installed on the phone, either on purpose or Alistair had simply forgotten to take his credit card information off the device before handing it to me. Either way, this driver would be receiving a very generous tip at the end of it all. I had a wool cap pulled down around my ears, and I'd found a hooded sweater a full size too large for me to wear over a t-shirt and baggy jeans with deep pockets. My attire didn't quite match the weather, but it didn't seem like a good idea to arrive dressed for war. Still, the loose clothing afforded me more opportunities to smuggle various tools, and in better hiding spots than would be picked up by the average pat down.

The first two pieces of my instructions were clear enough. I was to meet Margaux Brouillard at two in the afternoon. That was easy enough. However, I was to meet her under the Coliseum. I had to ask twice to make sure I'd understood him correctly. Was there a specific tunnel or special area? Alistair abruptly told me to figure it out, which indicated to me that he didn't know and wasn't interested in admitting as much. So figuring it out was all that was left, and arriving an hour early seemed to me to be plenty of time. And if it wasn't, well, perhaps he should have done his homework before sending me out.

There were no events scheduled for the day, so when I arrived, the driver seemed puzzled about our destination but kept any comments he may have had to himself. The parking lot was empty for the most part, not even a security guard that I could see, and when my driver pulled away, I was left to consider my options. Outside of just yelling Margaux's name at the top of my lungs, the only real choice was to investigate the Coliseum itself, maybe find a way inside.

The Coliseum is a landmark in Los Angeles. It's also been called historic, a monument, and full of character. All of which is to say that it is a decrepit old football field in an advanced state of disrepair. The structure itself is nearly a hundred years old and is shown the same care a puppy shows a nice pair of shoes. If it weren't for college football and the occasional concert, this place would be apartment buildings and a parking structure. The building deserved better, but that was none of my business.

I approached the front entrance of the structure, a thirty-foot archway topped with the words "Los Angeles Memorial Coliseum" and joined by the Olympic Rings, flanked by two bronze plaques of men who were likely important to the founding of this playground in some way. I was able to see the empty field through the gate and the various arches. The security here was abysmal. A locked gate, maybe ten feet high, that I could have easily scaled if I found that to be easier than simply picking the lock and walking through. I should be surprised, but then again, this was a place that even its caretakers seemed to have no interest in preserving. As I'd understood it, a local university held those responsibilities. Maybe they simply hadn't gotten around to it.

As I stood there contemplating my impending trespass, a stocky man with a bleach blonde buzz cut and a plain black suit that was so poor in quality it could have passed for costume appeared from behind one of the arches and met me at the gate, asking if I was that elf Alistair had sent. Lifting my cap to reveal an ear appeared to be a good enough answer, and after letting me through the gate and sloppily checking me for weapons—finding nothing, I might add—he announced my arrival over a radio. With the news that I was expected, he escorted me down through an old service walkway, leading into something more hidden, and down a long and winding staircase. I estimated that we were much further below the football field than earthquake safety guidelines would find comfortable.

My escort and I waited patiently in a tunnel, the sound of what I assumed was cheering coming from somewhere in the distance. Eventually, a much smaller man in a much more expensive suit joined us and dismissed the hired help.

"You must be Chalsarda," he said with a crooked grin that I'd bet he found charming. "Not quite what I expected, but I appreciate you coming all the same."

"I'm here for a two o'clock appointment with Margaux Brouillard," I said dryly. "Are you here to see me to my appointment?"

"The interim director is indisposed at the moment, I'm afraid," the man said, offering me a handshake. "Which makes me the appointment. Skip Santoro. Pleasure to meet you."

I cautiously took the handshake, locking my thoughts as I did, just in case he'd been able and willing to take my memories, but from what I could tell it was just a handshake. A little sweaty perhaps, but otherwise not threatening. "I see. So then, Skip, what exactly is it that you do around here?"

"Around here?" he said with a chuckle. "For all intents and purposes, I'm the boss! But for today, I'm the guy giving you your assignment, and if you play your cards right, maybe the cure for what ails you."

I took a moment to consider him now. I was a full head taller than him—stature wasn't his strong suit—but he projected himself well. His black hair was slicked back with enough product that it bordered on offensive and it had just enough pomp to straddle the edge of cartoonish. Aside from that, he was immaculately well groomed, but between the gold cufflinks and the prominently displayed Rolex watch, it all became just a bit too flashy to be still considered in good taste. The stupid grin gave me the impression he was someone who liked to call women sweetheart whenever he had the chance.

"Listen, sweetheart," Skip began.

Oh, bugger all.

"We can talk business later, but you're a bit on the early side, and I have something I need to get to. Care to follow me?"

I kept my poker face and followed him through a guarded door which opened up into what seemed to be a private box, prime seating considering this was an arena beneath the Coliseum. The thunderous sounds of hundreds of cheering men and women filled my ears the moment the doors opened. Skip motioned for me to sit and took a seat beside me as I scanned the chaos below. Littering the ground, dozens of besuited men and women lay still or struggled to get to their feet. And one man stood in the center, bare chest heaving with labored breaths and a firm hand gripping a scythe. I recognized him at once.

This was Bres.

3

I didn't trust this, but Skip was correct in that I'd been early. Whatever was happening here was independent of me. If that was the case, why was I called here and exactly what was happening? I had questions, but until I opened my mouth I wouldn't be in any danger of giving anything away, and so I followed Skip's instruction to have a seat, and I studied what I was seeing. Interestingly, the first thing I noticed was that none of the fallen appeared to be dead. Some had been wounded worse than others, many even gravely so, but they were all being attended to and helped out of the arena one at a time with the care a teenager would show the remains of a house party in the desperate hours before their parents returned home.

"I can see it on you. You recognize Bres, and you're wondering just what the hell is going on here, am I right?" Skip asked the question with such confidence that my face must have given away my thoughts, though I was certain I hadn't moved a muscle. "Don't feel too bad about it, sweetheart. Reading people is kind of my thing."

"You're not wrong," I hedged, still keeping an eye on the arena floor. I wondered absently how many more times I would allow him to call me sweetheart before I did something violent and unprofessional. "I have… an issue with Bres. And it's true that I do not know what is happening here, but it is also true that I don't particularly care. I am here against my will; I'm here to do a job. The particulars of which have not been made clear to me."

"Well, you are in for a real treat. Not only will all be made clear to you, I think you'll find the reason why you're here just, well, just a real eye-opener."

"Hey, boss man!" Bres called out loud enough to be heard over the roar of the crowd, walking in the direction of our box. "Is this really it? Is this the best you've got?"

"Pardon me, but this will require my attention for just a moment," Skip said almost displaying a hint of etiquette. He stood up and leaned over the box railing and looked down into the pit as the crown ceased their cheering, presumably to hear what was coming next.

"You should feel honored, Bres!" Skip attempted something like a decree, but he clearly didn't have the voice of authority for it. "These were some of my best men!"

Wiping away a bit of blood from his mouth, Bres stepped forward with a grin and called back, "There's your problem, boyo. To kill me, you sent men. You should have sent armies."

"Now, now, none of that. No one wants you dead, Bres," Skip responded. Seeing the look on his face and hearing the words as he said them, Skip corrected himself. "Well, *I* don't want you dead, at least. You and I are going to do great things together."

Bres sneered at that. "Don't get it twisted! You seem to be mistaking me for another soldier in your army. Let's get one thing straight before one of your fool assumptions gets you killed. I'm no soldier of yours. I'm a goddamn holy terror. And

I may not have chosen this life, but I make the most of it, and I've hurt people worse than anyone you can imagine. Thank your stars, lad, that I'm one of a kind because a wee pissant like you wouldn't know what to do with two of me. I just took the best ninety-nine soldiers you had, and I took them to places they might not come back from. So go on then, bring it out! Bring out your precious Battle Born, and when I plant them into the earth, I'm going to step over their body and walk out of here free. Through you, if I have to."

Skip blinked at that, shaking his head in mock surprise. "Wow, Bres. Wow. Did you write up that speech before you entered today or... no, it doesn't matter. Fantastic though, really giving everyone here their money's worth. But no, I'm afraid you're not facing a Battle Born today, you're—"

"I'm going to stop you right there before you go on making a bags of something you cannot fix!" Bres snapped. "If you try to cheat me again, I will be coming for you. And you will wonder every day and every night if this it. Is this the last time you put on one of your ridiculous suits? Is this the last time you take a drive in your fancy little car? And I don't want to worry you with how very different your life will be when I get my hands on you, so choose your next words with care."

"Good god, man! We've never cheated you!" Skip exclaimed. "We know how much the Fae love their precious rules. And our rules are simple, yet you've broken them every time you've had an opportunity here. First rule, no magic. You broke that one almost immediately. Second rule, no killing. And by god did you ever break that one in your second outing! No, we never screwed you, you screwed yourself. And if I can finish what I was saying before I was so rudely interrupted, I was getting ready to agree with you, Bres! You are indeed, one of a kind."

"What are you playing at?"

"Well, if you bothered to learn the rules, you would know

that nowhere does it say that a Battle Born is the last fighter in the gauntlet. Traditionally, yes, that's who we use, but the rules merely state that we may use one hundred willing participants. And Bres, someone as special as you deserves to go out on a high note! To leave here a legend! So without further ado, allow me to present you with your farewell opponent."

There was the crunching sound of large gears beneath our seats, and a thud as heavy wooden doors slammed open. And I watched as a towering man, one I nearly managed to mistake for an ogre, lumbered his way into the arena pit, a hush falling over the crowd as he did. Apart from his size, the man had to be just shy of seven feet tall; there was little else that was remarkable about him. He wore a white tank top tucked into beige slacks, the sort of apparel you might have seen on a brawler in the depression era, and that wasn't the only anachronism he displayed. His fiery red hair was oiled and combed over neat and tight in contrast to his mutton chop sideburns. Nothing special and entirely out of place, all at once. I couldn't see his face, but his body language was casual, almost bored.

"Hello, Bres." His Irish accent was flat, and his voice had the impact of dropping a slab of wet meat onto a linoleum floor.

For his part, Bres seemed equal parts amused and incredulous. "Balor, old son," Bres began. "Forget your sword?"

"Not gonna need it," Balor replied in the same heavy, flat tone.

Bres nearly cackled at that, just about doubling over with laughter. "Not surprised to see you here, truly. Even less surprised at your arrogance."

"Not arrogance, you're beat to hell. Stopping you won't be a challenge. But it's gotta be done."

"Does it?" Bres snarled, the illusion of amusement vanishing in an instant. "You're a bloody mouse is what you are! For all your power, you've never had an original thought of your own. If you thought it through for more than a second, you'd be with me."

Balor didn't seem intimidated. If anything, he seemed bored and began to lecture. "We all have a part to play. One of these days you'll grow up and accept that. In the meantime, here I am."

"Yes, here you are," Bres agreed. "The fearsome Balor, is it? Son of the worst, yeah? That's not what I see. I see one more body to drop. One task standing between me and freedom. Tell me now, what do you think I'm willing to do to you to get what I'm due?"

Balor shrugged his massive shoulders at that. "Guess you'll have to show me."

The ensuing battle was bloody and decisive, and to his credit, Bres took his pound of flesh. Probably literally. But the outcome was never in doubt. Balor struck with the force of a runaway truck, and if he felt pain at all where Bres carved into him, he certainly didn't show it. Whatever enthusiasm the crowd might have had before was gone by the time Bres had the fight taken out of him. Both men, if you could call them that, were stained in crimson, but only Balor remained standing. His demeanor was stoic, but his breaths were labored and even from my box seats I could hear a slight gurgling from his lungs with each one. The aftermath was grotesque.

"Come on; we don't need to be here for the rest of this," Skip suggested with a nod of his head. "Let's finish this conversation somewhere more private."

I agreed, not that I had much choice, and his guards led us to a makeshift office on another floor. Once we were alone, he took a seat behind a desk and said, "I'd apologize for you having to see that, but you've seen worse in the course of your career, haven't you?"

"I'm not sure how that's relevant," I replied.

"It's extremely relevant," Skip replied. "In fact, you've not only seen worse, but you've also been responsible for worse, haven't you?"

My patience was slipping now. "If you have a point to all of this, I suggest you get to it."

Skip raised his hands in surrender. "Hey, believe it or not, I'm not the enemy. And I didn't show you that horrible display for entertainment value. Hand to god, I didn't like seeing that any more than you did. I probably hated it even more, but it's not a contest between us. But you were here early, and I thought maybe showing you would speed up the process of explaining it to you."

"And what is it you intend to explain to me?"

"All of it," Skip replied. "Or as much as I'm allowed. I see no reason to be coy with you. If we're going to work together, I think we can both get what we want if we're both willing to be open and honest with each other. Truce?"

"You have my attention," I said cautiously as I took the seat opposite his side of the desk.

"Good enough for me. Now tell me, just for starters, what do you know about the Battle Born?"

"They're your muscle. Who you send in when you really want to make a mess," I said plainly.

Skip shook his head at that. "No, not that. That's obvious. I mean, what are they?"

I had to think about that for a moment, and if I was honest with myself, I didn't have a clue. They were tough, sure, but I suppose the thought of their origins wasn't one that had ever occurred to me. Skip took my silence as a cue to continue. "I'll give you a hint while I'm at it. What is Bres?"

"He's Fae, like me, except not," I said hesitantly. "He's not a god, but he's... something."

"I sometimes forget your former master wasn't interested in our arrangement nor was he able to accept even if he wanted to, but I still thought you would have figured it out at some point. There's the real Bres somewhere out there. Just like there's the real Balor. We've come to an agreement with them, as well as some of the other gods. Well, a lot of the gods, really." Skip sat up in his seat with an expression that suggested I pay careful attention to what came next. "You see, the gods, they're not from here, not really, they're kind of from all over the place. But they can get here easy enough. Well, most of them anyway. And it really grinds their gears that they can't add to their family tree. And that's where we come in."

"You make demigods?" I questioned.

"Not quite, but close!" Skip replied with mild shock. "No, no one and nothing can do that. Their past is a single solid record; they just sort of exist then, now, and forever. But what we've found is that those that travel have the winning genetic lotto numbers needed to reproduce with the gods."

"The Fae can reproduce, so I'm not sure what you're getting at," I replied skeptically.

"Certainly Changelings aren't anything new, I'll grant you that," Skip agreed. "But we're not talking about a housewife's fairy tales of a summer romance between a centaur and Karen from middle-of-nowhere Idaho. I mean, a Satyr is a lot more likely, but I digress. Fae plus human equals pretty baby as a story is one that's been told to death. No, this is something special. The gods, for all they can do, can't reproduce and it drives them wild. You see, once in a generation, the gods can produce something akin to a bad photocopy of themselves. Different, but with the pale shadow of their essence imbued in the offspring and bursting with magical energies. But you know how it is with the gods, and especially the Fae; they need to ask permission, they need to make deals. So we sat down at the negotiating table and made one hell of a deal. If one of ours, usually a Gardener, is willing, they can mate with one of theirs. But we keep the kids and raise them as our own. The gods could care less what happens them, and this at least keeps them alive. Once they reach maturity, if they desire, they have a chance every seven years to earn their freedom in the contest you witnessed today. Face a hundred willing participants in big old fight without killing anyone or using your magic, be the last one standing and badda bing badda boom, you're free to go. Most of the time, no one is interested. Every so often, we get someone like Bres."

I was trying—and failing—to keep my composure at this news, but I couldn't help myself. "Child slaves? How can you possibly be cavalier about this?"

"Hey, whoa, I'm just middle management!" Skip said defensively. "And like I said, I don't like it any more than you do! That's just the way it is and the way it has to be. And by the way? That wasn't our provision; the gods suggested that. Seems for the most part they care more about the act of making a life than caring and raising for one. And with the danger we face on a regular basis to keep the multiverse safe, those little godling bastards are a blessing. I guess maybe the gods want to see them earn their way out; I don't know. I just work here."

I took a breath at that, knowing full well that the whims of the gods were capricious and someone like Skip or myself couldn't stop them from doing anything that they wanted to do. Besides, he was feeling chatty, and I might as well get as much information out of him as I could. You never know when some of it might prove useful. "And I suppose the children are bound to the agreements of their parents by association?"

"Something like that, yes," Skip agreed. "But again, we give them a home and a place to belong, we make them feel special. They grow up liking what we do. They don't want to leave."

"And what does any of this have to do with the Battle Born?"

"What do you think happens if one of those kids is born without that bit of their parents in them?" As he asked, I felt a sick wave of realization. "They're born stillborn, magically speaking at least. No domain to claim, no Fae ties whatsoever. But they still have god blood in them, and that makes them extremely dangerous. Maybe they don't have that magical spark, but when you can bench press a bus maybe you don't need it. The gods themselves are sickened with this result, even the lowliest Fae has a perfect track record of passing on their magical essence when their kid pops out. So, they would prefer just to forget they ever happened. And that's the other part of our deal. They don't get names; they don't get to know their parents. They're raised for one purpose, and that's to be our personal weapons of mass destruction. The people in charge of that sort of thing, they tend to treat them well enough. Like a farm with plenty of space for a dog to run and play. But all in all, they're still treated like things, not people."

"So then it is child slavery," I fumed.

Skip sighed at that. "I don't want to make excuses for it and say no, but they don't actually fight or do any of our dirty work until they're adults. It's not perfect, but it's something."

"So why am I here?" I asked on the edge of my patience. "If the answer is to be disgusted, you're doing a bang-up job of it!"

"Our children have grown wild, it would seem," Skip said evenly. "And one of them has escaped. If it were up to me, hey, I'd say good for them. But it's not up to me, and the people above me want to put the word out. The Battle Born comes back dead or alive. We can't have something like that just out there on the streets. And if we don't bring it back, we set a bad example for the others, and things could get out of control in a hurry."

"It seems to me that you think I'd willingly be your slave hunter, and I can't think of a single damn reason why I'd do this."

"I can think of a couple," Skip said. "Your friend Ann being the primary reason. If you complete the task, I have the authority to tell you how to save her. As for what Alistair gets out of it, the bounty is either a half million or an enchanted dagger capable of instantly removing any glamour. Hunters choice."

He had a point. If I walked now, Ann would die, and unfortunately, everyone seemed to know I wasn't ready to let that happen. Still, it was starting to add up. Alistair saw dollar signs, and while he had a good lead, he was far too cautious to take on this sort of task on his own. The poor thing might break a nail. I'd rather it was a neck. "Why are you telling me all of this?"

"Simple answer? I like you the most," Skip replied. "I mean, you don't think you're the only one hunting the bounty, do you? The key difference is, you're not a monster. Alistair is a weasel and a real scumbag for putting you in this position. Right off the bat, I have sympathy for you and your friend, and out of everyone taking this job, you're far and away the one I want to see succeed. The others want to do this; you're the only one doing it for the right reasons."

I was taken aback by that answer. It made sense. I wasn't sure why else he would be so free with his information if his words weren't true, but he seemed to know a lot more about me than I knew about him. I carefully considered my response and asked, "Who else is out there?"

"Well, let's see, there's the Abbot of Kinney," Skip began.

I groaned in spite of myself. "Really? The cult leader?"

"He prefers the term Crystal Healer," Skip countered, then relented. "But yes, your description is more apt. He has a modicum of talent and probably, technically has the ability to travel. But his juice is just enough to patch up a skinned knee or cure a hangover. Idiot thinks he's Jesus, probably. Still, don't look past him. He's gained quite the following."

Skip brought up an interesting point. People with the ability to travel were also gifted with magic, but magic came a lot easier than traveling. To travel meant to break the skin of the world and walk in the Knowing, an infinite space between world where literally anything and everything possible. Some, like Elana, could enter at will and with little effort. Most however, would need to spend days, weeks, or even months getting in and that was even if they were aware of that place at all. For obvious reasons, people like Skip didn't like to advertise what they could do.

I gave him a small nod of acknowledgement. "I'll keep that in mind. Who else?"

Skip chewed his lip. "There's also Birdie. If I were you, I'd pray I didn't cross paths with her at all. She's psychotic, and when she's on the hunt, she rarely brings back the whole person. I've never met her and don't know much else about her, but on reputation alone, I'd bet a year's salary she's not human. Watch yourself around her."

I hated to admit it, but Birdie wasn't a name that I was familiar with, something that came as something of a surprise. If she was as notorious as Skip claimed, I was surprised I hadn't at least heard whispers about her. Either Skip was exaggerating, or everyone had just been too afraid to say her name out loud.

"I'll be careful," I replied.

Skip pursed his lips for a moment studying me. "Don't sleep on Birdie, I mean it. It seems like you might be sleeping on Birdie and that would be a mistake. You're not sleeping on Birdie, are you?"

"Please stop saying that," I asked, surprised at how quickly I was prepared to slap him.

"I'm just saying, I have two dozen reports of incidents involving her and every single time she makes an appearance it's like horror movie took place in a meat packing plant. Things don't generally keep their limbs around her and that includes a loup-garou. I've got pictures in here, hold on," he said fishing out a folder from his desk and displaying the graphic images for me to see. Sure enough, the pictures showed the headless remains of massive beast that had been carved with a fury that didn't look targeted, even if the decapitation did. Considering how quickly a loup-garou can regenerate, this was savage.

"Disturbing," I agreed, not taking too long surveying the carnage. "Though, why not just say werewolf? Are you trying to sound impressive for my benefit?"

"For one thing, this one was actually French, and for another there's a distinction. A loup-garou is an inherently magical creature where a werewolf is just some poor sap who got bit and infected. But you know this and you're testing me, aren't you?"

Skip had caught me, and I admitted as much. "Indeed."

"Well don't, I've been around," He remarked sourly.

I made an apologetic gesture and changed the subject. "So then Alistair, the Abbot, and Birdie? Those are the players?"

"Well, there's one more," Skip said. "Caleb Duquesne. Gunslinger, completely human, no magic or talents that anyone can tell. That said, he's the one that scares me the most. The Abbot has charm as a weapon; Birdie has bloodlust. Caleb, however, he has that dangerous combination of intelligence and integrity. Once he takes a job, he sees it through. For a guy with nothing but a couple of guns at his side, he sure seems to come out on top in a lot of unlikely situations."

Caleb Duquesne was another one that I'd heard of, but to hear that he was merely human was something of a surprise. I'd heard more than a few rumors about what he was, but humans didn't tend to survive the sorts of encounters that he willingly took on. "I know of Caleb by reputation only," I admitted. "Seems odd that he'd take on this kind of job, doesn't seem to fit his profile."

"Never underestimate the allure of epic loot." Skip shrugged. Ah, there it was. The man was a geek.

"This has all been very helpful, and very unexpected," I said, trying to simultaneously push down my disgust at what I had to do and acknowledge my gratitude. "And while I hate to ask, there's still just one more crucial detail. I don't have a clue about where to begin my search."

"I can do you one better." Skip grinned knowingly and leaned across the table. "I can tell you exactly where it is right now."

4

I fought down the immediate urge to demand, "Where?" and instead opted for another one-word question.

"Why?"

Skip studied my face for a moment, gently rocking back and forth in his chair. "Why do I have this information? Why am I giving it to you? Because I thought we already—"

"Why don't you just go in and get the Battle Born back yourself?" I asked, doing my best to keep my tone confident while I figured out this newest wrinkly. "You have the resources, surely. Send Balor or an army of Gardeners or even just two Battle Born. Two must be better than one."

"Ah. I was wondering when this was going to come up," Skip began. "It seems you don't know quite as much about us as I was led to believe. The simple answer is, well, those are the orders. Someone with a bigger desk than mine wants me to send a fistful of psychopaths at the problem; I open a little file folder on my desktop dedicated to terrible people. The longer answer is that if we start sending our own after everyone who goes AWOL, we can't control the narrative if we get our missing child back. Someone outside the organization does the job, then who knows how it happened? And if anything, it reinforces the idea in the others that the world is a desperate and precarious place full of individuals capable of hurting us and all the wonderful citizens we've sworn to protect."

The sarcasm was heavy in his voice, especially at the end; and he seemed to reflect a moment before he continued. "That's if you succeed, of course. You probably won't. I'll be impressed if any of you do, scouts honor, but no one is particularly counting on it one way or the other. There's a betting pool going. I stayed out of it. Nevertheless, there's the other half of it. If you all fail, none of our people had to get hurt in the process. None of the other Battle Born get any clever ideas of how they would get away. They stay here and get whatever story they get, and we try again. Getting the picture now?"

Pity touched my heart for nearly an instant before I was able to remind myself that for all of Skip's outward disgust and sympathy for the victim, he was still here by choice and he would continue to profit from this practice he would have me believe sickened him. I knew better than most that sometimes you had to do something unsavory for the greater good. Worse, I understood intimately what it was like to be used as a tool. None of this applied to Skip. You don't get a watch that nice and the authority to talk down to dangerous men if you didn't compromise yourself along the way.

Then again, who was I talk about being compromised? Even now I had a choice. I could stand up and call Skip out on his hypocrisy and cowardice. I could try to force the antidote out of him if I needed to. I could have likely broken the man in two before anyone outside was any the wiser. But I wanted his information. I wanted him to think I was on his side and indebted to him, grateful to him for his help. So instead I offered a curt nod, and in the most appreciative voice I could muster, I asked, "Where is the Battle Born right now?"

The sun was setting by the time I arrived at the Hawthorne mall. It wouldn't seem possible these days, that a place like this could exist, but seeing was believing in this case. Nearly twenty years ago, the vast shopping center closed up for good, standing as a monument to failure ever since. I had heard rumors recently that there were plans to revitalize it, but then again, there always seemed to be plans to revitalize it. I've had business here in the past. With the exception of a lone security guard and the occasional urban explorer, it was a rare unwatched location in the city, which made it perfect for transactions between discerning parties and for the temporary housing of things that go bump in the night. I'm sure some or all of the above contributed to its stagnation.

Walking around the building gave me enough time to regret that I didn't have more equipment at my disposal. A small set of lockpicks, a fistful of caltrops, and a bit of blinding powder that I had been led to believe was enchanted, but I've since learned was merely Magnesium something or other. It ignited briefly and produced a momentary flash when exposed to the air. Magic or no, it had a use, and I don't suppose I needed to know more about it than that. Still, between what I had at my disposal and my own set of skills, I didn't like my odds if it came down to facing anything with the blood of a god coursing through its veins.

I also didn't have a choice. Two teenagers in football jerseys slowly rode past on bicycles, not giving me much more than a glance, but the impatience I had for them to be out of sight served to remind me that every second I waited was an invitation for one of the bounty hunters to get there before me. I had an advantage at the moment, and if I didn't act now, I'd be squandering this rare piece of good fortune. For Ann's sake, I didn't dare wait a second longer than necessary. The current security guard, an elderly Hispanic man, was making a perimeter check, which allowed me to time my entrance. As it stood, it didn't appear that he bothered to walk along the railroad tracks behind the structure, which made it ideal as an entry point. No one was likely to see me from the street and I welcomed the low likelihood of being discovered.

Most of the entrances to the structure were boarded up with a handful of chains and padlocks on carefully chosen doors. The one I approached was attached to a loading bay behind some defunct department store. A Montgomery Ward, if I didn't miss my guess by the faded color patterns. A couple of thoughts occurred to me as I set to the task of maneuvering a shim into the lock. The first fleeting thought was gratitude to the security personnel for not letting their padlocks rust and thus making my job easier. I'd have the lock open as quickly as someone might have with the actual key. But that gave way for my second, and more alarming thought. If Skip's intel were correct, then it would stand to reason that the Battle Born would have had to remove one of these locks themselves. And even with the bare minimum effort the security provided here, someone would have noticed. A guard could be bribed or convinced to look the other way with a threat to their family, but this wasn't an arms dealer or shrewd businessmen. Arguably, this was the loneliest person in the world. Someone on the lam, a fugitive from a dangerous, clandestine organization. They wouldn't have an expired MetroCard, let alone the resources to make it unnoticed. That didn't discount the idea of a secret entrance or six, but you wouldn't know it your first time here. Hell, I've been here before, and I don't know of any hidden passages. So then, that left the question of the hour, bigger even than how Skip knew where to send me. How did they get inside without anyone noticing?

I unwrapped the excessive amount of chain which had been snaked around the handles of two of the doors which led inside. A good four feet of machinery grade chain links. Over-kill for a door, but then the door probably wasn't used often. Upon further inspection, it seemed clear that the chain was worse for wear compared to the lock. The lock wasn't brand new by any means, but it might as well have been compared to the chain which showed signs of rust. I took a second to con-sider this and it occurred to me that the chain might have been left over from the days when it would have been needed for heavy transport or some such, and it had been abandoned and then repurposed.

There would have been no way to rewrap the door handles after I'd entered and I decided to take it with me, wrapping it around my forearm over the sleeve of my hooded sweater, holding the end of it in my fist, careful to avoid as much skin contact as possible. I cursed lightly under my tongue that the chain had been made of iron for some inexplicable reason and didn't have the courtesy to be stainless steel like its friend, the padlock. I had, for lack of a better term, an allergy that would have made prolonged skin contact uncomfortable, to say the least. All of the Fae did. I didn't have time to stand around and lament all night, however. I opened the doors and slipped in-side. Anyone passing by would be far more likely to miss the detail of the missing chain than they would be quick to spot the lock and chain in a pile at the foot of the door. Besides, this gave me a makeshift weapon. Not enough to instill confidence in my chances in a fight, but it wasn't nothing.

The stench of mildew nearly overwhelmed me the instant I stepped inside. Years of neglect meant that the weather had taken its toll on the structure and stagnant pools of water were everywhere. The only light in the building was what managed to shine in through exposed holes in the roof from either the sun or streetlights. Thankfully my kind did just fine in low light, but I'd be just as blind as anyone in total darkness. I was hoping it wouldn't come to that. My eyes needed at least some external light source to take advantage of my elven eyes, and for the moment I was grateful for what precious little seeped in from above.

I didn't envy the task ahead of me. I was to search for a one-person army in the dark, more or less unarmed, in an unsafe environment that once housed over a hundred stores in the space of more than forty acres. I was a puppy looking for a hibernating demon bear with every intention of waking it and biting its ankles with no idea which cave it might have chosen for its slumber. This was a foolhardy plan for sure, but the one advantage I'd have is that so far as I knew, no one else knew I was coming and the Battle Born might be caught flat-footed. If was to have any chance of success here, it would be to hit early and hit hard.

My daylight advantage was all but gone after twenty minutes of searching, and I was no closer to finding my prey. The outside lights had kicked in, but they didn't extend to the entirety of the enormous shopping center, which made my already glacial-paced search slow even further. At this rate, I could be here all night, and I didn't know how long the Battle Born intended to stay or who else might be coming. I could move faster, but I risked exposing myself and I didn't dare. Slow as it was, I was sure that my movements had been devoid of sound, and Heimdall himself couldn't have seen me without at least squinting for a closer look.

On the other end of things, while I hadn't made a noise, I hadn't heard one either. Not just that I hadn't heard the sound of someone skulking about, I hadn't heard *anything* at all. Not rats or the less natural creatures one might expect to catch of glimpse of after dark. Nothing. I began to get the sense that not only was Skip's information on the money, but everything here had been frightened off by their natural survival instinct to be someplace the big bad murder machine wasn't.

I was on the second floor now, having yielded no results from below. As I made my way through a nameless, long forgotten store, my foot stopped maybe half an inch above a pile of trash. The lighting here was worse than it had been in most of the areas I had searched and stepping on this would have made quite the noise, relatively speaking. Crouching down to get a better look at the refuse, I stared at it with a measure of confusion. I needed the light of my cell phone, now dangerously low on battery, to get a look at what was I was seeing. Sprawled out in front of me, in no discernable order, were dozens of boxes of Little Debbie snack cakes. Swiss Rolls, Zebra Cakes, Nutty Bars; there was indeed no lack of variety. The snacks that had been eaten had the plastic wrappers left in untidy piles, but there were several unopened boxes as well. "This is fresh," I puzzled out loud to myself, rubbing a bit of cream filling between my thumb and forefinger until it was too thin to see. There was no dust on the boxes either. This was very fresh indeed.

"What are you doing here?"

I did my best not to jump at the unexpected sound, but my head shot up all the same.

The source of the question was shrouded in the shadows created by the dim moonlight that found its way into the store. The voice was feminine enough, but the figure was imposing. An inch or two over six feet with wide, muscular shoulders that possibly gave the illusion that the person was wider than they probably were. Currently that illusion equaled the width of cargo van.

"Just a bit of urban exploring," I said, standing up. It wasn't technically a lie, which is always the best answer in these situations. "I'm sorry, was this your food?"

"What is an elf doing exploring an abandoned mall after

dark?"

The tone was accusatory now, and covered ears or no, this person saw me for who I was.

"And does that make you the Battle Born, then?"

I wished almost instantly that I hadn't asked that, but my bad habit of answering with a question to avoid answering directly got the better of me. I had been taken off guard, and my mouth had been quicker than my brain.

There was an uncomfortable pause that was filled with a heavy silence. "I have a name," the woman replied. It came across as a threat.

"Forgive me; I'm sure you that you do," I said apologetically. "Please, hear me out. I don't want to hurt you."

There was a sound like the snort of a bull. "If you know what I am that almost certainly means that you know I escaped, so I'm sure that you'll forgive me if I don't believe you."

If I hadn't been watching closely, I might have missed it. She moved almost too quickly for me to react. I spun on my heel, hoping to land a spinning thrust kick into her stomach and take the wind out of her, but she slammed into me before my leg could extend, sending my body back into the shop, slamming into the wall with a loud crack that I hoped wasn't coming from me. My head was spinning, but instincts were taking over. If I didn't get up and defend myself, my life would come to a very abrupt end.

I'd been knocked down and getting back to my feet proved to be an extremely short-lived victory. A fist hammered down in my direction, and I raised my chain wrapped forearm just in time to avoid having my skull caved in. The chain absorbed some of the blow, but not much, and I was back on the ground less than two seconds after I stood up.

There must have been some reason there wasn't a follow-up attack. Maybe in the dark, I just looked dead. Or maybe the Battle Born just wasn't used to things still breathing after more than one strike. Whatever the reason, it gave me the chance to whip the chain out and wrap it just above her knee. With an effort, I gripped the chain with both hands, ignoring the burning sensation as I threw myself behind her and yanked for everything I was worth.

It worked. The Battle Born went down hard, her feet taken out from underneath her, and there was a wet, sticky sound like a watermelon being punctured. I let go of the chain the instant I was able, desperately trying to avoid going into shock from the pain radiating through my body. My hands were shaking, but I gripped them into fists, willing them to be stiff as I scrambled back in her direction and let loose with a rabbit punch to the base of her neck before she could rise. This was no time to fight fair, and if I were lucky, it would put her down in one go.

Lucky wouldn't be the word to describe me in the following moments, just like unconscious wouldn't be the word you'd use to describe her. There was a sucking, slurping sound as she stood up, and I saw that when she fell it had been hip-first into an exposed piece of rebar that had unfortunately for her punched a hole directly below her ribs. And unfortunately for me, this had all made her quite angry.

The rebar and block of broken concrete were hurled without a word in my direction, but I ducked it quickly enough, only to be shoulder tackled as I stood up straight, sending my body rolling end over end until I was outside of the shop. That had done it. With all the bits of glass and debris on the ground I would have been a mess of small cuts if not for my baggy clothing, and by the time I had lost momentum, my legs chose that moment not to work.

"Please, just listen," I said weakly. Every extra second she wasn't swinging at me could mean the difference between life and death at this point.

The Battle Born didn't seem keen on listening. She walked gingerly out of the store clutching her bleeding side. I managed to pull myself up into a sitting position, but that was about as good as it was going to get for the moment. She didn't slow down as she approached me, her free hand balled up into a fist. If I didn't think of something quickly, I would—

The blinding powder!

Looking away and shutting my eyes tightly, I shot my hand into the pocket of my hoodie and retrieved the tiny pouch, flinging it in her direction in one fluid motion. I saw the flash of red through my eyelids and heard a cry of surprise. I also felt like I'd been struck with a battering ram as gravity suddenly embraced me, my eyes opened wide to see the ceiling rush away from me as I plummeted towards the ground.

My people don't require sleep, not in the traditional sense.

An intense chill filled the air around me. I wasn't sure where I was or what had happened to me, but it must have been traumatic. I knew what this was. I was beginning to trance.

If you ever see an elf taking a nap, you can consider that their idea of a recreational activity. To recover, we enter a sort of inert state not unlike meditation. While our bodies rest, our minds expand, and we are capable of giving serious consideration to whatever matter is currently weighing heavily upon us. Once, when I was young, I had tranced for eight hours and considered what I should have for breakfast when I came out of it. Not every trance has to be meaningful.

But sometimes, if we weren't careful, our trance can take on a mind of its own, forcing us to relive moments or events that hold some sort of meaning for us. Negative or positive is unimportant, it's the weight of the thing. And I've been forced to live through far too much to ever consider taking the experience lightly. Unfortunately, somewhere out there in the world, something terrible must have happened to me because I could feel a very significant event coming on, hitting me with the force of a dam break. This was something that I've spent most of my life trying not to remember, and if something this repressed was finally breaking free, I could only assume that I was in an awful sort of way.

The thought that this might be the last thing I ever experienced seized me suddenly, the fear of it giving me even less control of the trance. There was no reigning it in now; I'd just have to ride it out and hope for the best. The process of experiencing days, weeks, or even years in the span of a few hours could be unnerving, depending on how prepared you were for it. I was not prepared. I knew exactly what I was about to experience, that I would see, hear and feel these things for the first time and yet I knew every second of every minute and I would have no control over the outcome. I was an unwilling observer of my own life.

My eyes open to see my lover watching me with something like bemused admiration. "I was starting to think you might sleep through lunch," he teases. Our bodies face each other as we lay on the soft bedding, our feet a tangled mess of gentle familiarity. The sun shines aggressively into our clay hut, suggesting that he wasn't entirely joking.

"Good morning yourself." I feel my smile tighten in spite of myself. "You know that sleeping is still new to me. Besides, do you have somewhere else to be?"

I lean in to give him the briefest of kisses, the joy I feel at his acceptance and love fighting for position in the pit of my stomach with the rising disgust and embarrassment I feel at knowing where this all ends.

"I can't think of anywhere else I'd rather be," he tells me, running a finger down my arm. I believe him and welcome his touch. The rage I feel never shows. This already happened.

My eyes widen suddenly with the knowledge that I was supposed to help my mother this morning, and I have no idea how late I am. Alistair teases me, then tries to coax me back into bed. I laugh joyously, regardless of the anxiety that normally comes from my mother's potential disappointment. I dress as quickly as possible while Alistair sits up and watches me with a look of contentment. "Fine, I surrender," he says with a smile. "But tonight I have something of vital importance to tell you. Promise me we can speak over dinner?"

"Promise," I tell him, hastily slipping on a boot.

"Promise-promise?" he asks.

"Yes! Promise-promise!" I nearly squeal. I lean in for another kiss before he can respond. "But I really have to go! Be a good boy, all right?"

He laughs at that. "I don't know why I'd start now!"

I throw his shirt at him, and he allows it to land on his head, covering his face. I blow him a kiss that he cannot see, and I'm out the door faster than he knows.

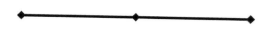

"So, what was it that you had to tell me?" I ask Alistair. It is dark now, and we are sharing a meal on a stone table, the warmth of a nearby fire pit staving off the chilly night air.

"It's not what sort of meat this is," he responds sardonically as he pokes his meal apprehensively. "I don't know that I want to know what this is."

"Quit playing with your food," I chide, taking another bite of my own. I briefly ponder if the meal is still vegetarian if the plant produces meat.

Boldly chomping into my food seems to embolden him to take a bite of his own. His face registers displeasure, but he powers with gusto. "I have to go," he says finally.

My stomach drops at the news. Just like that, no warning. Alistair is leaving me. He sees it on my face and holds up a hand to indicate that there's more. "This isn't bad news," he reassures me. "I've been here far longer than I was ever meant to be, and I have a job I must return to. You must have known this day would come."

I did, not that I ever wanted to admit it. "So, what happens now?" The question comes out of me robotically.

"Well, come with me."

"Alistair!" I exclaim, unable to help myself. "It's not that simple! If I leave, that's it for me. I'll never be able to return, never again be able to see my mother! I would never—!"

His hand covers mine, and I fall silent. "I know," he says gently. "This is not a small thing that I ask of you. But where I am from, it is customary that birds leave the nest. That is to say, you've grown beyond this place. This is it, Chalsarda. This is when you fly. Together, we can have our adventures, seek our fortunes. See the unseen!"

"But my mother—"

"Speak with her," he suggests. "And take the time you need to decide. I wouldn't ask you to do anything I didn't think you could do. I know this is right for us. We are in love, and a whole world is waiting for us out there. In the morning I will be gone, and I lack the ability to take you with me besides. But there is another who can help you. If you choose to stay, I will miss you dearly and remember you always. But if you come with, that is, if you come to me... Well, right, you've never been outside of the town, have you? Hold on."

Alistair is frantic as he runs inside, returning with charcoal and parchment. "This is the way," he begins as he draws a map, first of our town, then our roads and surrounding areas. "So, the road to the south of town winds a little bit down, about a mile or so away is a creek."

I tease him in spite of myself. "Yes, I know all this, we sell maps. Have you not noticed the traders?"

Alistair looks flushed with embarrassment at that. "Right. Yes, of course. Well then, this will be your special one of a kind map in that case, with something you might not have seen."

He goes on to explain that past the river there is a fork in the road. To the east lies plains and farmland, but I am to head to the west. About half a day's travel I will spot an enormous rock that looks like a crow. I ask him what a crow is. He waves it off and tells me that from there I must leave the path and venture into the forest. He will mark a path for me by way of string, but to be careful as the area is home to bears. I ask him what bears are. He reminds me of my rug, and I nod. We do not call them bears, but I don't press the issue. He is eager to finish his story. In a clearing some ways in, I will find a door. The door shall be held for me on the other side, a week's time and no longer. I do not understand what he means by the other side, but before I can ask further questions his fingers weave through my hair as his hands draw me into him and he kisses me. I am unable to correctly process the competing forces of revulsion and the sense that time itself has stopped.

"If this is to be our last night together," he says, brushing away a lock of hair resting against my jaw as he searches for something in my eyes, "then may we do everything necessary to remember each other forever."

It is lovely and romantic, and it's all wrong.

The days following are hard and pass by painfully; I'm watching them as they happened, playing out in my mind's eye now as minutes. But I remember the void left in his absence. I had

become accustomed to his presence, and just like that, he was gone. It is the fourth day when my mother approaches me. She knows even before I tell her.

I'm not ready.

This is the clearest vision of her yet, my attention focused solely on this memory and I'm not... I couldn't have prepared for... She is just so—

I miss my mother.

As she comes into focus, I take in everything I can the way one lost in the desert takes in an oasis. Her hair is the color of snow, not from age but from birth. Her pale, violet-colored eyes like sun-bleached amethyst, still vibrant but gentler somehow and they seem to brighten as they see me. Her eyes are one of the traits I did not inherit from my mother, those eyes lacking any white or pupil, just one solid and captivating color. My father, a different sort of elf, had eyes much closer to those of the humans, and I ended up with those. Her skin was also not quite like mine, reminding me of the palest of periwinkles but shone with the smoothness of stone polished by the patience only time itself can offer. In contrast to the paleness in other parts of her, her smile shines brighter than any sunrise as the human child eagerly accepts the poultices and salves my mother hands him, no doubt as part of a delivery. There should be nothing extraordinary about this memory, it is routine even, but I cherish it all the same.

It has been so long since I've had a memory of her this vivid and I want nothing more than for this moment to stretch out into eternity. That's not how this works, however. I am merely a passenger in my story, unable to stop myself or any of this. I will always leave, and even now as I try to block out my own voice, I hear it. I address my mother by her name, Aeleth, in some childish attempt to show that I am grown and capable of making this decision. It is time for me to say goodbye to the friendly roads of Verisia. There is more to be seen than can *ever be seen, and I can't stay here. She has taught me so much, how to mix elixirs to heal the infirm with that which has been given to us by the earth. How to defend the defenseless, and more importantly, why it is always best to help others in need. But most of all, she has taught me how to be kind, and the world can always use more kindness.*

I don't tell her my other reasons. I want to slay great beasts and revel in the glory as the names of Chalsarda and Alistair are sung about in taverns. That I want to have a grand love affair that will make poets blush and great lovers frustrated at their own envy. I want to get so deep into trouble with my beloved that the only light either of us will be able to see will be in each other's eyes as we laugh at the joke that only the two of us are in on. That when we get away, as we always will, our story will just be that much more impressive because of the odds stacked up against us.

I am a fool.

She doesn't try to stop me, of course. If anything, she says she always knew this day would come and wishes me well. Her path is not my path, but she will never forget me, and I promise to always remember her and to take what she taught me into the world beyond our walls. There's no further ceremony, no going away feast or speech in the town square. I'm up and gone as the sun rises the next morning without any tearful goodbyes because deep down I had wanted to leave so badly that from the moment I stepped out onto the road I had never stopped to consider where it was that I was going. I'm just filled with a sense of adventure, the nervous expectation that I'm coming for my love.

Alistair left adequate instructions, though he underestimated the pace with which I would travel, and I am over the river and through the woods well before the sun had its chance to reach the height of midday. I had not, however, expected there to be a literal door in the middle of a clearing, regardless of what Alistair had told me. It was a door, yes, nothing special about the wood, painted white. Brass handle on either side, but it was not attached to anything. No hinges, nothing on either side of it. I could simultaneously touch both sides of the door, and I did. I was meant to open it, surely, but what could that possibly accomplish? Did it matter what side I tried to open? If I pulled it open or pushed? And that's when a that's when a thought so obvious occurred to me that I laughed at the stupidity of it.

I knocked.

There was a beat, nothing but the sounds of the woods, and then a voice from thin air invited me to come in. Well, I had come this far, so why not? I opened the door and stepped through, and found myself in another world. Where there had just been daylight and serene forest, it was now twilight and vast desert. At the time, I didn't even know what desert was, but that was it. Nothing more for another moment, then soft tones played across a gentle wind, and behind me a voice. I turned and recognized what he was in an instant, though not who. Not elf or human or anything else. Something greater. He regarded me with a smile, knew my name. I must be the one Alistair mentioned. I ask him his name, but he assures me it doesn't matter. Even then, I know that is false, but not a lie. He apologies for the delay, then makes a wry comment that he hopes nothing else has come through. Enough of that, however, he says, we have business to discuss.

We are in something best described as the middle. The halfway point between my world and his. I can turn back now, and that will be the end of it. Alistair will be lost to me. Or I can accept a trade. An item of fantastic power that can take me to Alistair and back again. The description and the origin sound beyond belief, but I know the words ring true. The deal then is this. Alistair helps him on occasion, but the lives of humans are fickle. The item is mine forever, never to be with-

drawn and I may use it to visit his world. However, at such time as our relationship ends, likely after what humans would consider a long and healthy lifetime; I am to return to him to work in his service for such a time that he deems appropriate to the value of the gift, doing the tasks he feels that I am best suited for.

I am screaming now. I know better, I know that I cannot change what has happened, but I do not care. I know how this will end, and I am fighting it with everything in me, because just once I want to view another account of this. An account where I ask questions, an account where I am not taken in by the showy bauble, an account where I don't blindly believe an obvious serpent because he is promising to give me access to a life that I think I want and know now that I will never have. I have no form here, no legs with which to kick or arms with which to slam fists on the inside of my own skull; just thought and a voice that only I can hear. Not even a throat to rend raw with my screams.

So it's what I do. I beg and plead and shout every curse and offer every bargain as I watch myself accept the deal. As I look into those ethereal blue eyes, never questioning why they are so hungry. I reach my hand out to his, never questioning why it has been put towards mine so eagerly. I do this until the screaming isn't just my own, nor is the pleading, and I'm confused.

And then I'm awake and aware of where I am. Ann, my dear, dying friend who should be very far away from me, is pleading with me to wake up. And more importantly, pleading with universe that I am not dead.

6

"Why are you here?" It wasn't the most elegant or sensitive question all things considered, but the fact that I was forming words into phrases at all was a minor miracle.

Any annoyance Ann may have felt at the question was drowned by her concern for my well-being. "You called me, remember?"

"Early days," I replied sheepishly, squinting to keep the beam of Ann's flashlight out of my eyes.

"I rushed out here as fast as I could! You sounded like you might be dying or drunk. Or both," Ann continued. "And I think it was a J.C. Penney, not a Montgomery Ward."

I hadn't remembered calling Ann, but sure enough, I found my phone in my hand, now completely drained of its battery. "How long?"

"Just about two hours ago," Ann confirmed. "You're lucky it's a warm night, and you had that sweater otherwise you might have... Ignore that. What the crap happened here?"

An excellent question and one I wasn't entirely prepared

to answer yet, though it was all coming back to me in waves now. I was in an abandoned mall, looking up through a hole in a ceiling at a clear night sky, stars obscured from my vision by the surrounding city lights. I was also sitting in a shallow puddle of stagnant water that threatened infection should any of it seep into an open cut. I tried to sit up, and I was introduced to significant stiffness throughout my body, and that's when I remembered the entirely one-sided fight. 'Fight' might have been generous. But nothing was broken, so I'd have to count that as a win.

"I was tracking someone," I stammered, still not ready for more complex sentences. "There was a fight."

"Okay, well, who were you fighting? And why?"

Just a moment longer and I'd be good to stand. "A Battle Born. For you."

Ann nodded as if she was starting to understand. "This has to do with Alistair. And what's a Battle Born?"

"You met one," I explained, gingerly getting to my feet. "Whatever I just fought, I felt the same energy in Roger's office last year. They're very powerful, born of gods, but they're not gods themselves. It is difficult to explain."

Ann gave me an understanding look, and I knew that memory was still fresh in her mind, though our potentially meeting a Battle Born was likely the least memorable moment of that encounter. She'd had her mind transferred into an echo of a memory of the life of an old friend of hers, she watched Elana get punched through the window of an office highrise by a child with super strength, something Elana managed to walk away from, and the footnote would have been the Battle Born.

"Well, next time maybe you don't fight it then." Coming from Ann, it came out as obvious and sarcastic, rather than a suggestion.

I shook my head at that. "Might not have a choice in the matter. If I ever see it again, that is."

"Well, whatever you're going to do, we need to do it somewhere else. I wasn't subtle when I ran in here, and security is probably calling the cops." Ann was beginning to lend me her shoulder in case I had trouble standing.

"Wait!" I exclaimed, startling her and echoing my voice throughout the corridors. I knew immediately that waking up something in here would be a remarkably stupid thing to do, but the thought came to me so suddenly and urgently that shouting was the only reasonable reaction. "Shine your torch ahead of me and stay close. It should still be there!"

"What? What do you need that badly?"

"Blood." The bluntness of my reply visibly took Ann off guard. "Oh don't look at me like that, it's not mine."

Her face contorted at that, but she nodded in agreement, handing me her light and holding onto the back of my sweater as we negotiated our way up the decommissioned escalator. It took a couple of precious minutes to make our way to the room I'd encountered the Battle Born in, but it was still there, plenty of it in fact. In the spot where the Battle Born had been wounded was a fair amount of blood. Most of it had dried and would be useless for our purposes, but luck was on our side as much of what had pooled into a spot on the floor missing a chunk of concrete. The combination of the cold night air and the sheer amount of it may have very well been our salvation.

My sweater was off in an instant, and one of the dry parts was pressed into the pool, sopping up what I could into the absorbent cotton. "I guess your monster had a sweet tooth?" Ann asked, examining the refuse. "And what are you going to do with a blood-soaked hoodie?"

"Not me," I replied with a grin. "You. You are going to find her with the blood."

"Like I'm going to follow the literal trail of blood out of the building or like an augury?"

I shook my head, pressing the sweater into the ground.

"No, an augury would be a waste. We already know that finding her portends a bad day for anyone. No, you're going to scry for her."

"Me?" A genuine surprise came from that response. "I'm still super new to the whole magic thing, and besides, it looks like we could really use the extra help with whatever we're dealing with. I really think we need to get Elana involved with this, maybe just the whole crew."

"Absolutely not." I stood now to face her and said it more sternly than I intended, but I'd had a rough night. "Suppose we do as you suggest and involve Elana. What do you think she will do?"

Ann was at a loss for words but finally gave it a guess. "Magic?"

"And a lot of it, no doubt. But this is not a problem that can be solved with magic, not entirely. Allow me to tell you what I think Elana will do with the news. Upon hearing that her friend has been poisoned and that I need to capture a godling to find your cure, Elana will shake her rod over her head with righteous fury, making declamatory statements about beating up all the bad guys, and then run headlong at the problem. And probably die."

"Harsh."

"Perhaps, and I don't say it to disparage her character, but she is not what we need right now. More to the point, she's not prepared for what we are to face, and neither are we, quite frankly. But we are involved one way or the other. If anyone else gets hurt after we involve them, their blood will be on our hands." I looked at my sweater and realized what I was holding. "Metaphorically speaking, of course."

"Okay." Ann seemed to be musing more than conceding. "So just what are we facing here? Why did you of all people, run headlong at your problem and you know, almost die?"

The hypocrisy of my own words stung now, however justified I felt in making them. "Alistair is a traveler, like Elana. He also has just a bit over two hundred years of experience as a wizard on Elana which makes him extremely dangerous. But his weakness is not wanting to get involved directly. He's stayed alive all of this time by manipulating others into doing his heavy lifting, as he's done with me in this scenario. Alistair has decided that there's a bounty he wants to collect, one on a Battle Born, and I need to do it before anyone else if you are to get your antidote."

"Okay, that sounds bad." Ann began to lose her calm by inches as she continued. "Like, all of it. Hopeless even. I mean, a two hundred-year-old wizard? He could do anything he wants! And even if you manage to capture this person, and no offense, but yeah, we don't have any promise that Alistair will give you the cure. Or that I'll get it in time, or—"

"That's enough!" I snapped. It wasn't gentle, but gentle wasn't going to hold her attention. "This situation is a lot of things. It is ethically questionable, it is grim, and it is desperate. But it is not hopeless. Never that."

Ann's face flushed with anger for the briefest of moments at that, either from the tone of my voice or the embarrassment of being seen as afraid—likely both—but in that moment I could see the type of person she would grow into one day. I could see her standing up for herself and others. I saw her as someone who would refuse to give in when all seemed lost, and it filled me with pride. I didn't need to be a Sibyl to see that; I just hoped that she didn't lose the more innocent parts of her being in the process.

She wasn't going to respond, which left it to me to bring the conversation back down to earth before it rose to a level neither of us would be comfortable with. "We just have to be smart. Neither of us is dead yet and the Ann I know wouldn't give up this early, would she?"

Ann huffed at that. "Of course not, that's not what I was

saying!"

"Good, because just as badly as I would like to win, I want Alistair to lose. We will survive this; we just need to be smart and decisive."

"I get what you're trying to do, and I appreciate it," Ann said after a breath. "And I'm onboard; we go down swinging. Awesome. But let's be honest with each other at least. I'm going to be useless against an honest to god full-blown wizard, and after I heard about what happened with Freyja, you're lucky to be alive if you just fought anything even remotely god related. And if I'm reading you right, there's something else you haven't told me, isn't there?"

There was, but it could wait. Instead, I opted to address our most immediate concern. "She may have the blood of a god running through her veins, but she is still just flesh and bone. If she can bleed, I can kill her. Believe in me; I can do this."

There was a palpable stillness in the air as I said those words. Ann's breathing stopped as she stared at me with eyes that even in the dark were clear enough to fill me with guilt. "Why would you kill her?"

It was a fair and pointed question, and there was no way around it. "I've seen what they can do. I doubt I can capture her, and your life depends upon her return."

"Does she deserve to die?"

My stomach fell at that. "No. However—"

"Is she guilty of any crime that you would deem worthy of death?"

"No."

Another breathless pause. "Okay, I have one question for you, just one. And I know you can't lie, but as my friend, will you promise to answer me without trying to twist the words? Just a yes or no, that's what I need from you."

I hesitated, just a second, and I believe she was aware of what that pause meant. But I gave her the answer she wanted, and I'd hoped that counted for something. "I promise."

"Have you killed before? People who didn't deserve it?"

"Yes." The word came out of me softer than I thought possible, and it carried with it an enormous amount of shame. Memories I had wished to keep locked away forever.

Ann nodded a couple of times, more for herself than for me, I suspected. "I'm not judging you. I swear I'm not, and I hope you know that. You don't need to talk about it. I understand that for a long time you may not have had a choice, I get that. But you do now, okay? So if we're talking about my life, I don't want you to kill anyone you don't have to. I mean it, that's not what my life is worth. Whatever happened before, this is different. You can be different. You can be better."

Real tears formed before I could stop them, and I hoped they wouldn't be visible in the dim illumination of moonlight and streetlamps filtered through a roof in disrepair. Ann didn't know what she was talking about; there was no way she could have because if she had, I doubt very much she would have said that to me. I managed to say the only words that I could. "That's not fair."

"I wasn't trying to be."

I felt a rise of anger well up inside of me at that, the sort of instinct to bring harm to someone in the instant after they've hurt you. I wanted to use words like 'ignorant', 'ungrateful', and 'child', but that desire faded into the darkness around us as soon as it had appeared. Ann was treading over my past with all the delicacy of a military parade, and to make it worse, she was choosing now of all times to impose her values on me. But then again, if not now, when? After I killed in her name? If this meant that much to her, she would bear the guilt of not speaking up when she had the chance. Either way, I was too tired to argue the point any further. Tired and drained.

"Let's just get to your car." My words were heavy and left no room for debate. Not that I'm sure that anyone wanted to.

The two of us reached the street without incident, either from the local authorities or anything that may have been hiding in the shadows. Perhaps they had seen what I just fought, and the fact that I wasn't dead served as a warning to anything that may have seen us as fast food. Those things are few and far between, admittedly. Most things are smart enough not to draw attention to themselves and where they sleep. Kill one mortal, you attract the attention of the police who suddenly want to check every nook and cranny, and for creatures whose continued existence requires living in shadows, a forty-acre abandoned mall is about as good a home as they're likely to find. Still, that doesn't mean that something hungry enough or greedy enough to abandon common sense doesn't exist, which meant that in my dazed state I had invited my friend to take a stroll straight through a dragon's cave.

Not a literal dragon, of course, I doubt one of those would be caught dead in a place like this, but when you're squishy enough, there's no real measurable difference between a dragon and anything else with claws and teeth and the ability to rend your flesh before you can react. Maybe the lack of fire, but that was academic at that point. I decided against telling Ann how much danger she had been in or, bloody hell, how much danger I had been in with my extended break out in the open like that. She had enough to worry about for the moment, and something told me that she wasn't planning on going back in anytime soon.

We needed to secure a map of the area—a real one that is, not something on a screen, a task that proved more difficult than it ought to have been. Seven gas stations later, we tried an auto parts store a mere fifteen minutes before they would be closed for the evening, and we lucked out with our prize. It was a good thing too, as I was equally likely to throttle the next person who laughed at the idea of paper maps in the era of GPS as I was to burgle an arts and crafts store and create my own from memory. Ann must have sensed my discomfort as she took me home wordlessly.

The ride home was uncomfortable and silent; the weight of the situation had put a space between us for just a little while, where no conversation could survive. I had been beaten and forced to relive some of my darkest memories, and Ann had been forced to discover her friend and instructor looking like death warmed over and then immediately confronted with simple truths that she did not know she was not ready to hear, no matter how much she may have suspected. Once we entered the house, however, it was a different matter altogether. Ann was immediately her inquisitive self, perhaps believing that the long drive back was enough for me to get over our uncomfortable moment, or maybe that coming to my rescue and acting as chauffeur had earned her the right to answers when we were in the privacy of my temporary home. If that had been her thought, of course, she'd have been more or less correct. I wasn't keen on staying upset, and she'd dropped everything and run into the dark to help me. Of course, I was willing to speak with her.

"Okay, we have our Hercules blood, and the best cartography Triple A could afford on an entry-level salary. So what do you want me to do with it?"

"Getting right to it then?" I asked. "No time for a drink?"

Ann tapped her fingernail brusquely into her necklace, creating a sharp tapping sound as acrylic met ceramic. "In the past day, one of us was nearly pummeled to death, and the other was literally poisoned by an evil wizard, so how long of a break do you think we should take?"

My mouth opened in surprise at that, and I needed a moment to formulate a response. She wasn't being unreasonable by any stretch, but she had caught me off guard. "You are, of course, right. I don't know what I was thinking, let's get started."

Impatience gave way to frustration on Ann's face. "No, I didn't mean that, I just... ahhh!" Her shout wasn't exactly a battle cry, but it conveyed her meaning well enough. "I'm sorry, it's just been a really long night. I know you're doing all of this for me, I'm just not, I don't know, handling it well."

"It is as you said. You're trying to assist an elf in defeating a godling and along the way perhaps outwit the centuries-old wizard who poisoned you." I began, placing a reassuring hand on her shoulder, giving her the kindest look I could muster at the moment. "I'd say you're doing just fine."

Ann smiled timidly at that. "Well when you say it like, I sound stupid."

"Come on then, one more task for the night before we rest. We'll be no good on the hunt if we pass out."

I unfolded the map of the greater Los Angeles area in the middle of the living room, and I instructed Ann to bring the blood-soaked hoodie over to it. "We have one secret weapon at our disposal here, and that is you. I personally find Thaumaturers distasteful, but we're not using your blood, and this is not Thaumaturgy. Just, try to avoid working with your own blood. I'm not trying to be a mother hen about this, but—"

"I do solemnly swear not to cut myself open to perform magic unless I like, really need to. Now, what's the deal?"

My lips were pursed involuntarily at the notion that I'd become sidetracked, but also that my well-informed caution had been summarily dismissed. Now was not the time either way. "You're going to attempt to scry. As I mentioned, an augury won't tell us anything we don't already know. The extraordinarily violent person who doesn't want to be caught will do violence if we catch them. But with their blood, you should have no trouble finding them, and if we know where they are, we can plan accordingly."

"I mean, I can try, but I've never done this for real, and definitely not with someone's blood."

Her voice was unsure, but all the same, I encouraged her. Not just because I knew she could do it, but because it was the only play we had at the moment, and the fresher the blood, the better her odds. If she couldn't perform the scry, we would be back at square one, but I didn't anticipate any opposition to the scry. The being wasn't strictly magical by nature, and I doubted anyone would bother or have the means to provide any interference. Maybe an important task completed and a step in the right direction would be precisely the morale boost we both needed.

Ann began the ritual, and in watching her, I was reminded of just how little magical talent she actually had. Others had a well of magic inside of them; she may very well have had a puddle. Nothing close to someone like Alistair or Olivia; even Elana looked considerable next to her. I have no magical talent of my own, but I've been around it long enough that I can see it on someone, and my friend didn't have much. But Ann understood the process almost preternaturally; the mechanics of magic came to her like a second nature, and often times I've seen competency win where raw strength failed.

I watched in astonishment; maybe thirty seconds had gone by, and the scry was already working. I've seen them take hours to perform, so either Ann was exceptionally gifted at this task or the materials made it easy. A drop of blood formed from my ruined garment and floated lazily to the map before coming to rest in a community I was all too familiar with. For her part, tears streamed down Ann's face involuntarily, and she exhaled something like a relieved laugh. "I—I think I did it!" she panted, looking down at the drop of blood on the map. "But what does it mean?"

I studied the area, making sure I was absolutely certain of what I saw before I answered. "You know how I tried to tell you what I was up against, and you said there was something else that you were sure I wasn't telling you?"

"Yes?"

I sighed, holding the map up in front of my face with both hands. "Well, there's something else I wasn't telling you."

7

A nn took the news of our competition better than I
thought she would.

"Yeah, of course they are." She delivered the
line with such a sense of obviousness that I almost felt silly for
not telling her earlier. "They want to get paid; someone wants
to pay them. Supply and demand are a hell of a thing. At least
there are only three of them."

"About that," I began, pointing out the blood drip on the
map. "That's Venice. Meaning if the Abbot doesn't already
have her, he's well on his way. The man has more than two
hundred followers, a hodgepodge collection of the homeless,
vendors or employees, wealthy locals, and he has eyes everywhere. I think he might notice."

Ann chewed her lip thoughtfully for a moment. "Well,
maybe not. Think about it. Or, you know, think about it like a
story, which is what I've started to do with all the fairly recent
weirdness. So, this Abbot dude, you said his strength is mainly
charisma, right? Leading the flock and all that? And Venice
might be his stronghold, but that's fairly out of the way, and

it's not close to the other locations that you've been to. If we're assuming that the Coliseum was the location that the Battle Born actually escaped from and wasn't just a random ass spot where they made them fight, then you can only track movement between here and here."

Ann pointed out on the map the distance to the Coliseum from the Hawthorne Shopping center, which according to the map's legend was about a ten mile straight shot through South Central LA, more or less. "So, we have questions, sure. The first question isn't how she got from point A to point B. We don't know how long she had to get there or even if the Coliseum was where she actually escaped from. But! Look! Hawthorne to Venice! How far is that?"

Standing behind her and looking over her shoulder, I followed the trail she made with her finger from the abandoned mall to the little blood dot. "Maybe twelve miles? Assuming you go around the marina and you don't swim through it, we're talking fourteen or fifteen miles, so what?"

"So consider the clues! How did she get there? She's being hunted, right? So she's not going to sprint through the city, no matter what time of day it is. It's why she was hiding in the first place. And we know she doesn't have access to Lyft or Uber, no means of income to pay a taxi unless she mugged someone, so maybe, but for my own mental health let's assume not. No friends even, she's lived a life of captivity. And we know she wasn't in a hotel, she was in a condemned structure. And if you add the hour and a half it took for me to get to you, the hour or so it took to get home, and thirty minutes we spent chasing a map, we know exactly how long she had to get across town."

"And she was injured, besides, I poked a hole in her," I remarked.

"Yeah! If anything, that really should have slowed her down. So what do we know?"

"She couldn't have made it on foot," I thought out loud.

"Which means she either had help, or someone picked her up!" Ann exclaimed. "And don't forget, even injured she almost killed you. So what are a bunch of cult members going to do? It would make sense that the Abbot sent out his followers all over the city, but individually they don't stand a chance, do they?"

"No, but the Abbot himself might," I mused. "As little power as he has, he still possesses a measure of magic, and we don't know what sort of tricks he could have planned for this. So that means that the Abbot himself captured the Battle Born or…"

I trailed off, and Ann let the statement hang in the air for a moment before finishing for me. "She got a ride there! One more thing we both noticed. The food. Dozens of snack cakes! Where did they come from?"

"She could have grabbed a whole box of them off a delivery truck at a supermarket, not knowing what she was getting."

"Maybe. Or it could have been delivered."

I had thought that could be the case, but no, there was no evidence to support that. "Possible, but we should stick to facts, for now, so ignore the food. The Battle Born was bleeding out here, and a few hours later she's here. And she's not—"

I didn't feel my legs give out from underneath me as much as I experienced the sensation of losing a fight with gravity as I collapsed to the floor. Ann started to say something, but I waved her off before she could get too excited. "It's nothing, just a little weak from earlier. Perhaps this should wait until morning."

Nervous eyes scanned my body and searched my eyes before Ann offered a curt nod. "The map is… we don't have to worry about doing this again, it's tuned to her now. We can follow her anywhere she goes as long as it's on the map. Just… sleep, I guess?"

"Yes, bright and early tomorrow, I'll be good as new."

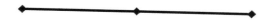

I was terrified of falling into another trance knowing what I'd see and remembering how little control I had with the last one, so I decided to fall back on that old adage: When in Thousand Oaks, sleep as the humans do. I didn't get more than four hours of rest, but it would have to do. At any rate, the couch wasn't as comfortable as I would have liked, and I was confident that I was awake before Ann. Hearing no noise from the bedroom at the top of the steps, I retrieved the now-charged phone, which was on loan from Alistair, from the kitchen counter, and I walked to the back door and looked out at pre-dawn colors and sparse lighting. This far out of the city, I was able to enjoy at least the idea of the sky. The descending color gradient of mostly starless black, fading into a navy blue with a thin horizon of a glowing golden orange with just a hint of burnt red underneath. It was calming. It wouldn't last. The sun would obliterate this portrait soon; the sun would come up despite any efforts to the contrary.

The phone made a sound effect announcing that its coming to life was a matter of some importance, and my eyes left the sunrise to the phone and then to the wards I'd placed next to the sliding glass door as well as the other doors and windows in the house. I frowned. They weren't set by a practicing magic user, no invisible webs of spells. Just blessed sprigs of holly and minor sigils etched into wood carvings. A whole lot of good they'd done to prevent my current situation. They may very well have even garnered the attention of someone like Alistair, and they wouldn't be needed for the things they'd actually work against. And for the things that may give me real trouble they'd be at best a minor irritant.

On the one hand, having never had access to magic, I'd never grown reliant on it. But when you're up against a remorseless, sociopath wizard, god spawns, and an entire bloody organization of reality-bending idiots, or to put it another way, up against the wall; it's easy to feel like a stick and string might not be enough, no matter how many times making pincushions out of enemies had worked in the past.

Just then the phone lit up for the second time, and when I answered, the voice on the other end of the line reminded me of exactly how satisfying making pincushions could be.

"Did you really have your phone turned off?" Alistair demanded. "Because last I checked, I asked you to be on bloody call! If I have to—"

"Oh sod off, yeah?" I exclaimed into the phone, temporarily forgetting the hour. I hadn't slept well and every bad thing that had happened in the last twenty-four hours could be directly attributed to him. "I'm in no mood."

"Well, you'd best get in the mood, because—"

"Because what?" I cut him off a second time, knowing exactly how infuriating that would be to him. "Because you'll poison my friend? A bit late on that one, eh?"

I could hear the controlled breaths through the phone before Alistair responded to that question. "Because it sure would be a shame if a certain bookstore burned to the ground in the middle of the night, and I'd hate to think that your courtesy was the sole thing that could have prevented that tragedy. Why, I even hear someone is living in there!"

A throaty laugh escaped my body in spite of myself. "Oh gods, I'd love to see you try, I really would! You mean to tell me you'd attack someone under the direct protection of Abarta? And that's not to mention the deal she just struck with Freyja, if you can believe it. And before you feign surprise, let's not kid ourselves and pretend you didn't know. Come to think of it, for as much of a crash as she might be headed for, Elana Black may very well be the safest person in the world at the moment. That goes for her friends, by the way, in case you thought of a second clever plan. No, you're greedy, but you're not suicidal."

"If any of that were true, then why aren't the gods raining hellfire and plagues all around me right this minute, eh? Where's that white-hot fury you're so keen to promise me?"

The frustration and anger were rising in Alistair's voice, and if he hurried, those levels might just reach mine. This wasn't the conversation he expected when he called, but it was undoubtedly the one he was getting. "No, you know what? I'm glad you asked because there's something you'd better know from this moment on. The only reason I've agreed to your deal is because what's done is done. By the time you've been relieved of the burden of having limbs, I'll be chancing that I can save my friend without your antidote and that's not a risk I'm willing to take at the moment. You enjoy this small victory while it lasts because this is the only one you're going to get. If you so much as dream about any of them after our business is concluded, there won't be enough of you left over to dust off of my boots! Are we clear?"

I gave Alistair a whole four seconds to respond, and all he managed were a couple of angry snorts where words had failed him. "That's about what I expected. Now if you're interested in my getting back to work, I'll thank you to hang up and maybe get into a staring contest with a gorgon if you still feel the need to bother someone."

The screen glowed as I took the phone away from my face and hung up the phone before Alistair could respond. I was certain he was incensed wherever he was; he might have even come up with a clever comeback by now. There was something cathartic about telling Alistair off and taking away whatever sense of power he might have had. The mere sound of his voice or the mention of his name was enough to make me tense up and ready to chew through a cinder block. And yet, putting him off his game, letting him know that he didn't hold all the cards was, well, it was the sort of dull endorphin rush you might get from popping a dislocated shoulder back into place.

I missed the sunrise. At least the best part of it. I'd been so focused on the call that the brief, almost insubstantial amount of time came and went. Two minutes that would have made the day that much more tolerable came and went. Perfect timing on Alistair's score, if that was his intention. It wouldn't surprise me.

"Telemarketers?" Ann called from the top of the stairs with a yawn that she made no attempt to hide.

My face flushed at that and I sighed, tossing the phone onto the counter without a care for its state when it landed. "I'm sorry, my friend, I didn't think I'd wake you."

"For real? I wouldn't be surprised if they heard you in Venice."

"It was Alistair," I admitted.

"Yeah, I gathered. So we're up now, I guess. Besides coffee, what's our plan?"

"Our plan?"

"Yeah, our plan. How are we doing this?"

"We aren't doing anything," I said bluntly. "Unless you've lost your reservations about dying before thirty, you're staying put. You're already dying, so let's not expedite the process, shall we?"

"Oh hell no!" Ann's voice rose in a challenge that nearly took me off guard. I still wasn't in the mood to deal with anyone, but that didn't slow Ann down in the slightest.

She stomped down the stairs, trying to put as much of her weight into each step as she could. "This is still my life we're talking about, isn't it? And I know you're not a hypocrite, so you must have an excellent reason why you overruled Elana last year when I wanted to enter the Knowing for the first time, but now you're saying it's not my choice."

"That was entirely different!" I exclaimed.

"Yeah, totally different!" Ann shouted back in mock agreement. "That was a god powered nightmare shaped like a horse, and this god powered nightmare is shaped like a person! Are you kidding me?"

"Enough of this!" I roared back. "You're the pupil, I'm the teacher, and you do as I say, understand?"

"Like hell!"

Well, if there was one thing to be learned here, it was that Ann wasn't going to just back down from a challenge, and I clearly hadn't done enough to put the fear in her.

"You see this? Look at the necklace! I'm already down a petal, so I guess it's getting real now so no, you're not going to scare me with loud words. The clock is ticking, and I'm not going to debate this with you. My life and I'm in. And if you want some real talk? As far as I'm concerned, having to wake you up in the middle of Hawthorne after you nearly had your head knocked off your shoulders tells me that maybe this just might not be something you can handle on your own. Which means I'm not only backing you up for your sake, but for mine. Because if you die, I also die and then we both died for nothing. And besides, say you get the cure and can't get back to me in time? I don't know how long I have, so I'm sticking close until this whole thing is done! And...! And...!"

She was really on a roll there for a bit, and I didn't expect her to run out of steam so quickly, but she either couldn't leave well enough alone or her mouth just hadn't caught up with her brain. "And?" I asked, crossing my arms.

"And I have a car!" The enthusiastic retort lacked the confidence of everything else she had said.

Some of the tension left my shoulders as I stifled a laugh. "You have a car? That's it?"

"Well, yeah! Think about it. You just yelled at Alistair. How much longer is going to let you run up his ride sharing bills?"

It was a valid, but an unexpected point. "I can drive, you know."

"And what? Does the DMV issue driver's licenses to centuries-old mythical beings?"

I could have told her that I had an entire fake identity set up, complete with a social security number and a credit score, but I was starting to feel an odd mixture of generous and willing to prove a point the hard way. "You know something? You're right. You want to come with me and face down lunatic cultists and who the hell knows what else, then why not? Maybe you'll show me how it's all done and I'll learn something from you for once."

"Maybe you will!" Ann yelled back, and the two of us stood in an uncomfortable silence followed as we stared each other down.

Ann was the first to break the silence with a shout that lacked some of the fury of earlier parts of our debate. "I'm not actually mad at you, and I didn't expect you to agree with me, and now I don't know how to move forward!"

I laughed at that with genuine mirth, all traces of authority wiped clean from my face. Ann nearly laughed at my laughter, looking unsure of how to not be fierce. "Oh gods, I don't know why I agreed to train you!" I said, shaking my head.

"I don't know either!" she agreed.

"You're an absolute maniac. In some ways you're worse than her, you know? I thought Elana was bad, but I don't think she'd yell at me like that."

"That's because Elana is Gabrielle, the well-meaning sidekick and I am Xena, the badass warrior princess!"

"Oh really?" I asked doubtfully.

"Yeah, I can almost fire an arrow and everything. Soon armies will tremble at the name Ann Bancroft."

"All right then, while you get the map, I'll get the coffee.

Does the warrior princess still take cream and sugar?"

"Ooh! No! Hot cocoa if we still have it! With whipped cream, please?"

Incredible. I shook my head incredulously as I looked through the cupboards. Ready to fight for her life one minute and sounding like a kid on Christmas the next. Challenging me at the crack of dawn as we're getting prepped to hunt a one-woman army while she's literally dying of an unknown poison, about to fight the gods only know what or who in the process, and she wants hot chocolate.

"The blood hasn't moved," Ann called out from the living room. "So, we're going to fight the god blood person now?"

I carried our mugs back into the living room, Ann's complete with a floating dollop of whipped cream precariously bobbing at the rim. "Eventually, perhaps, but not right away." The end of that sentence clung to the air as I took a deliberately slow sip of my coffee, watching the anticipation build on my friend's face. I knew how much the second half of my statement was going to excite her, and I wanted to savor the moment. "First, we're going to see a witch."

8

"I am sincerely regretting telling you that she is a witch." I wasn't technically trapped in the car; I was almost confident that I would survive a leap out of the passenger side window. Seventy miles per hour, give or take. I could sit on top of that big rig and just see where it took me.

"Okay, yeah, but I know that you can't lie, and you said she was a witch and that means she's a witch!" Ann was unusually enthusiastic about the possibility of meeting a witch, something I was at least a little surprised by. She'd bartered with a sorcerer, one of her oldest friends was an adept traveler who had made a deal with Freyja herself, and not that it's on par with those examples, but I was the first elf she'd ever met, and I'd been training her for several weeks. And the mere mention of a witch was what excited her. I wondered if it would always be this way; if Ann would be excited every time something new entered into our lives. It wasn't a bad thing, not exactly. I envied that sort of lust for life. But at that hour and with everything else happening, at the moment it bordered on annoying. And now Ann was on the other side of the border and residing as a naturalized citizen.

Whatever frustration I'd been feeling was lost to Ann, whose continued smile threatened to produce legitimate sunshine if left unchecked. "How many different ways do I have to tell you? She's not an actual witch, that's just what she calls herself."

"Are you buying magical items from her or not?"

"Yes, potentially."

"And she made these magic things all on her own with magic or whatever?"

"More magic than whatever, yes, but Ann, she is not a witch!"

Ann slapped the steering wheel hard with the palm of her hand, her face registering something like a eureka moment. "Oh my god! Can she make potions?"

"Yes, and of remarkable quality, in fact, but you could make potions as well if you'd set your mind to it. That doesn't make her a witch."

"I don't know dude, she does magic, makes potions, and you called her a witch," Ann replied, unconvinced, as she shook her head. "Sounds like a witch to me. And I mean, if she's not, why did you say she was?"

"Dramatic effect!" I exclaimed. "I thought you'd be excited!"

"I am!" Ann shouted in turn, still smiling. "We're going to see a witch and peruse magical wares. My life is incredible!"

"The whole reason we are out here in the first place is that you're dying and I'm being coerced by an asshole wizard!" I exclaimed, beginning to lose my temper. "How is that in any way incredible?"

Ann's face returned to something of a more neutral expression, and the car rolled along quietly for a moment. "I'm sorry," I said after a moment.

"It's fine," Ann replied but said nothing more. My guilt

was getting in my way of reading her expression. A couple of minutes passed, and she spoke up. "No, actually, it's not fine."

"I deserve that, I was out of line," I agreed.

"No, not that," Ann said as we made the switch from the 405 to the 10 freeway. "You've been extra grumpy lately. You doing okay?"

I slumped into my seat. "You spend the majority of your life forced to observe ancient and arcane rules of etiquette whenever you're not fighting for your life and let's see how short your temper is when you're off the clock," I deadpanned.

"I think that's the first time I've ever heard you say asshole," Ann observed, drawing a chuckle from me. "And look, it's cool, I promise. We're both dealing with things; I haven't forgotten. The psycho ex who's stalking you is the same one who poisoned me, so trust me, I get it. But you know, just trying to keep a positive attitude. See the silver lining in every cloud or whatever."

"Those are probably just the nephelai."

"What?"

"You know, cloud nymphs."

"What?" This time it came from Ann as disbelief rather than an actual question.

"No wait, those are just clouds." I smiled at her as I said it, and for a moment, the tension seemed to subside.

Venice was a place I might have liked if I wasn't so intimately familiar with its dark history, both secret and public. The entire city has been an amusement park, an oil field, and in one unfortunate year in the seventies, a battleground. These days it's home to the wealthy and the unfortunate in equal measure. It also happens to be a hotspot for grifters, pickpockets, and imps. Well, not just imps, there have been other problematic beings here, but if I had to choose the most significant issue to deal with around here, it would be the imps. The phrase tourist trap might apply to the city more on the nose than the mortals might like.

These days, Venice was home to the headquarters of a couple of billion-dollar companies, and just like that, the city was changing once again. Thrift stores now charged upwards of seventy dollars for thirty-year-old t-shirts. The Bank of Venice is a bar and grill. At least the canals still have sharks in them. Leopard sharks to be exact, and they're about as harmless to people as slightly overfed goldfish, but it's just fun to imagine the locals aghast over the word shark while remaining utterly ignorant of the real danger around them on a daily basis.

Even at the early hour, Ann was lucky to find a parking space a mere four blocks from our initial destination. If this had been the summer or even just an unusually sunny weekend, we'd have been better off walking here. I retrieved my bow and a quiver of arrows from the backseat as I felt my brow furrow and my lips tighten. I didn't know that I'd be needing these just yet, but I didn't like the idea of having to run back here if I did. And this was still a densely populated city. I'd need to keep them covered to avoid being stopped by any local police, and coated or no, walking around with a bow was just as good as spinning a sign on the corner that read 'I'm armed and danger-ous and not from around here!'

"Think you'll need to shoot anyone?" Ann asked with a hint of accusation in her voice. She shrugged a backpack up onto her shoulders as she looked at my weapon.

"No," I replied, dodging the question. "It's probably best that I left it here. For now, at least. Just until we're certain of our situation. And you? Do you have everything you need?"

Ann nodded confidently in response. "Absolutely. Pepper spray and a spell book. Let's find a thing."

I must have misheard her. "You don't say? And when did you get a spell book?"

"Right after New Year's, I guess? But I've been working on it ever since."

"I remain unconvinced. Show me." For a moment I wondered if I was just imagining this conversation and I was suffering from an undiagnosed concussion.

Ann looked at me with an expression of disbelief, and it didn't take a telepath to see why. She was treating me as someone who just refused to believe that she owned a drawer full of spoons and forks. Her backpack slung back down from her shoulders, and she turned it around to her front, unzipping it and producing a college ruled composition notebook, marked with doodles and perhaps scorch marks, and it had the handwritten title on it, *Book of Ann-Chantments*. I didn't think Ann actually knew any enchantments, but I've yet to meet anything that has been capable of stopping her from forcing a pun if she thought she could get away with it. "That's adorable, but it's not a spell book." I realized how I sounded as soon as I said it, but my patience was still running at all-time thin levels, even for the people I liked.

Ann's face flushed slightly at that. "I mean, it's not some dusty old leather-bound tome or whatever, but I have my spells in here."

"You have your spells in there?"

"Okay, not all of my spells, but a couple of them! Besides, you know how many spells I can cast without writing them down? Not many. I can't do what Olivia and Elana do, okay? I need help."

That got my attention. "Okay, that's more than fair, I'm just understandably surprised is all. Maybe walk me through it. How did you create this spellbook of yours?"

If that was meant to calm her down, it had perhaps the opposite effect. "Dude, I don't know! I just figured this stuff out! I take a spell, and I look at the different parts of it that make it do whatever it is that is does. Kind of like computer code in a way, or how different notes added together at a certain speed make up a melody. But not either of those on their own, I think it's somewhere in the middle of those two. The exact why doesn't matter, just knowing what the pieces mean seems to be half the work. And if I can vocalize the sounds as I write them down, it doesn't use up all the, I guess, magic inside of me to do something. So okay, you want an example?"

This was all fascinating and felt like something I should have heard before, but I urged Ann to continue all the same. I must have been wearing my serious and interested face because Ann was starting to calm down by a matter of degrees.

"So you know how Elana and Olivia can just cast a wind spell with their minds or their hands and like, it ain't no thing?" she asked.

"I wouldn't say it's nothing to them, but yes, go on."

"Yeah, so if I try that I'd be lucky to mess up someone's hair. And then I'd need a nap. But if I try it from the book..."

Ann turned away from me and flipped through a couple of pages before she made a sound like air escaping from a tire while at the same time making an impression of an agitated duck. A modest gust of wind seemed to emanate from her, rustling some tree branches and causing a parked motorcycle about fifty feet away from us to topple over with a crash of metal and fiberglass against the asphalt.

"Oh shit!" Ann cursed louder than I would have expected. "I did not mean to do that! Just, all right, come on. We have to go."

I was practically pulled down the street and around the corner laughing loud enough to alert all of Pacific Avenue, laughter that only seemed to frustrate Ann to an unfathomable degree as she rushed us away from the crime scene. The shrill chirping of her car alarm acted as a vocal witness to our escape.

"Will you stop laughing?" Ann hissed at me once we were out of sight.

"Oh, that was incredible! I needed that!" I exhaled, allowing the laughter to subside into giggles. "But you should know, sincerely, your spellbook? You should not be able to do that."

"Yeah, well, no one told me," Ann deadpanned.

"This is good! You should feel very proud of yourself," I reassured her. "From what I've seen, spellbooks are created only after someone has mastered a range of languages and practiced those spells for countless hours until they have been burned into their minds. And reading from one is even more impressive, understanding the meaning behind the magic burned into the pages is a skill all to itself. And you've just re-verse engineered the whole process to allow the magic around you to flow through you, rather than out of you. I don't know that I've ever heard of this happening before!"

"Dude, I just wrote dumb noises down in a composition book. It's cool, but I'm positive someone's done it before. Chill."

Impressive or no, Ann wasn't going to be able to hear it just this moment, and we still had plenty to accomplish. Now might not be the best time to get her head inflated besides, and so I began our walk down Pacific Avenue before making a turn for the boardwalk. It was the morning, and in broad daylight, I didn't think we'd have much to worry about in our immediate future, but I was keeping an eye open all the same. Again, I knew what lived, and I'd have liked to avoid coming there if at all possible. The city was packed with about ten times the peo-ple it ought to have had in the first place and was home to the weird, both intentional and otherwise, which made the job all the more difficult.

"You doing okay? Relax, we're at the beach. No boss bat-tles just yet. The blood on the map hasn't moved, so unless I screwed the scry, we should be safe." Whatever concern I had was clear enough on my face that Ann could pick up on it. I was less concerned for my own safety as I was for hers, how-ever. Still, I muttered an apology which Ann waved away. "Don't apologize, just maybe try to enjoy the calm before the storm? Bold move on the ears, by the way."

My ears! With all the stress and confusion, I'd managed to prepare for just about everything except attempting to disguise myself. "Never mind that," I said dismissively. "We're in Venice, anyone who sees me will mistake me for a... What's that thing you do where you pretend to be other people, and you hit each other with foam swords and throw paper towels at each other?"

"Huh?"

"The thing where you all go camping, and one of you pretended to be a cat, and you ended up getting drunk?"

Ann flashed me an unreadable look. "You mean LARP? You think someone is going to think you're in a costume?"

"Yes, precisely."

"That's not really my thing, that was something Jason and Logan used to..." Ann trailed off at the mention of Logan. Damn it; I hadn't meant to bring him up in all of this.

"Well, when Logan returns, I'm sure he will be an even better LARP." I had hoped that the words were a comfort. From what I understood, Logan was in Alfheim. I did not envy him, but his sacrifice was noble, and though I'd never been clear on the details, it sounded like Freyja had assured Olivia of his return. I had no way of knowing for sure, but that's not what Ann needed to hear.

For her part, Ann seemed quick to move past the topic. "I just meant that if someone is looking for an elf, maybe the most defining aspects of an elf would have been better off covered up. Headphones, a hat, maybe something with your hair?"

She was right of course, but I wasn't willing to concede the point. "I doubt anyone is looking for me specifically, just yet. Anyone looking for the Battle Born will be—"

"I'll show you what's in my birdcage for a dollar." It was a woman's voice, discordant and strained, but the fact that there was a woman there at all took me by surprise. We had taken a turn to make our way out onto the boardwalk, and slumped up against the side of one of the shops was a homeless person covered in an odd looking coat that could have been made exclusively from old feathers and dryer lint. I'd like to think it was because I'd been distracted, but I hadn't registered this person as even a person, and I felt a twinge of guilt at that.

Next to the woman was a birdcage, covered by a stained piece of blue velvet that was likely torn away from a more significant portion of the material. It was frayed along the edges and whatever sheen it once held was long faded by sun bleaching. For her part, my olfactory senses were assaulted by her scent. Something like rotten fish and stagnant water clung to her. Ann didn't seem affected in the slightest.

"Oh! Uhh, let me see what I have!" she said, immediately digging into her pockets, producing a ten-dollar bill. "Sorry, that's all I have, I hope it helps."

The woman raised her head now to look at Ann, excited but jaundiced eyes looked at her hand, and she eagerly outstretched one of her own. It had a layer of grime, and her fingernails were reminiscent of talons, and there was the unmistakable matte black of dried blood on them. With that coat she had likely become a breeding ground for mites and fleas, and her exposure to the elements, my guess was scratching at psoriasis scabs constantly.

"Oh, my! This is so much more than I asked for!" she said as she took the folded bill. "For this generous sum, I need to show you something very special! Yes, you deserve a show! But not now, no. No no no no! No, we must be patient!"

"Don't worry about it, I promise," Ann said gently. "Just get something to eat and have a good day, okay?"

"Today looks to be a very good day indeed!" the woman rasped, making a sound that sat somewhere between a cough and a laugh. "What may I call you?"

"My name is Ann; it's a pleasure to meet you." At the

edges of her eyes, it looked as though Ann was rapidly becoming uncomfortable with the length of this conversation, but was letting it play out for kindness sake.

"I will find you, Ann, and I promise to give you a show." The woman smiled, and her dry lips threatened to crack she did. "You have my word. Your pretty friend, too, even if she doesn't say much."

Ann took that brief opening to thank her and keep moving, and there was the fleeting sense of stepping into another world as we rounded onto the boardwalk. "There," I said, pointing a just a couple of shops away to a sign that read:

The Gem and The Moon
Books, Holistic Remedies, Metaphysical Supplies

"Cool, let's do it."

"Actually, I'd like you to go in first, give you a chance to meet the witch for yourself."

Ann eyed me with suspicion briefly but shrugged as she walked inside through the already open door, pushing aside the wall of beads that acted as the only barrier to the outside world. I stayed back at the edge of the doorway and listened.

"Bright blessings!" a cheerful voiced called out. "How may I guide your journey this day?"

"Sup?" Ann replied. "Hey, super quick. Are you a witch or nah?"

"That is correct. You may call me Ariadne. I am a Hedge witch and a devout worshipper of the fair one, the luminous goddess Freyja."

"For real? Rad! That actually makes this a lot easier. One of my best friends works for Freyja, y'all might know each other."

There was a sound like someone trying and failing to prevent an object leaving their grasp, the very brief noise of small objects scattering. "What did you just say?"

I took this as my moment to enter the store, drawing the attention of the woman the instant I did. "She's telling the truth," I said with a grin. "But of course, you already knew that, didn't you?"

9

"Well, this makes more sense." There was a look of exasperation from our host as she saw me. "I would have thought you'd be hiding on the other side of the world by now."

"Ann, allow me to introduce you to Wilma Baxter, proprietor of this establishment and the best magician in Venice Beach. You're how old these days? Seventy? Eighty?"

Wilma was a hearty woman with blonde hair that flowed messily to her waist. Despite my comment, she appeared to be no older than thirty due to her magic. Magic slowed or halted the aging process for all, but it hit everyone a bit differently. Wilma had looked to be about thirty for at least forty years. Beyond that, she was dressed in innumerable patchwork scarves, robes and bits of cloth and silk that I wasn't even sure were attached to anything. Her neck and wrist, as well as in her ears, nose and who knows where else held a tacky amount of jewelry of various metals and stones. All of it served as camouflage to cover up one specific charm. To anyone who didn't know better, she'd look like nothing more than a friendly neighborhood hippie.

"You take all of the fun out of this for me; you know that? All the theatrics, the pageantry; it's all that makes my front of the shop work tolerable. Let me say I'm a witch if I want to say I'm a witch." Wilma's tone was turning south towards the genuinely annoyed now.

"If you're going to do that, at least get your words straight," I chided. "Ariadne is Greek, Freyja is Norse, and she takes that whole devotion thing pretty seriously so you might not want to go throwing it around. Besides, why would a hedge witch worship Freyja in the first place?"

Wilma actually scoffed at that. "Like you'd know the first thing about Pagans or Wicca. Hedge witches can worship whoever they'd like. I should know, I probably sell a book or two that says something along those lines."

"I know enough about them that I don't sell them garbage!" I shouted, motioning to her visible stock. "Hell's teeth! You're not a hedge witch! You're not any kind of witch!"

"Umm, excuse me, but what the actual hell is happening here?" Ann interjected herself into our conversation with a little annoyance of her own.

Wilma turned to stare at her as if she'd forgotten she'd been there in the first place. Then she turned back to face me. "Her idiot friend knowingly went to work for Freyja? Does that mean Freyja is literally, physically in town?"

"It's a long story, but yes, and that idiot is also a dear friend of mine, so be careful with your words."

Wilma made the barest motion of an apologetic gesture with her hands. "And your story is equally long, I take it? Making the jump from a god to a goddess? I would have thought you'd like the time off."

I barked a laugh at that. "By association, perhaps, but it will be a peaceful day in Tartarus before I go making any more deals like that. Are you telling me you never did anything short-sighted in your youth? I seem to recall—"

Ann stood directly between us now and waved her arms above her as if making sure for our benefit that we could still see her.

"Yes, what is it?" I snapped.

"What's going on, why are we here, and how is she eighty? I mean, take this the right way, but she looks to be your age. Or like, what age you'd look like if you were human." This time it was Ann's turn to snap at me, but her frustration lost steam as it found the intersection of confusing and semantics.

"Oh, you just can't keep your yap shut when the adults are talking, can you?" Wilma laughed sardonically. "Do you have any idea who you're talking to?"

Ann blinked at that and adjusted her glasses to look from me to Wilma. "Wait, do you mean her or you, or like, both of you?"

"Everyone relax, I'll make the proper introductions this time," I tried to calm the room down, knowing full well I was getting away from our reason for being here. "Wilma, meet Ann. She's a trusted friend and as of now, my apprentice."

Wilma snorted at that. "And here I thought I was your only friend."

I continued. "Ann, this is Wilma. Like you, she's a magician—"

"No, I'm not," Wilma interrupted.

"—and over the years she has become a reliable resource and a trusted colleague."

"Umm, I'm not a magician?" Ann's voice was somewhere between a question and clarification.

"Neither am I," Wilma agreed. "And admit it or not, we're friends."

Since cutting and running didn't seem to be a good option, I decided which fight I was willing to dive into just then.

"Wilma, you know as well as I that there are names for things with good reason. What you do falls squarely under the title of a magician. You only say you're a witch for the tourists, why can't you accept what you are?"

"I never agreed to any rules."

"Neither did I, come to think of it," Ann chimed in. "And are we talking like card tricks or sleight of hand or...?"

I wanted to make the argument with her that by accepting my training she was subject to whatever rules I deemed she needed to follow, but I decided to table that particular conversation for later. "I give up, Wilma. You're a witch, and Ann, you're a basilisk if that's what you want. What do I care?"

"Excellent!" Wilma concurred without protest. "And with that out of the way, what can I do for you today?"

I took the half second I needed to completely let the previous discussion go before I continued, hoping no one noticed. As helpful as Wilma had been in the past, she had a habit of getting under my skin. "Before we get into all of that, I have to know one thing. Have any of the Abbot's people been through here?"

Wilma's lips curled slightly at that. "Those chumps with the Symphony of the Attuned? No, we steer clear of each other for the most part. Muscle Beach is our unofficial border. They stick to their side of the boardwalk, and I stick to mine. Oh, east is east, and west is west, and never the twain shall meet." She recited that last sentence from memory with a prideful flourish. Just so long as she didn't continue to the rest of the verse, I was content to take her meaning.

"Really? You've never seen any of them around your shop and your customers? I was under the assumption that the Abbot took a measure of pride in having eyes and ears everywhere in Venice."

"And that's the trick, isn't it?" Wilma asked. "You could have passed half a dozen of them getting to my door, and I wouldn't have known. How could I? I don't see any of their obvious members at least, the ones chanting on the beach with their crystals, doing their yoga in the sand or whatever it is they do. But the Abbot has the numbers, far more than just the pets he keeps in his home; an army if you believe the compound is real. If it is, and if he really wanted to, he could make one phone call and just run me right out of town. But he knows what I do and who some of my clients are, and I suppose that makes him content to steer clear of me just to be on the safe side. Is that what brings you here? The Abbot?"

"Him, some fighting if I'm unlucky, and maybe the Salt and Straw if we have the time." Wilma was mostly trustworthy, but she didn't know about the existence of a Battle Born, let alone the price on its head or who was after it. She wasn't likely to get me intentionally killed, but I couldn't be sure she wouldn't repeat the information. Something this big might be something she'd try to leverage later.

Of course, there was also the lie detecting charm around her neck.

Unfortunately for her, it didn't work on a spectrum. It heard a lie, or it didn't. If she asked you if you'd like to include a dollar on your tab to support the spiritual awakening of Venice Beach charity fund, and you say you just donated when you bought your Venice Beach fanny pack and t-shirt combo on your way here, she knows you're lying and not just because she made up that fundraiser to scam a few extra bucks from the normies and tourists. But it had to be specific. Leaving out information, keeping it vague, or even just being sarcastic would get around the charm. It's why Wilma had been so surprised when Ann mentioned that Elana made a deal with Freyja. Getting no alert was the biggest surprise she could receive.

"I see. And you're here to shop?"

"Yeah, but we'll skip the candles and essential oils if it's all the same."

Wilma's face contorted with something like annoyance and she moved to lock the front door. "The secret menu it is then. I hope you brought a list and you're not just here to browse. And I hope to high heaven you can pay this time. This is why we make appointments; I need to close up shop whenever we do this."

Having locked the front door, Wilma made her way into the backroom first to take down the various wards that were set up to keep anyone who wasn't herself out. Like myself, she didn't use invisible strings of magic, lacing the room with evocations as traps. She stuck to the old-fashioned way of doing things; her wards were more of a repellent. I could have probably crossed them if I'd really wanted to, but I'd be violently ill for the rest of the day. I always wondered why she didn't use magic, and my best guess was the mere inconvenience of the thing. There's only a certain amount of energy anyone has access to at any given time, and with the crafting she did for a living, it may just have not been prudent to cast and recast every time she wanted to bring by a customer. Or maybe she was just afraid of a crowd of tourists being too much for her to keep track of, and then she's having to explain why one of them was immolated while looking for the bathroom. Easier to explain why they have the runs.

For a backroom filled with riches and wonders, it was surprisingly drab. For all of the splendor and showmanship that filled the main room of the shop, there was none to be found here. Barren white walls that would have fit better with an accountant's office and plain shelving and tables housed various scrolls, amulets, potions, and a few bags that I probably didn't want to open.

"Dude! Really?" Ann's mouth hung open in amazement. "Okay, if she can do all of this, I'm inclined to call her whatever the hell she wants to be called."

"It's impressive, no question," I replied as Wilma moved

some boxes to make standing room for us. "But remember, you've created a spell book. You could create anything in this room given enough time to learn how."

Wilma immediately stopped what she was doing and sighed, uttering a swear under her breath before speaking up. "You created a spell book?"

Ann nodded in agreement. Wilma's question came with a level of frustration that seemed to prevent any unnecessary conversation immediately.

"Do you happen to have it with you?"

Ann nodded again.

"Well, may I see it?"

Ann looked to me for approval for some reason, and after digging through her pack, she produced her spellbook and handed it over. Wilma raised an eyebrow at the title and began to flip through the notebook, her brow furrowing in interest or concentration as she did. I started to offer some explanation, but she waved me off without looking up before stumbling over the pronunciation of Ann's written onomatopoeia. A moment later a dozen or golden motes of light floated up and around the little room before popping in brief bursts of light.

"I quit," Wilma said flatly.

"I'm sorry?" Ann asked.

Wilma turned her attention to me. "The girl created a working spellbook. And I can read it! How long has she had her magic?"

"Two months?" I said with a shrug, looking to Ann for confirmation. She tried it on for size and seemed to agree.

"Give or take, yeah. I'd say two months," she agreed.

"We can call it two months," I said definitively.

"And let me guess: Self-taught? No, don't answer that. Can you see how this is not okay? I mean, it's fine, I-I'm not going to… you know what? Let's just move on."

"No, don't be like that," I offered. "Everyone has their

own talents; I'm sure you'll make a spellbook one day."

"I said it's fine. What did you need?"

I thought about it for a second and realized that her ego didn't need coddling so much as it required stroking, so I got right into it. "A ghost whisper for starters would be helpful, maybe something to help with defenses? Potions would be great; whatever you have there is just fine. Oh, and if you have any of those beads from before, the ones with kinetic energy stored in them. What did you call them?"

"Kinetic beads," Wilma confirmed.

"Right! Yes! Exactly. If you can spare any of those that would be brilliant. But most important of all, and I need you more than anyone else for this because no one does it better. I need a couple of glamours. Top shelf, best you've got."

"Christ, Chalsarda, what are you really fighting?" Wilma exploded. "Because this is not all for the Abbot, and don't try to dance around the answer."

"It's not," I admitted. There was no sense in pretending it was, but dancing around the answer happened to be a specialty of mine. "I've heard from a reliable source there are a couple of dangerous people who may try to hurt us, bounty hunters named Birdie and Caleb Duquesne."

"I've heard of them both," Wilma said slowly. "But neither of them is the type to work with the other. In fact—"

"It gets worse, Wilma," I interjected, cutting her train of thought before she could piece together anything from that bit of knowledge. "It's Alistair. He's back. He threatened me, and he hurt Ann. Poisoned her. Alistair knows I'm free and I think he's toying with us simply because he can."

Wilma's eyes snapped to me as if I'd slapped her. They'd grown full with something a half-step removed from fear. "He contacted you? Directly? He's here?"

"Yes, to all counts, I'm afraid."

Wilma blew out her cheeks and seemed to look off into

the middle distance. "You'll need a lot more than your shopping list to deal with him. But there is one thing that's bothering me in all this, though. One thing you seemed to leave out intentionally. You're going to see the Abbot. Or lay siege to his home, I'm not sure which. But you haven't told me why."

I chose my words carefully. "He has something that I need, and I don't think he's willing to give it up without a fight. And more importantly, it's something that can help Ann. What he did to her is a one-of-a-kind sort of deal, and it can't be cured by you, me, or anyone. So this is something we have to do ourselves. Ann's dead if I don't."

I hoped that Ann didn't take those last few words too personally. That didn't make them any less accurate, but I felt terrible exploiting her all the same. If only because she was in earshot.

Wilma seemed to consider this. "Fair enough. I'll outfit you. But not for free."

"I never expected anything less. What do we owe you?"

"There's what you will pay me, and there's what it will cost you." Wilma made sure to emphasize the difference between the two.

I sighed as she said it. "I thought we were past the dramatics. Can't you just ring us up?"

"No dramatics here, I'm deadly serious. Unless leaving the service of a Celtic god comes with a nice severance package, I don't think you can afford a single item in here. Unless of course, you'd like the friend discount?"

"I suspect we're not walking out of here without it," I remarked.

"It's a shame the friend discount only applies to friends. So before we move forward, I'd like to hear that we are friends. Or, if we're not, I'd like to hear that as well. My little charm aside, you and I both know you can't lie. So beyond what you will pay me, this is what it will cost you: An honest answer."

"Oh dang, what?" Ann whooped from behind, momentarily taking the air out of the situation. "She got you though."

I whipped my head around in response, shooting her a look that did nothing to dissuade her heckling. Wilma was still waiting for a response, however, and time was a factor. "Okay then, this is my answer. I have been slow to trust any acting as an agent or a contact of my former employer, and for that matter, I have had precious few people that I would consider a friend. Not only in my past service, but in my life. Given the nature of my charge and for reasons I hope you will understand, I have refrained from ever calling anyone I worked with a friend. However, of anyone I have worked with on a professional level I can say that you are the most trusted person I've ever encountered, you are someone who has become the closest thing to a friend that I have allowed myself to have."

Wilma nodded her head at that. "I'll take i—"

"I'm not finished," I said, putting up a hand to stop her. "While I'm telling you the whole truth, I would be remiss if I didn't also add that you are one of the single most obnoxious, frustrating, cavalier charlatans I have ever been forced to endure!"

We held each other's gaze after that for a tense moment before we both burst into laughter. Ann studied us quizzically, apparently not in on the joke. "Y'all are weird," she said to herself, gaining no reaction from either of us.

"I'll consider the cost settled," Wilma began, after regaining her composure. "Now for what you will pay."

"The answer isn't 'Dearly' is it?" Ann questioned.

Wilma finally showed her displeasure at being interrupted. "It is not, but since you seem intent on being a part of this deal, welcome to the conversation. Chalsarda has covered her half, and I'll allow you to cover the other. This is for your benefit, after all. So tell me, how much cash do you have on you? And I'll remind you not to lie to me."

Ann looked nonplussed at the question, but she pulled out her wallet all the same. I remembered the tenner she had given to the homeless woman, but apparently, that wasn't everything she had on her, just what she had loose in her jean pockets. She produced a series of crisp twenty-dollar bills and counted them to herself. "I've got two hundred forty bucks."

"There you have it, Chalsarda. A magical boon for the low price of two hundred and forty dollars." She locked eyes with Ann as she said it.

My friend's face fell knowing she had to foot the bill but that she wasn't in a position to complain or barter.

"Chin up, you're getting a bargain," I commented.

"That was my rent money," she sulked as she handed it over.

"You have cheap rent," Wilma replied, folding the bills in half without counting them and stuffing them away.

"That was part of my rent money," Ann clarified.

Wilma grinned and added, "At least it wasn't your pudding money."

Ann looked to me for some kind of hint as to what Wilma could have possibly meant by that statement, not finding the idea of two-hundred-and-forty-dollars' worth of pudding plausible or humorous in the least. Wilma's grin faded into disappointment as her joke or reference fell flat. "Watch the front of the store while I get you loaded up," she said by way of transition. "I won't be long."

Not long translated into ten minutes or so and, when she returned, she held several small drawstring pouches. "Okay, here we go. The blue bag is the Kinetic beads. I don't have to tell you, but I'm going to tell you all the same. Do not let this bag spill unless you want to make a spectacular mess. One at a time should be plenty for most people. The white bag is the potions. I'm giving you five of them because five is the number of samples I had left over. I stored them in those little mini liquor bottles you get on airplanes, but don't let that scare you. They're all clearly marked, and one-hundred percent guaranteed to work."

I opened that bag to examine them, and sure enough, she was right. The glass clinked as I opened it to reveal our prize. I grabbed a couple to get a closer look. A pair of fifty-milliliter bottles, the first a Goldschlager with a sticker placed on its front that read Steelskin, the liquid swirling inside of it resembling mercury. And another potion, a bottle of Grand Marnier that read Slumber. Purple milk would be the most accurate description I could come up with. The red color of the glass obscured it, but I'd seen it before. I'd examine the rest later.

"And finally, in the red bag, we have your ghost whisper. Don't open it until you want to hear it."

"USA! USA!" Ann quietly chanted. Seeing our expressions, she added, "Because of the colors? Like our flag? Then again, those are also the colors for France. And Yugoslavia. And even North Korea. Okay, sorry. Please continue."

"I think we're good here, actually," I said quickly. "Once again Wilma, you have my sincere thanks. You have been most generous."

"Well, that's not all. Your glamours, right?" Wilma opened up a fist over my hand, and two minuscule scrolls fell into my palm. "And I don't need to tell you, but only use any of this as needed. Your new friend here may not know the value of this work, but I'm sure you know exactly the kind of deal you got today and why I probably can't do this for you again for a while."

"I'm aware," I agreed as Wilma crossed around the counter to open the shop again. "But why are you helping us? To this degree, I mean?"

The door chimed as she opened it and turned to face me. "Because Alistair is a prick. Because Ann created a spellbook without trying and I'd hate to see that potential go to waste. But most of all because as much as you can be thick headed about who actually cares about you in this world, I want you to know that I'm your friend, and if you died out there I would be upset for reasons that didn't involve the loss of a customer. So understand this: I'm not going anywhere anytime soon and hopefully, neither are you. So that means you gotta back here in one piece and maybe return the favor sometime. Good luck, my friend."

nn's expression remained sour as we left The Gem
and The Moon, but I suspect not for the reasons I
might have typically had. Doubtless, the idea was that
she walked away with less of her pocket money than she anticipated. Wilma hadn't even so much as given Ann the chance to
barter, or even given her illusion that bartering was an option.
In truth, for the amount of money Wilma had received, she may
as well have just given us her stock for free. An owed favor
from either of us would have been worth far more to her than
mere money, but I suppose she was looking to make an example for the future. Still, Wilma wouldn't have to deal with
Ann's pouting the rest of the day, so maybe this was her subtle
punishment to me as well. Two for one on her end, I suppose.

"Oh, come now," I began to say to my friend as we began
out onto the boardwalk. "It's really not that—"

Hands clutched to her chest with white knuckles, Ann's
face flushed red from strain, and she tensed and began to fall. I
planted my feet into position on instinct and managed to catch
her before she could hit the pavement. She left out a small cry

of pain, and just as quickly her body began to relax, and her breathing seemed to resume. The whole event lasted no more than a second; I didn't even have the time to ask Ann what the matter was before she managed to tell me she was okay.

"Your chest! Let me see it!" I demanded.

Ann withdrew her hand to reveal the necklace. One of the petals looked to be drained of all color and now held a dull black finish akin to a charcoal briquette. And as if the direction of the petal was pointing the way, a jagged scar of raised skin about three inches in length marked her chest. The ruined petal crumpled and fell away as I watched it.

"No! I'm not ready; this is too soon!" I swore under my breath.

"Is it? That's good news, I suppose."

I looked into Ann's face, and she smiled weakly at me, waiting. "I meant... the poison is spreading faster than I would have hoped. It would appear Alistair was telling the truth, at least. I recognize this."

Her eyes lit up at my response, but her reply was still weak. "Rad. If you know what type of poison this is, we can maybe just get the antidote on our own."

I shook my head. "I'm afraid not. This abrasion is a death line. Or a dead line, depending on who you ask. Whatever caused this is exotic and not of this world. Chasing after the source is a fool's errand, I'd wager. But on the bright side, this is just the second petal to fall. We have time. Are you sure you're okay to continue?"

Ann collected her notebook from the ground and stood up straight with a thick, reassuring breath and said, "Peachy."

I'm a fool. I was so wrapped up in our immediate task that I had managed to lose my sense of urgency for her condition. Well, if it wasn't real before, it indeed became real to me now. Ann's life was in immediate danger, and if we could assume that the timing of each petal would hold constant, she had maybe a week until it was too late. Something told me that the Battle Born had less time than that, one way or another. I regarded my friend for a moment, and for whatever her words told me, she was not, in fact, peachy. What she needed was a distraction. Something to take her mind off her impending doom.

"Ann, what do you say to a little fun?"

Ann looked at me with mild disgust that I could tell was more for our situation and less for me personally. "No. Thank you, but no, let's just get this over with."

"Come on, trust me," I coaxed. "And if it helps, consider this a lesson from your teacher and mentor that will just happen to be a little more fun than having your ear pulled for insubordination."

"Fine," Ann said, resigning herself to my suggestion. "What do you need me to do?"

"Just follow my lead," I said. "And for goodness sake, try to have fun with it. That's an order."

The Venice boardwalk was a beacon if nothing else. Like moths to a flame, the very nature of the area attracted all sorts. You'd never find a stranger class of citizen anywhere else in the area for one thing. Some were just trying to make a quick buck and didn't know where else to go; some just didn't know another place where they might be accepted. It certainly attracted merchants. Just about anything you could think of to purchase was available, often hidden in plain sight. Looking for a weapon? Try an incense merchant. Drugs? Maybe the henna artist. A lovely, aromatic candle? Sorry, I couldn't help you, I've always made my own. Maybe Wilma?

If there was one thing Venice attracted in abundance, however, even more than tourists, was its hustlers. Some were more criminally minded than others. There were the pickpockets of course, though an outright mugging was rare in the area. Then there was the "damaged" street art. If you touched or otherwise moved too close to a street artists work, they would claim you damaged it and would demand money, going so far as to make a scene. The ring scam still happened as well, the idea being that some poor soul would be approached by someone, usually speaking poor English, who would give the tourist a ring, claiming they dropped it. Before the tourist could protest, the seemingly good-natured individual would run off, and a moment later the mark would be confronted by the apparent rightful owner of the ring, who would make a big scene about how they'd been robbed by the tourist. Of course, the tourist would have no recourse. If they weren't the thief after all, why were they holding the ring? Or phone. This was also used with phones nowadays, too. Anyway, give up some cash or answer to the police.

It didn't take me very long to find something a bit more common and lower on the complexity scale of common scams, but an effective one all the same. I watched as a man standing in the center of the boardwalk with a stack of cheaply produced compact discs handed one without a word to an obvious tourist as he walked past. A few steps away was a much larger, much more imposing man insisting that the tourist hadn't paid for his purchase of the CD, and currently owed them twenty dollars. The man with the stack of discs now approached the other man from behind as a means of intimidation. This was where I came in.

I fell forward into all three of them, making as big a scene about it is as I could, knocking the disc out of the tourist's hands and forcing the larger man to either absorb my weight and catch me or nimbly leap aside and allow me to fall onto the pavement. The more massive man was not nimble. "Oh gosh!" I exclaimed doing my best impression of a clueless and earnest teenager, bending at the waist to pick up the disc and giving the tourist a wink as I did. "I think you dropped this!"

I handed it to the man with the stack of discs, interposing myself between the two men and the tourist, who decided that my two-second distraction was enough of a reason to leave immediately. The hustlers looked incredulous as their mark escaped but before they could say anything, I feigned surprise and continued with the same mock voice, "Wait a minute! Oh gosh, you two weren't trying to scam that poor man, were you? You know, my Daddy is a police officer, and he told us about something like this! Saffron, don't you remember?"

Ann chimed in from behind them, and they both turned in her direction. "Lavender! Oh my god, are you okay? Did they try to steal your phone?"

Ann's voice screamed 'Rich kid' even worse than mine, and I had to suppress a smile at how quickly she caught on. "No! But I think they're running like, some kind of con or something!"

"You two better knock it off! My pop-pop works at the DA's office, I know like, the law or whatever! I'm going to call him right now!"

Ann pulled out her phone and began to dial. I pulled out my own phone and held it up like a camera. "I'm recording you! I'm recording you!" I loudly announced.

The pair of them never saw us coming and were off in a panic before they ever had the chance to offer a single word of protest. A second after it had happened, the boardwalk moved on as if nothing had happened. I kept my composure until I was satisfied they were out of sight and I pulled Ann around a corner, where I allowed myself a sharp laugh. "Lavender? That's what you decided was a good name for me?" I asked, still smiling at the absurdity of it.

"You called me Saffron!" Ann protested.

"Well, either way, it worked."

"What? Saving some poor Midwesterner from having to listen to some terrible mixtape?"

"No," I responded, tossing her a billfold. "Distracting the thieves long enough for me to do my own thieving."

Ann caught the money and examined it in disbelief as I continued. "I have his wallet as well, but I wouldn't hold onto that. I'd hang onto his ill-gotten gains and quit while you're ahead."

"You mugged him?" she asked, her mouth agape.

"Technically, I robbed him. I think mugging involves the direct threat of violence."

Ann looked as if she were prepared to protest, so I stopped her. "Ann, you have three choices as far as I see it. You can return the money to the two men who we both know have been steadily stealing from people who don't know any better. You can spend the rest of the day looking for anyone with a CD in their hands they don't want and give them a twenty-dollar bill. Or, more practically, you can accept the money as an offset from your recent financial setback."

She pursed her lips, knowing she wanted to keep it, but felt guilty for reasons she didn't understand. "You should have told me what you were planning."

"Yeah, but where would the fun have been in that? Besides, this—"

I almost didn't see him out of the corner of my eye, but there it was.

"Besides what?" Ann asked.

"Not now. Stay close," I instructed my friend in a hushed whisper. "We're being followed."

Ann blinked twice at that. "Followed? Are you sure? Who's doing the following?"

"I'll give you three guesses," I replied tersely. "Come on."

The quickest way to discover if you were being followed was to take three left turns. Anyone still behind you after that was following you. That method, unfortunately, didn't apply to a boardwalk, and even if it had, my general sense was that with the Abbot's network of spies, it would have been a fruitless gesture all the same. Wilma may not have seen the prying eyes

107

on her side of the fence, but she didn't have my eyes. And our little stunt made sure anyone looking for something unusual was sure to find it. I'd been careless, and the only thing for it now was to get off the boardwalk and make our approach before anyone else could join them.

With a companion in tow, however, exiting the boardwalk didn't afford me many options. All we could do was walk straight ahead until a path back out to the street opened up. We would be easy to follow until then. I considered a distraction, but that would only draw more attention and Ann wasn't particularly fleet-footed besides. So at the first chance we had, I dragged Ann into the speedway and made an immediate second left onto an alley barely wide enough for a car but somehow given the name Westminster Court. The suddenness of it all would put the young man on high alert, but it would provide us with a precious few seconds to ready ourselves.

"What are we—?" Ann began.

"Play with the bag and make yourself nice and noticeable. You are, unfortunately, bait," I remarked quickly, scaling the backside of an apartment building. There were plenty of windows here, but people rarely looked into their alley for the view. And being a good thirty feet above the ground or so gave me the advantage of seeing the young man make his approach. This was as much privacy as we were going to get.

"Oh boy, I can't wait to try out all this magic stuff!" Ann remarked unconvincingly and louder than needed. I watched then as the young man quickened his pace and removed a blade from behind his back, which had been tucked into his jeans. Ann saw the blade and something like an inability to process the moment crossed her face. My face went hot at that, and before I realized it, I was upon him more viciously than I had initially considered. I brought my full weight down on his right shoulder, feeling it crumple into worthless meat as I did. His weapon fell to the ground instantly, and to his credit, he neither went down with it nor did he make much of a sound. All the same, I was furious, and he was no match for my speed besides. With my left forearm, I moved to pin him to the wall while I kicked the blade up into my right hand in the same fluid motion and moved to drive it into his head.

"Ahh!" Ann bellowed, something that had meant to be a word but only came out as a sound. Either way, it caused me to stop in my tracks half a moment before I ended this poor bastard's life. "Jesus Christ, Chalsarda, what are you doing? Look at yourself!"

I caught a glance of myself in the reflection of a car window. My face was twisted in anger in a way that I couldn't remember ever seeing ever before. A glance back at the young man showed no fear, despite the fight being driven out of him. At that moment he should have been afraid.

"One chance!" I growled at him. "How many others are with you?"

His expression never changed, not even as I gave a swift jab of the blade's handle into his forehead, rendering him unconscious. He was making it clear that he wasn't going to talk and this was no time for a lengthy conversation. "I'm keeping the knife," I swore under my breath, only just then realizing how heavily I'd been breathing.

"What happened to not killing anyone?" Ann asked in a huff.

"Does he look dead to you?" I sneered.

"Almost, kind of, yeah!" Ann retorted looking at the young man's broken body. "And if I hadn't—"

"If you hadn't what?" I suddenly snarled. "Hesitated? Maybe you could have beat him up with magic? I saw you; you were just going to let him gut you open if he'd been so inclined!"

I couldn't have reproduced that expression on Ann's face if I punched her in the stomach. "That's... that's not... I didn't expect him to…"

Ann stammered the words out, and a wave of regret crashed over me. "Oh gods, Ann, I'm so sorry, I didn't mean it. It's not you that I'm upset with, it's just…"

My excuse remained incomplete, and Ann, nearly puffy eyed now, shot back, "Just what?"

"I can't watch you die, all right?" I shouted back. "It was different before. I was in service, I could detach myself from the situation. But now? Now I owe nothing to no one, and yet here we stand. We have chosen each other, and every time I allow myself to have a friend, they all leave me, one way or another. I have been teaching you to defend yourself. Because you asked me to, certainly, but also because there is so very much in this world that can take you from me and I am not ready to see you leave. Not yet."

Ann took a moment to respond. "So when you saw me freeze up, you lost control."

"Yes. Quite."

"But you don't lose control," Ann remarked softly. "You're supposed to be the one in control."

I let the unasked question hang in the air, in no rush to answer it.

Ann spoke first. "It's fine. We both lost our heads for a moment. It happens. I just don't understand how you can get to a place where you're ready to kill someone without a second thought."

"As I recall, you drove me here," I answered wryly.

"Not funny," she said coldly. "I'm serious. You are stronger than most of us. Faster. And you have entire lifetimes of experience to draw on. In many tangible ways, you are better than most of us, and you have a responsibility to act like it. I need to know that you'll find a better way, even if that way is more difficult. I didn't ask this before, because I didn't think I had to, but I'm asking you now. I don't want anyone to die just so that I can live. No killing. Will you promise me you won't kill anyone while we're doing this?"

My blood ran cold at that. An impossible question. One I desperately didn't want to answer. But if she wanted me to be in control, then so be it. I squared my shoulders, facing her directly now. She craned her neck slightly to look up at me as I looked her dead in the eyes and delivered my answer.

"No."

11

Anger and shock became evident in Ann's face as she stared me down. "No?" she yelled, her voice echoing in the claustrophobic alley. "You seriously can't promise me that you're not just going to go around killing folks?"

I raised my voice in return. "You honestly want to have this conversation out in the open and in front of your would-be assassin? Fine by me, let's address your concerns! For as much as I may want to believe otherwise, it is evident to me that you are still a child. You deal in absolutes, and what's worse, you think you have the right to demand anything of me. You either want to live, or you don't, but what about me? You're willing to let me fight this battle for you, but what happens when I arrive at a moment where it is them or me, hmm? What then?"

"There's a hell of a lot of difference between you defending yourself and what you were about to do to this man right here!"

I sighed impatiently. "Yes, there is. But that's not what you asked me for, is it? You asked me not to kill anyone during the course of our mission. Because you didn't think about your words. Because even now, you don't actually know what you want. That man could have just killed you, and that would be the end of all of this, wouldn't it? No one would else would have to be hurt. And you know that you and I are only just beginning with this. I almost died once already. You picked me up off the ground. You have to know that there is plenty of pain and suffering to come, all so that you can live, and deep down you're okay with that. I am too. I am willing to harm and be harmed for you, willing to do whatever I have to do for you, because of how I feel about you. But creator's mercy, Ann! What if I had said yes, just to appease you? What if you had bound me from properly defending myself? Do you have any idea of what that's like?"

Ann turned away from me at that, refusing the answer. I strode over to her, spinning her around by her shoulders to face me and gave the answer she may or may not have known. "No, you don't. And you likely never will, gods willing. Because you, Ann Bancroft, are stupidly, beautifully, impossibly human. Congratulations, I hope it lasts."

"What do you want me to say, huh?" Ann shouted back. "That I'm sorry for what you've gone through? I am. That I want to have anyone fight this battle for me? Because I don't. I don't know the right answers here, but I'm not going to just go along with... whatever this is!"

Ann pointed sharply at the unconscious body as she struggled to finish her sentence. I sighed heavily, suddenly feeling tired. "Listen, I don't have time for this, and I don't believe you're going to get the answer that you want. So, this is the best I can do for you. I don't want to kill anyone, I truly don't. And I'll do what I can to avoid taking a life, but I'm not going to make any promises. Especially not out here in the open like this. So you can come with me, or you can go home. Your choice. But the matter is closed for the moment as far as I'm concerned. Go home if you like. In fact, that might be the for the best. I don't know that you can handle doing what needs to be done, and I can't worry about keeping an eye on you, so, no more distractions."

I turned away from her as I said it, not waiting for a response, and as I walked away, I didn't get one. It was just as well. I really thought that maybe Ann could have handled this, that the two of us together could have figured this whole thing out, but she wasn't up to the task. Worse, she'd begun to anger me, though at least in part, I was to blame. I've barely started to train her, and as my student, I'd treated her too much as an equal, not enough as a student. Perhaps that's where she found the nerve to make demands of me that she couldn't possibly understand.

I liked Ann. I liked her enough to put my life on the line for her and betray my principles to save her life. I liked her enough to not immediately put an arrow through Alistair's heart for her. But for reasons I couldn't fully grasp, I was on the verge of strangling her. If I was being honest with myself, I'd been off my game from the moment Alistair appeared. In my time I'd seen many things that people would mistakenly refer to as evil. What people usually mean when they say evil is frightening or violent or something otherwise showy. A rampaging orc can be brutal and dangerous, but it isn't always calculating. Maybe it has a thought in its head, perhaps it doesn't, but either way, it is a product of what it knows. Big, dumb, and strong; but not truly evil.

Alistair is evil. Everything he does, he does without regard for the lives of anyone but him. He lies with more ease than it takes him to breathe. And whenever he has had the chance to hurt someone, he has done so with glee. It could be physical, or it could be otherwise, it didn't matter to him. It wasn't even that that he liked to see others hurt, it was that he liked knowing that he could hurt someone deeper than anyone else could.

He is sadistic in the most sincere sense of the word.

And maybe that's what was getting to me about Ann. Even with the shroud of death hovering behind her, and even with everything I was about to put myself through to prevent that untimely death, she was still making demands of me. For the most part, I was willing to blame it on her youth and inexperience, but there was another part, much smaller, that said maybe she was treating me like I was the help. Like this was the only reason I was around. I didn't believe that, not truly, but it was hard to shake. And maybe it was all just me, that I was just not doing the job of communicating how dangerous this all was for her.

Getting away was for the best, I thought, at least for the moment. If I was being honest, I couldn't hear and see what I needed to while I was watching her back. Ann and I should have never ended up in that alley in the first place. And for that matter, it could have gone so much worse. What if instead of just watching, someone decided to put a knife into one of us in passing? I'd like to think I would have caught it in time, but would I? Already I was making my way towards the address revealed on our map, and I'd managed to spy half a dozen of the Abbot's lookouts who had no chance to spot me, let alone any idea of how close I was. Wandering around Venice with Ann was drawing more attention to myself than a mother with a screaming baby in a crowded theater. This was more my speed. I still wasn't sure what would happen when I got there, but at least I would get there quietly.

The Abbot's house wasn't anything I needed help in finding. The moment I'd seen it on the map, I didn't so much as need confirmation or a closer look. I'd been here before, and even if I hadn't, all you had to say by way of direction was to keep an eye out for the biggest and most obnoxious house in Venice, and you'd find it. It was long enough that you could have fit two moderate sized homes on the lot of land that he owned, and incredulously it was three stories tall and boasted a basement and the privacy of a high walled backyard, all of which was a rarity in the area. And still, even with this total eyesore of a house, it was easily forgettable the second you turned the corner. That's just the way it was around here. All of the homes in the area were expensive, all of them were gaudy. Some were just a bit gaudier than others.

Broad daylight on a residential street was not what I'd call the ideal conditions for surveilling undetected. But like I said, I'd been here before, and thankfully the good people of Venice loved their trees. Well, the good people north of the canals who liked to pretend they weren't a beach community, that is. And as I sat perched in one of the lusher trees on this particular street, watching the house, it was impossible not to recall my earlier experience here. The first thing that stuck out to me was that the Abbot always had a guard out front. Always. The nature of his guard was concealed, of course. At a glance, you would merely see someone gardening, perhaps meditating or a couple of members enjoying a cigarette together. But anyone who watched them for long enough would see what I knew to be true: If you crossed their threshold uninvited and they didn't like your reasons, you might not make it back out.

There was no guard this time. No activity from the house that I could notice at all, actually. Highly unusual, given everything I knew about this place. The last time I'd been here, there was a minimum of three people watching the front at any given time, and that was to say nothing of the activity going on in the rest of the house. Abarta had sent me to watch the house some ten years ago. A teenage runaway had been caught up with the Abbot's cult, and he thought they might be useful to his plans. I was to extract them if he decided they were worth the effort. He did not. I insisted on saving them anyway, and I paid for my insolence. Insolence was a fancy way of saying that I should have known better than to have an opinion of my own. I didn't want to think about how I paid, and I didn't want to think about what happened to that child.

No, it was best to shrug off that particularly disturbing memory and focus on the task at hand. I climbed down from the tree, still unsure of what to make of the absolute absence of activity around the house. If I hadn't known better, I would think no one was home. But I did know better. I knew that the Battle Born was inside and I knew that the Abbot wouldn't leave his precious home unguarded unless... did the Battle Born just kill everyone inside? That doesn't match up with my working theory that the Abbot's people had managed to capture her, but then again, not much was adding up at the moment.

I reached the ground and crossed the street without incident. There was nothing to stop me from entering, save maybe an alarm system or wards, but as far as I could tell, there were no signs of either. There are really two types of wards. The first being physical, like the sort that I'd used in my current residence. The upshot for that sort of ward was that really anyone could use them once they'd been created. In some faiths, it can be as simple as leaving some salt in the corner. I knew a pagan once whose ritual lasted an entire day and involved a large number of specific stones, candles, symbols, and a lot that I'm probably not remembering. As far as I could tell it was sufficient. Personally, I've found that getting a priest to bless a bit of holly did wonders. It was an old Celtic trick, and I'll give you three guesses where I picked it up. The simple truth was that there was no one right method, and it really came down to the faith of the person doing the warding. I don't know that the Abbot believed in anything beyond himself, but I have no doubt he could find someone to help him out if he wanted. Maybe believing in himself was enough. The downside to these wards, however, is that they were static and really only focused on pure evil. If you knew exactly what you wanted to be kept out of your home, there were options for that, but then again, that took more effort than most people were willing to put in.

The other option was to magically weave a ward. If you knew what you were doing and you were mean enough, you could hurt whatever you wanted with whatever you spell you fancied. Elana had recently started warding her bookstore with increasing severity against anything that was not human or elf. One day something was going to wander into her store, and it was not going to enjoy the ensuing fireworks display. From what I knew of the Abbot, he may have a bit of magical talent, but nothing close enough to weave a proper ward. A smaller percentage of people with magical talent than you'd think had the kind of power to make a ward worth taking notice of, and Elana was only able because of her rod.

So wards didn't seem like a reasonable concern, and the only real way to find out if I was wrong was the hard way. That left a security system, and with no prep time to research if there was one active in the house or which one it was, I was left again to gamble. My best guess was that with everything that no doubt went down beyond his doors, the Abbot wouldn't want the local police showing up for a visit. Maybe he had something that would alert him personally, but if he wasn't already at home, where would he be?

It was at this point that I realized I'd walked right up to the front door without a thought for what to do when I got here. It was the middle of the day, not exactly ideal for breaking and entering. I could kick in the door, but I'd leave a busted door for any passerby to see. I could scale the side of the house, get a better look around, but there were a lot of windows on this street, and I'd have a hard time explaining that away. Picking the lock was an option as well, but again, I'd have to be quick about it. It was then that I considered, for just a moment, what Ann would do in this situation. And with no immediate options otherwise, I did just that.

I tried to open the front door.

Somehow, I didn't like the fact that the door was un-locked. I felt my skin flush hot at the annoyance that I was now for the second time in as many days walking into a situation with the same person who by all rights I didn't measure up to in a fair fight. This wasn't how I liked to work, but Alistair had put me in this position. I knew walking into this house was a stupid idea, but what else could I do? Everything was time sensitive. Ann was dying, at least one of the other bounty hunters knew where she was, and every moment that passed meant my chances got worse. This was the same situation as the aban-doned mall. I knew where the Battle Born was and I had no choice but to follow her and hope for the best. Well, not entire-ly the same. I knew firsthand now how strong and fast she was. I knew that she was prepared to kill me. But more importantly, I knew that I could hurt her as well.

I slipped inside before I could change my mind, quietly closing the door behind me and took a minute to study the room, now that I'd finally made it inside. The expansive living room felt and looked more like a new age spa than any kind of home. In place of any traditional furniture, the room was dotted with rolled out thick, comfortable looking mats and plump, cir-cular meditation pillows. There was no television or any other form of entertainment, which wasn't a surprise. There were altars against the walls, end tables with every inch of table sur-face covered in various crystals and the occasional odd succu-lent. And at the end of the room, on the other side of the tall glass door windows, was a lush green garden and an outdoor room at the far end of the yard, a wooden structure with sturdy white curtains and pillows not unlike those in the living room.

The small chirp of the radio was the first confirmation that I'd walked into a trap.

The second, of course, was the emotionless faces of the cult members revealing themselves outside in the yard, from around corners in the house, and the six-and-a-half-foot tall meat slab of a man who slammed open the front door behind me. Looking past him, I could see he had something of a twin close in tow. I set my feet and caught his wild swing, twisting my hips and rolling my shoulders as I did, sending him spinning across the room with a crash.

Here's the thing about us elves. Or at least, the thing about me and the sort of elf that I am. Anyone who has ever seen us fight is quick to assume there must be something supernatural about us. We're stronger, faster, and more agile than most humans. And to a certain point, that's true, but we're not quick to correct anyone who wants to give us more credit than we're due. I can lift more than the average human with ease. And when it comes to running and leaping, humans just couldn't compare. This is to say nothing of my dexterity. I was born nimble in a town where children could often cartwheel before they could speak. All of this just meant that in a fair fight with the average human, you'd do well to bet on the elf.

But it was becoming more evident by the moment that I wasn't in a fair fight, and certainly not with one person. More faces were starting to appear by the moment, and any second now there wouldn't be a way out.

No killing.

Ann's voice rang out in the back of my mind, causing me no small amount of annoyance. My preoccupation with her was what had led me to this moment in the first place. My lack of focus was how I'd found myself surrounded and in a fight for my life. I was very much in a kill-or-be-killed situation, and all I could think about was how much I'd be letting her down if one of these people didn't get back up. I didn't know that I could survive this fight otherwise, but not knowing wasn't the same as impossible. The frustration building in me would need a release, I guess.

Damn it, Ann. Fine. I will do this your way.

I pirouetted towards the fallen man before he could stand, bringing a heel down hard against the side of his knee with a rebellious crunch. The smart move would have been to stomp down on his neck, but I hadn't been smart in at least a couple of days, it would seem. He howled in agony, but at least he could howl. Two more people came at me from the kitchen, both of them women and both of them wielding steak knives. One of them earned a broken foot and a rolled ankle for her troubles, the other merely received a sharp elbow to the side of her head. They went down, but the one became two, and the two became four.

My training took over, and suddenly the parameters of the fight became clear: Defense if I must, offense while I can. Several more cult members went down and in a variety of creative ways. A dislocated shoulder here, broken ribs there, and most of the front teeth of one particularly eager young man, but if anyone was wary of my capacity for violence, no one was showing it. They all kept coming until I made sure they could not. When the numbers became too many, I leaped up over the banister and dashed to the second floor, only to discover that my presence caused a wave of them out of the halls and from behind doors. There was no room to maneuver, and in the face of a dozen or so of them, I was promptly knocked back down to the first floor.

Recovering in mid-air was easy enough; I twisted my body and planted my feet into the chest of the pot-bellied man unfortunate enough to be directly beneath me. Still, that bought me less than a second, and all pretense of offense was officially gone. I was fast, I was trained, and I was present. And it wasn't enough. For all of my defense, the punches were starting to land. I wasn't focused on who went down by this point, only that I managed to stay up. It didn't last. Minutes that felt like hours passed before I was lifted to my feet and pinned to the wall. Two particularly bulky men on either side held me back, and two more people I couldn't see held my legs. They needn't have bothered. I knew the fight was lost at this point, and they must have been ordered to take me alive. I didn't bother to struggle; it was wiser to conserve my strength in case those orders didn't hold.

The crowd of people began to part wordlessly as a silk-robed man slowly made his way into the home from the back-

yard. His dirty sneakers, which clashed with the rest of his outfit, seemed to deliberately crunch the broken glass around the
room as he approached. His face was an uneasy blend of features both young and elderly, making a guess at his age impossible. A golden surfers tan and the full head of hair flowing
down his back marked him as young, while the crow's feet
around his eyes and the large gray patches in his messy beard
exposed signs of aging. As he drew closer, he knelt down absently and waved a crystal over some of the wounded, and their
pained expressions faded almost instantly.

His eyes met mine as he rose, deliberately and slowly, and
with a forced smile, he let his first words languidly fall out of
his mouth. "Hello, Chalsarda. I've been looking forward to
meeting you."

"You'll forgive me if I cannot say the same, Samuel."

He chuckled softly at that. "Why would you call me that?
Samuel. Why that name?"

"Am I supposed to call you the Abbot?"

Samuel, the Abbot; whatever, knelt down beside another
small gathering of his followers, three people with broken legs
that I'd put down in quick succession, to repeat his perfor-
mance. One by one before my eyes, their injuries healed in a
matter of seconds.

He stood after a moment and looked at me as he continued. "I never said you should call me anything; I merely asked
why you called me by that name. Why do you call yourself
Chalsarda? Why does anyone call anyone anything?"

"It's my name, you dolt." At this point, I wasn't sure if I
preferred death or the philosophy lesson.

"Yes, it's your name. But who gave it to you? Why does it
hold meaning for you? Why do you call a tree a tree? You've
just accepted it. But is that who you are? Am I just a Samuel?"

"This feels like an odd way to go about gloating before
you kill me, Samuel. So if you're hoping for murder here,

maybe a ritualistic sacrifice or something, might I suggest you get on with it?"

His eyes grew at that with mock surprise. "Why ever should I kill you? Simply because you broke into my home and assaulted my family? I'd dare say the only one doing any violence here today was you. I am seeking to correct some of your wrongs if anything. But I digress, if you don't like that question, let us move onto another. Why are you here?"

"Is this just going to lead to some deep answer about why any of us are here, cosmically speaking?"

"No, I meant that in the present tense. Why have you broken into my home?"

"Oh good, a real question," I sighed. "Finally, I wasn't sure how much more of your nonsense I could stomach. I'm here for the Battle Born, of course."

"You mean Debbie? And what would you have with her?"

I blinked at that. "So you're not even going to bother denying it? And you've given her a name?"

"Why should I deny it? Of course she is here, but to your other point, no. I would not presume to name her; she has named herself."

He had me on this one; I hadn't expected him to be so blunt about it. "I don't understand."

"Oh, of course you do! If only you think about it, it makes perfect sense. Chalsarda, my words and my abilities are for those in pain, even you. And my home is for all people with nowhere else to go."

"No, you've captured her, you were sent to collect a bounty!"

He raised an eyebrow at that. "And why should I do that? Do I look as if I need mere money? Or trinkets? No, do not presume to put me into the same foul category as you. Debbie is safe here, with me. After all, you're the one who inflicted grievous injury upon her person, and now you're here to finish the job."

This was becoming more frustrating by the moment, and I didn't have time for it, but I didn't have a lot of choices either. "If you do not intend to turn her in, then what do you want with her?"

"The same thing I want with you, my dear. I want to show her peace. I want to help you heal your wounds."

"Have your goons let me go, and I'll give you some wounds of your own to play with!" I spat.

He laughed softly to himself as he approached. "You know so little of my power. Physical wounds are but one sort of injury to be healed. And before I even walked into the room, Chalsarda, I could tell that your wounds ran deep. Allow me to show you just how deep."

With an outstretched fist clutching a glowing crystal, he moved to place it towards my forehead. The terrifying idea of having unknown magic visited upon me suddenly seized me, and I struggled to break free, but it was too late. I was pinned tightly in place as the crystal—

He fell back and away from me like someone who took a sucker punch to the stomach, dropping the crystal as he lost his balance on his feet. I suspected that I got the worst of it. My senses were overwhelmed in an instant, more pain and relief than I could have ever possibly anticipated filled my being. Guilt and anger and regret and emotions I didn't have words for flooded to the surface and close behind them, mixing horribly, were the hints of acceptance and understanding and a soothing that was not enough to keep up with the sudden torrent of pain. There was only the knowledge, as terrible as it was, that I was in terrible pain and somehow I didn't know how badly I'd been hurt. It was the feeling of a bad tooth being removed from your head without anesthetic or the moment of adrenaline wearing off after realizing you'd survived a terrible accident; I was as-saulted with the sensation. And slowly, far too slowly for my liking, it began to evaporate. Suffering and fear faded from my being, replaced with a warmth I had almost forgotten.

My body began to relax as the feeling of muscles I hadn't realized were tense began to soften and relax. Deep-seated pains, physical and otherwise, started to smooth over and my legs went limp beneath me. The men on either side of me were no longer holding me back but were now holding me up, and my eyelids became heavier than anything they were responsible for keeping aloft. The Abbot was excitable, babbling as he got to his feet, but if whatever he had to say was important, I'd never know it. I was checking out of this conversation, and I didn't have any closing remarks.

Trancing again. Wonderful. I'm not ready to fight it now, despite knowing how this story ends. Even here I am weary. And more to the point, I've long since passed the part in my story where it has become too late to change my fate regardless. The deal has been struck, and I am now clutching my prize, incorrect in my assumption that I am ready for the world to come. I watch myself as I make my way to the shoreline, rushing to meet my love. I know how badly this will end, but for once I'm not going to resist. I will let my mind show me the last good and pure moment I would have for a lifetime to come, and when I get to the punchline, let me feel the blow as it lands without flinching. It may have been enough to break me once before, but I've since learned how to take a punch.

Abarta had opened the way into Alistair's world, and with my prize in hand, I crossed over without hesitation. I am in a small village. So small that I am confident I can see its border in any direction from where I'm standing. The men wear thick, dull black woolen coats and the women are clothed from neck to toes in multiple layers, bodices over corsets over outrageously big dresses; none of which matched the pleasant warmth in the air. Everyone wore tall hats, something I certainly had never seen back home. The looks I received and the comments whispered about me were immediate. I didn't care back then, and I don't care about them now, though getting the chance to relive the moment has given me the opportunity to chuckle internally at the phrase 'Devilish apparition.'

No one is of any help, but in my excitement, I follow the road to a larger town nearby, one visible before I even begin to venture forward. My request for Alistair brings sour faces, for the most part, one even spits at the sound of his name. For the first time, I'm becoming aware that my appearance, my ears and my attire, even my way of speaking are unlike anything anyone here has ever seen. Not everyone is ready to welcome an elf into their community, it would seem, but again, I don't care. Now it is for other reasons, the petty and spiteful side of me sarcastically thinks it's because everyone there has died due to their painfully short human lifespans; but then? Only because I had no intention of staying. I intended to see the world, and from what I could tell this was the most insignificant corner of it. Finally, someone recognizes the name. He's expected today on a ship known as Faith at Port Talbot, which is apparently not far from here. My heart soars. He has more to say, but I'm gone before he can tell it, sprinting for the ocean. And as I arrive at the cliff's edge, that's when I see it. That's when I feel it!

The ocean! Oh merciful gods, the ocean! In my excitement, I never stopped to think that I might see it one day! Salt from the breeze gently burned my nostrils, and I closed my eyes and inhaled deeply, welcoming and savoring the new sensation. I opened them again, more delighted and filled with wonder than any child. Before me, infinite and blue, was the ocean. Grey clouds dotted the sky but threatened no rain. Waves gently lapping the shore creating a rhythmic beat which the universe had decided that, at least for the moment, was a concert exclusively for me.

But what brought me joy, more joy than just the freedom from the borders of Verisia, was the knowledge that it was the ocean that connected what would be all of my adventures. That someday soon, Alistair and I would set off across it, disconnected from everyone, and wherever we landed had better be ready for us, because Alistair and I were coming to leave our mark. It was the life I wanted. It was the life I was sure that I had deserved and earned.

I tried to hold onto this portion of the memory like gripping sand with both fists. I wanted to embrace the beautiful feelings that came with such optimism. I leaned into the lie because I knew it wouldn't last. And it would be so very long until I ever felt good again.

I've spotted the port now. Dread is creeping over me in waves far more turbulent than are on the shore. They overwhelm the elation I felt at the time. My instinct is to fight the memory, but I force it down. This happened, and it happened to me. Pain is coming, worse than anything I'll experience for a very long time to come because today is when I learn about betrayal and heartbreak. Part of me hardens today, and I lose something I may never get back. And for reasons I can't pin down, I want it this time. I need it. I know intrinsically that I need to be hurt even if I cannot say why. Even if I'm disturbed by that very need.

I find running in the sand to be an uneven and perilous experience, but I laugh all the while, making a game of not falling down. When I arrive, the dock workers exchange glances in my direction, and whether it be from my appearance, my attire, or my unbridled glee, I do not care. It is not an understatement to say that I am unable to contain myself. It's coming, Chalsar-

da. It's almost here. You can take the punch. I squeal when I see the ship marked Faith. Don't you dare flinch. You are stronger now, and you do not run. You couldn't run even if you wanted to besides, so you will face this head-on.

I realize now that even preparing myself for what is to come is in itself, a defense mechanism. I'm dulling my senses against what was for what it is. I stop and remind myself I am merely a passenger in my own mind, and I quiet those thoughts as I see him.

Alistair Wright. Windswept and perfect. My hero.

He spots me soon enough. The surprise is evident on his face, even with the sun in my eyes. He moves to meet me, but I move to him even faster. "You're... you're here?" he asks in disbelief. I embrace him and kiss him in full view of everyone, drawing sounds of approval. His face beams as he looks into my eyes. "You're here!"

"I am," I concur. "And I am never leaving. Not without you."

"About that. Quickly, we need to talk. In private."

He leads me away from the glaring eyes of the public, around corners until at last, we stop. "So the deal, you made it?" he asks excitedly.

I nod my head in approval. "I did. For you. For us!"

"Tell me everything, what did he say? What was the bargain?"

It never occurred to me then why he was so eager to hear these details, and I try to watch with the same eyes I once had, ignoring what I now know. "Abarta gave me the means to travel to your world, just as you traveled to mine. You and I can live our lives together, and until our time has come to an end, I am free to be with you. After, I am to work for him, but that's not important now. What matters is that we have the rest of our lives! You and I! Worlds could not keep us apart!"

Alistair laughs softly at that. "Chalsarda, this is wonderful news. More than you realize. You see, because of what you just did, because of what you just gave up for me, I finally have the chance to tell now, from the bottom of my heart just how truly..."

I am expectant of his every word as he stares at me, letting the sentence hang for one more cruel moment. "*Just how truly disgusted you make me feel.*"

I know I couldn't have heard that correctly. "*Oh, you heard me, though I don't know that disgusted really encapsulates what I'm trying to say.*"

"*What?*" It's all I can ask. I simply do not understand.

"*Oh god above, how can you be so blind? You're an elf! Is there anything more unnatural? Did it honestly never occur to you to wonder why I, a human, would have taken an interest in you? You simple-minded cow, use your mind for once and piece it together! Did you not think for one mere moment what I might get out of all of this?*"

"*You... you had my love.*" I am breaking apart inside now, the large pieces first. The smaller cracks would come later.

"*You were a job!*" he exclaimed. "*Oh heavens, this was too easy. I could have just as easily fooled a puppy. Very well, pay attention to this. You are only free for as long as we are together, is that right?*"

There it is. There's the gaping, bottomless dread.

"*Then let's get this over with, shall we? Chalsarda, you and I are—*"

"Get up." I know I am being commanded. I know that voice from somewhere. My eyes open, and through the haze of watery eyes, I see a familiar figure. Imposing and dangerous. It is a woman, and her gaze itself is danger. She has another command.

"You and I are going to talk."

13

"The Battle Born," I muttered as my eyes began to adjust to the land of the waking.

"I told you before; I have a name," she growled.

I considered her carefully before I continued, but it was impossible to do that without considering the cold iron cage surrounding me as well. Given the Fae reaction to the touch of cold iron in general, this seemed excessive. Or given how much I fight I had in me when I got here, maybe just a bit cautious and otherwise wholly appropriate. "Yeah, I remember. Debbie, right?"

Debbie shifted slightly at that. "That's right. Got a problem with that?"

I let out a sigh at her aggressive tone, trying to get a better look at the windowless room. The basement, no doubt. "No, no problem. Just surprised, is all. Sort of how I'm surprised that you're willing to actually talk all of a sudden."

"You tried to ambush me, and whatever your words, you and I both know why you were there," Debbie scoffed. "Why would I think you came to talk?"

"Because it's better than fighting?" I sighed. I had no energy at the moment and certainly wasn't up for a debate. "I suppose it was too much to think you could even talk at all in the first place, wasn't it?"

"That right there! That is my problem with you! With all of you!" Debbie suddenly roared, and the ferocity of it made me sit up and flinch, even with the cage between us. "You think you know a damn thing about any of us! As if what we're called is what we are. The Battle Born, good for fighting and that's it, right? And what about you, Chalsarda? You think I don't know about you?"

Inside, my body was like a battery that couldn't hold a charge. Even her burst of excitement only roused my attention for an instant, but even with that accusation, I couldn't be bothered to press back. "I'm sure you do." It was all I could muster.

Her words came as accusations. "Blood soaked thief? Manipulator? Abarta's assassin?"

I stirred at the last one and responded softly. "I don't work for him anymore."

"No, but you came after me anyway. Yeah, I know all about you. It's in our namesake. We're born for battle, nothing else. But only a fool can't see past our physical prowess. We know our enemies, and I was taught much about you. You'd be shocked and sickened by what I know."

"Then you know about Alistair?" I asked. "You have to know that much. And if you did, you would know what he is. He poisoned my friend and the only way he spares her life if I bring you in for him. It wasn't personal, and I don't like that I'm doing it."

"I can believe that. But that makes all of this that much worse, doesn't it? You have resources and connections. Did you even try to find another way before you attacked me? No, you didn't, did you? Because violence is what you're good at, it's who you are. And you didn't stop to think about who you had to hurt in the course of who you wanted to save."

"So now what?" I questioned, turning to face her head on. "I hurt you. One unarmed elf against the big, scary Battle Born, and I found you. I hurt you. And I found you again. And you know I have every reason to come for you again and again until you put me down, so what are you going to do about it? You have me weakened and surrounded by cold iron. If you were ever going to kill me, you'd never get a better chance at it than now."

Debbie was seething now and gripped the bars of the cage in frustration. "Oh, I could do it! And I wouldn't need a cage, a weapon, or any advantage at all. You only think you know what I am and what I'm capable of, but I promise you that hurting me should not have happened and I'll never let you do it again. If I really wanted to, I could tear through this cage and bisect you where you stand. I could end you completely."

I didn't so much as blink as I responded. "Then why haven't you?"

She released her hold on the bars and took a couple of steps back. "Because I don't want to. Everyone has always expected one thing from me, and that's it. Violence. And I don't want to fight. Not you, not anyone. I just want to be free. And to be left alone. I am fine with not knowing my parents or having to name myself, or with having everyone I've ever known living to be an instrument of destruction. But I didn't ask for it, and regardless of how often I'm reminded that it's the only thing that I'm good for, I don't want it. I'd rather be useless than be used."

And just like that, the one thing I was hoping wouldn't happen suddenly did. I began to relate to her. "So that's why you're here," I began, the pieces clicking into place. "You were never captured, you sought the Abbot out intentionally. You wanted to get away, and you thought he'd make some kind of deal with you. He hid you, fed you, and after our fight, his people picked you up. But you have to know he accepted a contract for you; you cannot possibly trust him."

"You're not entirely wrong. But you're not entirely right, either. We never made a deal. It's like he's said, his home is for anyone with no place to go. I didn't offer him anything, and he didn't ask. The short answer? I'm just happy to be here. This is a place of healing, and he is a man of peace."

"No, you're wrong." I wanted to scream this, but I couldn't find the energy to raise my voice. "You're seeing what you want to see here, but he is not a good man. I know things—"

"And I know things too!" Debbie interrupted. "Don't think for a moment that I'm here because I'm ignorant and desperate. It is so easy for everyone to overlook this community and dismiss them as some nutjob cult. But there is power at work here, and the Abbot has one of the rarest gifts of all, the power to heal both the body and the mind. I'm not here for personal growth or spiritual enlightenment! I'm here to forget! I'm here to be something else. As long as I live like this, I will always have the urge to fight, to hurt anyone I see as an enemy or a threat. The Abbot can remove that part of me. When I'm wearing the robes or handing out pamphlets or meditating in the garden or whatever, I'm not going to be of any use to anyone; I won't be any kind of danger. And people like you will be out of a job."

Debbie didn't understand why the contract was out on her, but that had to wait. "Please, listen to me. Some years ago, there was a child, and I tried to help her, but the Abbot—!"

"Thank you, Debbie, for taking care of my guest." That voice belonged to the Abbot, and I could see him now, slowly descending the stairs into the dimly lit basement. "Would it be quite all right if I were to speak with her?"

Debbie backed away from the cage with a sneer. "Of

course, teacher. Not that she has anything worth saying."

I noticed it then, as she left the room. When she ascended the stairs out of the basement, her footing was uneven, and her hand instinctively twitched in a half motion to her side, though it never entirely made it. The Abbot's eyes never left Debbie until she was out of the basement, and only then did he cross the room and sit on the ground opposite me outside of the cage. Unlike the living areas above, this room was not decorated and it felt intentionally like a prison, though if he was bothered by sitting on the unfinished concrete floor, he didn't show it.

"You didn't heal her," I observed.

"Physically? No, no I did not," he confirmed.

"Why not?" I asked.

"Does it matter?" he asked innocently. "If I have a reason or I do not?"

I gave up the debate at that, laying my head down on the concrete to stare at the bars on the top of my cage. "What do you want?"

"I'm afraid you'll have to be more specific."

I turned my head to shoot him a look of annoyance. "With me, you insufferable—"

"Ah, of course, you," The Abbot said with a smile that approached something resembling sincerity. "I want to save you."

I don't think it was possible for me not to roll my eyes in that moment. "Mission accomplished, oh wise one. I don't think your people can get to me in here."

"Not from them," the Abbot said with a small shake of his head. "From yourself."

If I didn't think I had the energy for his nonsense before, now I was sure of it.

"All right then, go ahead and do it. Kill me. I'm sorry to cut this short, but I'm getting the sense that's where this was going to end up regardless, so, in your own time."

He rose to his feet at that, a look of impatience crossing

his face as he began to pace around the room. "Who do you think you are?" the Abbot snapped. I was taken aback by the question as much as the tone and my expression must have conveyed as much. "I'm serious now, that's not rhetorical. Who are you?"

The Abbot crossed his arms behind his back now, glaring at me expectantly waiting for an answer. He wasn't going away without an answer, and I finally told him, "Chalsarda."

"No, that's what you're called." He chided. "Someone decided that was who you are, and you've gone along with it. Let me ask you instead, why am I called the Abbot of Kinney and not Samuel or some other name? It's a silly thing, don't you think? I'm not stupid; I know what an Abbot is. That's not what I am, not really, so why say it?"

If I had more energy, I could have come up with a suitable response about precisely what I thought of him, but I was utterly drained and listless. The fact that I had so little energy was itself starting to become a concern, but with everything I'd been through recently, it could have just as easily been magical in nature as any number of other reasons.

The Abbot looked annoyed at my lack of response and continued. "It is because no one wants to follow a Samuel. It is because I've become something more than a Samuel. The Abbot is a symbol, something to follow. My message is far too important to go unheard, and the people cannot hear it from someone ordinary. The Abbot is who I've chosen to be because that is who they will seek out."

"And what? You amass an army and take over the world or something?"

He shook his head sadly. "No, the more people I reach, the more I can help. The way I've helped Debbie. The way I could help you. The way I would like to help Ann."

My blood ran cold at that, and I stiffened. How could he have known about Ann? All things considered, it was a recent event, and not even Debbie had known until I mentioned it to her. If he hadn't learned it from Debbie, and he couldn't have, then that left just two people. Now wasn't the time to let my surprise show, so instead, I asked, "Can you really help her?"

"Of course I can, don't be silly. Assuming you can see reason, of course. All of this can be over. No more tears, no more suffering. You can all be freed from your burdens. You and Ann and Debbie—!"

"And Wendy?" I ask, and for the first time, he showed something like genuine surprise.

"What did you just say?" he asked hesitantly.

"Wendy Sinclair," I clarified. "How's Wendy?"

The Abbot was studying me now, his confidence replaced with suspicion and a hint of defensive anger. "How do you know that name?"

I managed to sit up now to face him fully. "What happened to Wendy?"

Nothing for a long moment. "Wendy was supposed to be... more," the Abbot began carefully. "She was not—"

"She was sixteen," I seethed through clenched teeth.

The Abbot gave me a look of understanding as the pieces came together for him. "Ah, I see. That was you. The guardian angel who flew away without her."

It took every bit of strength I could muster, but I spit in his face through the bars. He didn't flinch. "I've seen what your help does, and for all your talk you have no actual interest in helping anyone but yourself. Those people up there? You feed on them. You exploit the desperate and the sick!"

"Oh come off it!" the Abbot shouted back. "Something you and I both understand all too well is that the point of dancing is to dance, the point of painting is to paint. The meaning of life is to live. You have been given a second chance to do that, and that is what I'm offering you. The people you're talking about? They're not dazed because of anything I did. If they're mindless, it is because they were given an opportunity to be alive, and they decided that it was too hard, or they didn't see the point, and in any event, they gave that life over to someone more deserving of managing it for them. Me! I am alive! I can bring a measure of worth to a gift they were wasting!"

I was on my feet now, though it felt like keeping my balance was all I could do. The ground itself began to insist that I visit it and enjoy an extended stay. I held it together and resisted the offer. The Abbot was a madman, worse than I had anticipated when I made my way here. I thought he had merely been a craven fraud, maybe even sadistic, but indeed he had been an opportunist. What I hadn't planned on was him believing his own hype. I could see it in his eyes. There was no remorse for anything he had done to anyone unfortunate enough to seek his aid. He felt if he could take it from you, you didn't deserve it. And I think the anger I felt at his callousness is what kept me upright.

"Is this really what you want to do? Do you want to waste the life of your friend because of some idiotic notion of pride or morals? Think about this. The longer we go on, the more likely it is that Ann will succumb to that poison. And that's the whole reason you're doing all of this, isn't it? Then come on. Help your friend by helping yourself. Disagree with my methods all you like, but do it when everyone is healthy and whole."

I didn't trust him to help Ann or anyone else for that matter. He didn't want to amass a following or even a congregation. What he wanted was an army. If I accepted his help, I wouldn't be in any better place than I'd been with Abarta. If anything it would be worse because in time I wouldn't even have my own mind. I've been possessed before, body and soul, but my mind was my own. Living in my own head may be a painful and scarred place, but it's still my own. I will never be anyone's tool ever again, and I would be damned if I walked Ann into that fate. I didn't want her to die, but if I took this help, she certainly wouldn't be living.

With an effort of will, I stepped up to the bars of the cage, close enough to the iron that the skin on my nose began to tingle. "I'll tell you what I want," I began coldly. "I want to get out of this cage and put my hands around your throat and squeeze until I am certain that no one will ever have to live with your help ever again."

"Very well."

I watched in astonishment as the Abbot unlocked the cage door and let it swing wide, leaving nothing between us. "What are you doing?" The question came out of me in a huff.

"I don't believe you know what you really want, but here's your chance to prove me wrong. Throttle me. Choke the life from my body if that is what you truly desire. You have my word I will take no action to stop you. End my life, and nothing will stand between you and Debbie. Whenever you're ready."

Every fiber of my being wanted to reach out, to make him pay, but even as he stood in front of me, no more than a foot away from me, I couldn't make my arms work. No, it was worse than that. I didn't have the will. As quickly as I was flooded with the desire to dart out of the cage I was filled with indifference and fatigue.

"Is that a no?" the Abbot asked, taking a step in my direction, and as he did, my knees buckled, sending me to the ground in a heap. "Disappointing, but not surprising."

The door closed, slowly and quietly, making a barely audible click to indicate that I'd once again been trapped. The Abbot took his time just then, studying me a moment longer before he continued. "So few know what they want, you know. You're not alone. It's all right, my child. Rest. You no longer have the burden of making this decision. I will make it for you. You don't have to join me to be of use, after all. You will be of just as much use to me as a sacrifice."

14

I didn't let myself sleep for fear of what I would see. I remained on the cold concrete of the basement unmoving, unable to tell how much time had passed. The discomfort eventually morphed into pain, and I was glad for it. I shouldn't have come here, at least not the way that I had. The pain helped me to focus on what had happened up until this point and thinking and considering would make slipping into unconsciousness less likely. There was magic at work here, no question. The Abbot had to be responsible for my fatigued state, and not just the initial blow that knocked me into a trance. His proximity was a part of it; I'd hardly been able to stand when he got too close. But was it a conscious effort or something passive once he had his hooks into me? The latter would make sense with the people in his home. Focusing on so many people at once might become too much of a strain and his cult already grown too big for that.

But that wasn't the only thing at work here. It shouldn't matter how distracted I was, I should have noticed those people before they attacked, and a lot sooner. Either they were magically concealed from my vision, or I really had no business adventuring ever again. The cloaking was well done, too. I've learned to spot the subtle changes in the air when something like that was nearby, though I could attribute my mind being otherwise occupied with painful memories and worrying about my friend to not spotting the illusionary magic. Between the various magic tricks at play and his recruitment of a Battle Born, it would track then that the Abbot would have recruited one or two others who might have their own measure of talent.

That would also explain Wendy Sinclair.

None of this did me any good at the moment, of course, but if I was going to survive this hornet's nest, piecing it all together could make all the difference in the world. The Gardeners, even a milquetoast little scab like Skip, presumably wouldn't have hired the Abbot if they had any indication about what he was up to, which meant that he'd managed to keep a lot of things secret from a lot of dangerous people and for a very long time.

I was thinking about what Skip would send after the Abbot for his betrayal when the basement door opened, and the sudden noise in the otherwise still room caused me to flinch. Heavy footfalls, and more than one set of feet coming down the stairs. I didn't need to see the Abbot to know that he was among them. I could feel his approach like a magnet with an opposing pole pressing down on me. Having a better idea of what was happening may do me some good in getting out of here, but at the moment I didn't see how.

"Go on, get her up." The Abbot's voice was hard and charmless. I didn't look up to see his face. The door to my cell swung wide, and the rough hands of unseen assailants gripped my arms, pulling me limply to my feet faster than my mind was ready to process.

As we exited the basement, my eyes adjusted to the sudden light and I got a look around. It looked as if everyone in the cult had gathered outside in pale pink robes, creating a circle around two of their members whose more colorful garb and that they were standing in the center of the circle led me to believe they were possibly lieutenants of the Abbot, for lack of a better word. Where everyone else had been looking down, these two stared at me intently. Each of them held a crystal roughly the size of a bowling ball with the care one might show a newborn. On the left was a tall, rail-thin man with bronze skin and a shaved head, his gaunt facial features reminded me of someone very sick and in their final days, but his imposing body language suggested otherwise. And on the right was a woman, shorter, but not by much. Hawk-nosed with cropped, wiry jet-black hair save a small streak of white, and thin lips that curled up at the edges just shy of a grin. The more I watched them, the more I sensed they were hungry.

The Abbot dropped me into the center of the circle. Not forcefully, but then, he didn't have to. With my body in a heap, he stepped back to address the crowd. "Friends, I address you today as those who have been found. Among you are many who had been teetering on the edge of destruction before fate delivered you unto me. And now, you have been given life anew. You drink deeply of my power, and I give it freely. Those who have been attuned to the way of the crystal know peace and contentment. You see life as the song that it is. Your days make notes, your weeks make lyrics, your years make up chorus and verse! But even now, I share beyond my limits. I do so without complaint and would do so until my end. For you. All of you. My children. But do not cry for me, but rather rejoice! Today is a grand day indeed for today my power shall be replenished with the sacrifice of one who is generous beyond measure."

The Abbot turned back to me then, looking at me with the gaze one might give a calf before slaughter. "Chalsarda is no mere human; she is an elf. She has been gifted with energy no human has ever seen, blessed with years we can only measure in generations. And rather than hoard these years to her own selfish ends, she gives them to us. And for this, we give our thanks. We bow our heads in reverence, for to give your life for another is the greatest gift of all, and one not received lightly, nor is it to be squandered. My disciples, will you begin?"

There was a nod from the gaunt man as he stepped toward me. "Exalted Chalsarda, I offer Seraphinite to honor the wholeness your sacrifice will instill in us all and to aid in your journey into the earth so that your spirit may rise to us all. What has been is what shall be and what shall be will show us the light."

There was a sense of awe in his voice as he said this. He knelt with great care and placed the crystal near my chest before backtracking to his original position, his head bowed. The woman then approached me much as he had, though her voice carried something closer in it to amusement. "Exalted Chalsarda, I offer Carnelian to honor the courage you show in your sacrifice to us and to signify the confidence we have in your life essence as it leaves you and flows through us. May the fires burn away all that is not pure. What has been is what shall be and what shall be will show us the light."

The woman left the gemstone at my feet and returned in the same manner as The Abbot nodded his appreciation to them both. "I thank you both for your gifts. If any among my children feel these gifts are not adequate, come forward and speak now and you may give yourself in their place, you may add your energy to us all."

The group remained quiet for several moments, proving that blind followers or no, there was still a shred of self-preservation among them. Or from a more disturbing perspective, it was possible they didn't actually care one way or another about their own lives, but genuinely thought the fancy rocks were fancy enough to kill me.

"It is settled then," the Abbot continued. "And lastly, my

brave elf, my precious child. Exalted Chalsarda, I offer Iolite to…"

He trailed off at that, his ears perking up for a moment. I heard it too. The screech of tires heard faintly from the street, the foreboding sound of a car wildly thumping against a curb before a thunderous crash served as the peak of a hideous crescendo to the music of Ann's blue Nissan finding its way into the living room. The sudden noise and dust seemed to shake everyone, some more visibly startled than others.

Ann, the triumphant warrior princess that she had earlier insisted she was, nearly lost her balance on shaky legs as she got out of the car, coughing into her forearm.

"Grab her!" the Abbot shrieked to no one in particular. His composure was gone, but to be fair, so was the front of his house.

Ann threw a tiny bottle at the staircase with her remaining strength, and an instant later there was a sound like a half a ton of bacon being dropped into a lake of boiling oil. Small fires rose up as a section of the house seemed to disintegrate before our eyes, giving everyone more pause than even the car crash had.

"Stop right there!" she commanded. It was meant to convey authority, but her voice cracked ever just so near the end. "That bottle was marked 'Melty'. Let my friend go right now, or we get to find out what happens when I throw the one marked 'Boom Boom' and just saying, I'm pretty curious what that one will sound like!"

Ann held the mini liquor bottle over her head as if to emphasize her point. The Abbot held up a hand to keep the crowd in the backyard at bay as he took a couple of steps towards the house. "You can't possibly think you can win, can you?" he asked with a sneer. "Look around you! How many of our number do you expect to destroy before we overtake you? And how much worse for you both do you think it will be if you force us to?"

Ann took a challenging step forward of her own, standing on the remains of a coffee table and straightening her posture to make herself as tall as possible. "Oh, but I don't have to, now do I? I just drove my car into your house and if you're not careful that fire is going to spread quicker than not, right? I think someone's going to notice, don't you? So you can let us be on our merry way, or we can sit here and explain this all to the police when—!"

Ann collapsed suddenly with a brief, but unnerving, cry of pain as thick black veins spread from her chest to her face momentarily before receding. Dead Lines. And I still couldn't make a move to help her. Internally my body ached with fury and wrath, but none of it would translate into action. At that moment I hated myself, but I hated the Abbot a whole hell of a lot more.

The Abbot for his part sighed in frustration. "Bring her to me. Throw her into the circle with the elf," he commanded. Then, remembering himself, he added, "And will someone tend to those damned fires before our entire home goes up like a tinderbox?"

Several of his followers jumped into action immediately, removing their robes to pat down the fires, even as the robes themselves seemed to slowly dissolve after making contact with the acidic liquid remnants from the bottle. The man from the circle left us to go into the house towards Ann.

"Stop this!" I finally managed, weakly enough that I wasn't sure the Abbot would hear me.

He looked down at me then, and asked, "Whatever would I do that for?"

I managed to prop myself up onto an elbow, but only just barely. "Can't you see? She's dying; she needs help!"

"And what of it?" the Abbot asked. "Who told you that you were allowed to live forever?"

A shout came from inside the house. "Master! The young woman had these in the car with her!"

He held my bow and quiver up over his head for the Abbot to see. "Bring them along with the girl. They can all burn together for all I care. Quickly now, we haven't much time!"

The gaunt man smiled in agreement, slamming the car door shut before grabbing Ann by ankle and dragging her roughly over the debris and through the house with his free hand. Ann was awake now and protesting, though still too weak to do much about it. Both she and my bow and arrows were dropped roughly near my worthless body as he returned to his spot, trading a look with the woman. The Abbot then knelt down beside me with a look of barely contained murderous intent. "Enough with the formalities, elf. You are proving to be more trouble than you are worth. But before I incinerate you and your wayward friend here, I will let you in on a secret. You see, you pretend that what you do is important, or more accurately, you pretend that what you have come to do is justified. Perhaps even heroic. But here's the trick. You, specifically you, are worthless. Your actions are meaningless. The world, in fact, the whole universe, is indifferent to your pain, your sacrifice. What you think of as right and wrong, good and evil, that sort of thing comes from a belief that there is some grand overseer. Maybe even a whole bunch of them, a pantheon of sorts. But there are no gods, at least not in the way that you think of them. There is no cosmic lawmaker who cares what you eat or how you dress or even who you kill. That god never existed. I am God. Myself and the enlightened few who understand that this is all there is and have the courage act on it. God is what everyone is afraid to be because once you know what you are, what is there to stop you? The past, present, and future are meaningless to the likes of you, because you see, in a moment when I reduce the two of you to ash, none of them will have mattered. Your works, your dreams, will have mattered for naught. And in what I expect will be a very short period of time, none will even mourn you."

The Abbot stroked my hair at that, almost lovingly and re-iterated. "No one. Just like Wendy... whatever her name was."

He stood then, addressing the crowd. "Fantastic news, friends! We now have a second volunteer! Today shall be bountiful for us all! As the gift of everlasting life will be—!"

Everything that happened next went by in a terrifying split second. Hot blood sprayed for just a moment, some of it smear-ing across my face as I was too slow to prevent it from striking me. A sound like a tarp flapping in the wind grew in intensity above us, with cacophonic laughter like dying chickens filling the air in concert with it. The unsettling noise of a zipper re-tracting from all too close to me. And then there was scream-ing. Enough to wake the dead.

A headless corpse collapsed in front of me, an enormous pool of blood already staining the ground as the Abbot leaked and twitched. The woman in the circle was screaming an order to retrieve the Battle Born, though who was rushing to obey the command and who were fleeing for their lives was utterly un-known. With a considerable thump and the sound of talons dig-ging into roof tiles, the unseen attacker perched to admire their handiwork.

But throughout all of this? Life!

In an instant my strength was restored in its entirety, the hold the Abbot had over me was now lifted, and I sprang to my feet, bow in hand as I did. Ann felt something too; her face a portrait of shock as she gasped deeply. I knew what this was. Magic does not die easily; it always goes somewhere—either the world or the nearest possible host. It would not be a perma-nent boost, but for at least a few moments Ann would be filled to bursting with the pure and unfiltered good stuff before it would dissipate back into the universe. There would be no time to check on her though, in the middle of this madness. I needed to assess this situation immediately.

"My, but that was incredible!" a familiar, horrible voice called down to us. Ann was getting on her feet now, looking up in disbelief at what we were both seeing. "Hello, Ann. I did promise to give you a show, did I not? You and your friend. And I always keep my word. Come to think of it I also promised to show you what was in my birdcage, didn't I?" As she said this, the bottom of her birdcage, which was connected to a rope and had the outline of a sharp and menacing saw blade, opened suddenly to drop the blood drained head of the Abbot of Kinney to the ground near my feet.

We could see it now, it was the homeless woman from before, though I was kicking myself for not recognizing it at the time. It wasn't a feather coat at all; those were wings. And the smell of blood and rot and all of it, those weren't the smells of someone derelict. That was the stench of kills long past but never washed clean. And with her wings now open, we had a full hideous view of the creature underneath. Calling this person a woman might have been correct only in the most technical sense. Depending on your point of view, this was at least half a person.

"What the hell am I looking at?" Ann breathed in disbelief.

"I'm pretty sure this is bounty hunter number two. Birdie," I said, not taking my eyes off of her. "And Birdie, it would seem, is a harpy."

The situation grew more chaotic by the moment as cult members fled in a panic around us. There was already at least one death in this situation, and I had the sense that more were on the horizon if we didn't figure something out. I had to get to Debbie, she was within my grasp, but I couldn't ignore the fact that Birdie watched me with a hawk's gaze. With the two behind me gathering power, with the growing panic, I was the one she wouldn't take her eyes off of.

"Well, is the harpy our friend or foe?" Ann asked hesitantly.

"I get a distinct impression that Birdie isn't exactly willing to let us do what we came here to do, but she did just save our lives, so at the moment I'd call it a wash. Though I expect that this might change shortly one way or the other." I never broke eye contact with Birdie as I answered. "How about you? If we give you another tenner, do you think you could just forget this whole thing?"

Birdie offered something like a laugh. "And miss the opportunity to kill one of the god's forgotten? I wouldn't do that for anything less than twenty."

The gaunt man from the circle earlier stepped forward, power now radiating off of him in steady pulses. If I could feel this much with no magical talent of my own, I could only imagine what Ann was sensing. "Foul creature! Murderous abomination!" He challenged in a voice I wouldn't expect from a man of his frame. "Your cowardly attack on the Abbot shall not—!"

Even seeing it coming, the man didn't stand a chance of getting out of the way as the blades from the birdcage sank into his neck. At least he wasn't decapitated.

Ann looked like she was going to be sick, and I didn't know if that was from the sudden gore or from experiencing the death of two magic wielders in her proximity in such a short amount of time. I caught a glimpse of the woman who interestingly enough, rolled her eyes at the death of her comrade. Interesting indeed.

"Quiet, dearie. The women are talking." Birdie tsked at the fallen man. "You know, I never got to know his name. I'll bet it was something really neat too, like Pyrus or Xerxes or—"

"Birdie?" I interrupted.

Birdie shrugged. "Nicknames stick. No one in this town pronounces Greek names correctly anyway."

"What are you doing?" I finally shouted impatiently. "We're both after the same person, aren't you concerned about —"

I don't want to think about what would have happened if I'd taken my eyes off the harpy. The cage shot towards me at a disturbing speed, and I only just got my bow up in time to intercept the blow. My bow was carved from an Ain'thond tree, incredibly rare and nearly indestructible, it was perhaps my favorite bow. Birdie's saw managed to cut halfway through it. So the blades were no ordinary metal, either. That complicated things. Before she could retract the cage, I snatched the rope with my off hand, in an attempt to pull her down to ground level.

I immediately regretted the decision.

I yelped loudly, equal parts pain and surprise. My hand burned as hundreds, if not thousands, of tiny shards of some kind dug their way into my palm. I glanced up in time to notice that something more important had grabbed Birdie's attention as she retrieved her cage and flew to the other side of the house.

"I've indulged enough of this," the woman said from behind me, impatience evident in her voice. I'd nearly forgotten about her for just a moment, and I turned towards her just in time to see a shimmering wave of air tinted with a bluish hue explode in front of me with a rising hum. Pure concussive force propelled me backward, tumbling through a stone garden as the woman strode away.

Ann rushed to my side with something like shock and panic on her face. It would be a moment before I could reassure her. "Chalsarda! Are you—what should I do?"

The wind had been knocked out of me, but with an effort, I managed to force out a couple of words. "You... need to go..."

"I am not leaving you like this!" She nearly screamed in response.

I vigorously shook my head, given that it was easier than speaking at the moment. When I'd gotten a bit more air in my lungs, I added, "Not what I'm asking. Get... get to your car. If it will still drive, try to keep an eye... on Birdie. I'll catch up."

Ann looked at me hard for a split second but didn't argue, and instead bolted for her car. To my relief, I could hear the engine turn over, and with a horrible grinding noise, the car managed to reverse. A couple of tell-tale thumps later and it was gone. I managed to get back onto my feet but now faced a dilemma. Do I follow the deceptively powerful magic user or the insane harpy? And more importantly, did I have it in me at this point to fight either of them?

It was a simple answer, and not just because fighting someone practiced in magic would be foolhardy on the best of days. No, it was simple logic. Presumably, the cult members wanted Debbie alive, one way or the other. Birdie wanted her dead. If fighting a cruel and bloodthirsty harpy wasn't a big enough problem as it was, I had to contend with her flying out in the open without so much as a glamour. Most non-humans tend to keep hidden with excellent reason and the longer she kept this up, the more likely we were to find out exactly what that reason was.

The yard having emptied at this point, I took an extra moment to collect my arrows and examine my bow. Ain'thond wood was legendarily strong, but my bow wouldn't be safe to pull in this condition. It might fire, but it might just as easily explode in my face. Still, if Birdie were airborne, I wouldn't have a choice, should I choose to fight her. Which meant I'd need a plan. A plan, a lot of luck, and about a week to sleep off this headache.

It, fortunately, did not take me long to find something I could use, more specifically a rather long length of jute rope. I presumed the rope was meant to tie me down for whatever ritual they'd had planned for me, but the sheer amount of bundles gave me the chills. I could guess that I had not been the first, and I was not intended to be the last. Still, I only needed the one. I didn't trust my bow had more than one good draw left in it anyway, and more likely not even that, but I intended to make that shot count.

I removed a broadhead arrow from my quiver and left the rest of them behind. The rest of the arrows weren't about to do me any good, besides. I tied one of the ropes to the arrow's shaft and the other to an improvised hold in my trousers. Wherever this arrow went, I was going with it. On shaky legs I readied myself and scaled the house, looking to the skies. I saw her at once. She looked like a gargoyle the way she was perched on that telephone pole a couple of blocks away, watching the streets below her with some interest. It was too early to take my shot, but I couldn't chance her getting away. Without giving it a second thought, I took a running leap from the roof of that house and onto the next, making each of my jumps without allowing myself to feel pain or fatigue.

I was maybe three houses away when Birdie decided to acknowledge me and chose to head for the skies. This was my moment. She was airborne and dangerous, but at her most vulnerable during her ascent. Using all my momentum, I angled my leap towards the street, and at my apex, I unleashed my shot in time with where I felt her body would rise to. The bow groaned with a hideous creak, the string raked viciously across my exposed forearm, but I was not disappointed with the result. The arrow tore through the sky and didn't stop until it was halfway through her shoulder with a sickening thump. I landed awkwardly on a telephone pole of my own, dropping my bow as I did, and when the rope tugged as Birdie tested its length, I took that as my cue. With every bit of remaining strength in me, I pulled her down with both hands in one massive tug.

It had worked. Birdie had lost control of her flight, and the torn muscles in her shoulder and sudden blood loss had robbed her of her ability to stay aloft. Even her birdcage went loose from her grasp in the process. The harpy plummeted towards the earth and directly into the path of a moving van, too slow and unaware to stop for her in time. There was a screech of tires as Birdie smashed into the windshield and bounced off into the street. To my dismay, she began to rise to her feet almost immediately, but I wasn't about to give her the chance to recover. I made the twenty-foot jump to the ground below, planting both feet into her back. The blow was enough to send her into the pavement, but it was like landing on a parade float. Her body was thin and light, and the wings sprouting out of her back seemed to absorb much of the kick.

I rolled to my feet half a second before she managed to get to hers, a look of fury and hunger touching her face before a sick grin replaced it. And behind her, I could see the driver of the van was terrified out of his mind as he threw the vehicle recklessly into reverse, sideswiping several cars before he sped off and around us. This was it. Out in the middle of the street, neither of us whole. And about to fight for our lives.

Birdie was breathing heavily as she began to circle me, eyes scarily fixed on me. "I assume this wasn't the entirety of your plan. You wouldn't think something like this would stop me, would you?"

"I'm still here, aren't I?" I asked, assuming a defensive stance.

"You are, and I'm not surprised by that the same way I'm not surprised that you didn't put that arrow through my heart," Birdie responded. "See, I know all about you. But what do you know about me?"

Not much, I had to admit to myself. And even less about what Birdie was capable of. I knew about harpies from stories and reputation only. This was my first time fighting one, and I wasn't confident that I would survive the encounter.

Birdie took the silence as an opportunity to rake two claws at my face, and when I managed to avoid them, she spotted a weakness and sent me stumbling back into a parked car.

I composed myself and continued to keep an eye on her. This fight had deadly implications. She was at least as fast as I was and twice as vicious. Between her clawed hands and the talons on her feet, I could be gutted in the blink of an eye if I made a mistake.

Birdie continued, matching my gaze. "I can see it in your eyes, you know. And you see, I want you to look right back at me, deep in my eyes, and realize that you don't have what it takes to stop me. And I'm not in a rush to get out of here. I'll find the Battle Born again, and next time I won't have you around to annoy me."

"But why are you so intent on killing her?" I pressed, looking for an angle to get her off her guard. "Isn't the reward enough?"

The harpy's face managed more of a sneer than I had expected. "Yeah, I was right. You don't know shit about me. You think I need some trinket? It's a hunk of metal to me; you can keep it. And the money? What can money do for me? Nuh-uh, money just brings problems, makes you lazy and weak. No thank you, I'll take what I need when I need it. No, I don't want the prizes or the reputation or any of it! What I want is that mistake of a creature's bloody head in my hands and—!"

It was my turn to capitalize by way of interruption, and I shot into her bad side where the punctured arrow was still dripping blood and went to stomp on the side of her knee. I was half a second too slow, as her leg raised just a hair off the ground, preventing any leverage I might have had in buckling it. I tried to follow that up by pivoting behind her, but a wing flapped open and shoved me away with a shocking amount of force.

"Maybe there is something to you after all," Birdie pondered aloud, circling me again, this time to protect her bad side. "But I know you're not supposed to be here. I know something went wrong with your master. Something very wrong happened if you're befriending humans. I can kind of relate. I'm not supposed to be here either, but here I am. I was never supposed to be anything but loyal to Zeus, but he's not here. I was never supposed to leave Tartarus, but the underworld gets along just fine without me. But that's the difference between us. You were made to love trees and commune with nature, I was made to do violence, but when I do what I'm supposed to do, I'm a monster? Is that right?"

I rushed in just then, closing the distance on her, pushing

her out of the street and into a tree, pinning a forearm under her chin. "Yes! You are a monster, and not because of how or why you were created, but because of how little you care for life!"

"Good! So you understand me then!" Birdie rasped back at me. "And I'm going to keep killing my way up the food chain until something puts me down or until I get to Zeus himself and there's nothing left for me to kill! So how about it? Are you going to stop being prey long enough to put me out of my misery? Or am I going to have to use your pretty corpse to send a message that I am not screwing around?"

I lost my temper and removed my forearm long enough to swing at her face and wildly miss. I tried to turn on my heel to follow up, but I was too slow and knocked back again by a wing flap suddenly opening up into me, sending me into a parked car hard enough to shatter glass. The movements of Birdie were fluid despite their chaotic appearance. No sooner than I slammed into the hood than she dove at me, claw extended. This time I wasn't quite fast enough, and even though it was a grazing strike, the tips of her claws opened up my arms with a razor's precision. It burned, and that burning told me that enough was enough.

If she could fight dirty, so could I. Birdie had overextended herself with that attack, and rather than trying to get away, this time I reached up and clutched at the arrow still sitting in the meat of her shoulder, and pressing my feet into her chest, I pushed her off as hard as I could.

If you're shot with an arrow, the best you could hope for is that it goes clean through. If you have one resting in between a large clump of muscle, your best option is not to move it, maybe get someone to cut it out of you and patch up the hole. Birdie had already been moving around quite a bit with my arrow inside of her. And now, I just showed her exactly why you don't want to pull a broadhead arrow back the way it came.

She howled a bestial sound, the kind of noise that makes

even skeptics lock their doors and shut their windows. I could hear the barbed tips rend muscle as she fell away, the blood coming out of that wound no longer a gentle drip but a steady pump. Clutching the arrow in my fist I willed my body forward, knowing instinctively that someone like her was going to be far more dangerous injured than not. I was on top of her before she could react, and with a sound of my own to rival her previous howl, I slammed a knee into her wound, pinning her to the ground.

It was just then; arrow raised over my head as I prepared a deathblow that I heard it. From down the street, Ann's car, now significantly more damaged than it had been this morning, came toward us, picking up speed as the two of us came into her view. And it was at that moment that I hesitated. Everything that I had been conditioned to do up until that moment told me that I had exactly one second to put this harpy down or else I might not get another chance before she and I traded positions. And yet, something stopped me. I didn't want to kill anyone, not even someone as vile as Birdie.

And I hesitated just a moment too long.

I had somehow managed to completely forget the rope I'd attached to the arrow was still connected to me. All at once, my wrist was somehow pulled back, and the rope tied it over my head and to my shoulder. My back arched in sudden strain as the remainder of the rope went up and over a tree branch in a flash, pulling me awkwardly to my feet. Birdie spun on a talon in my direction, and in a miracle among miracles, I managed to twist my body just enough to avoid a puncture wound. The back of her leg still caught me behind my ribs, however, and that hurt more than enough.

Birdie looked at me for a moment, helpless as I was tied up in the tree. Then at the approaching car, and I knew, deep down, that Ann wouldn't make it to me in time.

16

I kept waiting for the final blow to land, and for an instant, I thought maybe Birdie had been just as hesitant to kill me as I'd been to take her life. But my optimism was given a quiet reminder that I was not dealing with beacons of morality when I saw it in her eyes. The blood loss was becoming too much for her to endure, and she must have figured she couldn't kill me and survive Ann before passing out, because Birdie turned away and began a somewhat drunken-looking jog away from me, scooping up her birdcage as she did. For my part, I tried to reach up and untie myself, but now that the rush of the battle was starting to fade, I realized how useless my arm currently was. Moving it caused blood to pour from those razor-like cuts, and I couldn't close my hand without feeling those splinters dig deeper into my flesh.

I didn't need to wait more than a couple of seconds anyway for Ann to pull up and practically fall out of her car to reach me. Her hands fumbled wildly as she tried to get the rope untied. "Jesus! Are you okay? Can you hear me? Where's Birdie?"

The rope came loose enough that I could pull myself free and I shrugged off Ann's attempt to console me as I stumbled towards her car. "We have to go. Now. Drive." My words were approaching something like a slur. The blood loss may have been getting to me as well.

Ann dutifully followed me, getting in the car and shutting the door with an extra bit of enthusiasm that was no doubt brought on by her anxiety from all of this. "Okay, but where?" she asked. "Are we going after the vans or Birdie or—"

I shut my eyes for a second, shaking my head. "No, home. And we need to get out of Venice right away unless you want to explain two horribly mutilated bodies to the police."

Something flashed across Ann's face; my guess was that the possibility of police involvement slipped her mind during the last few minutes of excitement. She started the car, and before she decided that what we needed was to crash through barricades and launch the car over rivers, I added, "Back the way you came. Drive normally but stick to the side streets. We don't know if they're looking for your car or not just yet, but we don't need to give them a reason to pull us over."

The car reversed and made a three-point turn before Ann got us off that street and twisting down alleyways and side streets. I could hear a siren in the distance now, but just the one, which was a small comfort. That meant there wouldn't be anyone looking for us immediately. It also meant that they had no idea what they were about to discover. The thought of all of that blood made me realize we were probably about to ruin someone's day, but then I caught a look at my arm, now coated with a sleeve of dried blood, and any pity I had just went out the window.

"There's a sweater in the back if you want to, uh, do something." Ann's eyes kept darting from my arm to the road and back again.

I obliged her, instantly ruining the garment as blood seeped into its fibers. It stung, but I pressed the sweater into the wound and tied it off as tightly as I could manage. "This is important," I started to tell Ann. "You need to keep me awake. Keep me talking."

Her eyes widened in response. "Oh wow, is this a concussion thing or something?"

I briefly considered the possibility; that woman's burst of magic had rattled me, but I shook my head. "It's not that. It's just that I can't be alone in my head at the moment."

"Well, anything you're itching to talk about?" Ann asked, but something in her voice told me she had her own list of topics.

"You came back for me," I said it plainly, getting the simple truth of it out in front.

"Well, it wasn't too hard, the map showed me exactly where to go. I just figured you'd be—"

"Not what I meant," I said, cutting her off. "You saved my life."

I slumped into my seat slightly and watched Ann's expression. Several uncomfortable moments went by before she asked, "Is this the kind of thing I need to respond to so that you don't fall asleep?"

"I'm merely acknowledging that it happened," I said carefully. "Whether we speak of it or not is up to you. Just know that I appreciate what you did."

Ann seemed to tense up at that. "I wasn't about to just let you rush into danger alone like that, of course I came for you. But that doesn't mean I'm happy about any of this."

"I know, I know. I messed up," I protested with all the energy of a mewling kitten.

"Dude, you messed every dang direction," Ann retorted. "But so did I. And look, I'm not apologizing exactly, and I'm not asking you to either. Because if we just keep going down that road of apologizing and fighting and apologizing some more, I think we're both going to wind up dead."

"Fair enough," I conceded sourly. "Game faces it is then."

"Don't be like that," Ann chided. "It doesn't mean we aren't friends, it just means that the two of us table any hollow apologies until I'm not dead."

I was silent then until Ann made it to the freeway. We hadn't been pulled over by now, which was just about as free and clear as we could expect for the moment. But my silence had nothing to do with being vigilant for the long arm of the law. I just wasn't excited about what I had to say next.

"I've been in a lot of pain," I said with a hard swallow, finally.

Ann quipped to try and hide her apparent discomfort. "Yeah, no shit! If I were you, I'd be crying my eyes out, no question."

"I don't mean physically," I continued. "I mean to say, that is, I never finished my story from earlier about how I got here. It's why I can't fall asleep and why I've been snapping at you and why I didn't recognize Birdie as a harpy and just... all of it. I need to tell you some things. And some of those things are painful. I haven't said them to anyone else in my life. I need you to understand me, but only if you're up for it."

Ann did her best to look at me and the road at the same time. I'm not sure if it's me or everyone, but she is utterly incapable of hiding her emotions. And for as tough as she would like to be, I could see her heart break at the mere idea of my pain. And so when she told me that I didn't have to ask, that part of being her friend was that she would always listen, it made the idea of telling her that much worse.

I took a deep breath before I went on. "Ann, when Alistair came for me, he'd had designs on me from the start. All of his confessions of love, the promises to see the world; they were all lies designed to lure me away from my home. To take me from my mother. I told you what it meant for me to leave, but he'd done his job so well, I didn't stop to think about what I'd been giving up. And I hadn't known that Alistair had been working for Abarta."

"The magic Irish god that Elana was working with?" Ann exclaimed.

I made a half-hearted and ultimately failed attempt to snap my fingers in response. "The same. A trickster god. He'd made use of Alistair's talents to recruit someone like me. Alistair was only in it for the reward. And some reward it must have been, because Alistair is disgusted by elves. Anything non-human, come to think of it. But at the time he'd made certain I knew how he felt about my kind."

"That racist dick," Ann fumed. "You're beautiful, by the way."

"Well, the way the deal had been worded, I was given freedom to be with Alistair for as long as we'd have each other," I continued, unsure of how to respond to compliments at the moment. "He was a wizard, and I am an elf, I was certain we'd be together forever. But when I found him, met up with him…"

"I'm so sorry," Ann breathed, not needing me to finish the sentence.

"My half of the deal complete, I was bound to Abarta in his service after that. I was taught to lie, taught to steal, and yes eventually I was taught to do more than that. Many things that I am not proud of, things I don't want to think on too long." I shuddered in spite of myself. "I told you before that I've killed, but you need to believe me when I tell you that I am not prepared to speak about that. Not now, perhaps not ever."

"Of course."

"I was his tool for most of my lifetime. It didn't matter if he'd needed someone charmed or filled with arrows, I was to do as he asked without question. He could force me sometimes, because of our Fae nature. His name for example. While I was under his employ, I was forbidden to speak it unless he allowed it. I physically couldn't speak it! You have no way to know what that's like, you know. I'll let you in on a secret. That's the gift of humanity. You always have a choice. You can be threatened, coerced, but unless someone breaks your mind—and that sort of magic is forbidden in most respectable circles—then you always have a choice. The Fae can be bound by their souls easier than you'd think. I don't care if it's being bound by your soul to wash the dishes, it's agony."

"So when I asked you for a promise earlier?" Ann pressed.

There was a part of that answer I wasn't ready to tell her yet, for her safety as much as mine. Still, I answered in a way that she wouldn't question. "You'll often hear that the Fae don't do favors, they make deals. That is because if we aren't careful, we could be giving up much more than we bargained for. A pact with a Fae creature isn't inherently meant to take advantage, it is meant as insurance. But after a while, asking something in return, bargaining, it becomes second nature. Most can't help themselves. My issue with Abarta was that I'd never needed to ask for anything in my life. He knew that and took advantage."

"Chalsarda, those things you had to do," Ann started carefully. "It doesn't sound like you had a choice. It's not your fault."

"Oh, you're wrong about the choice, my friend," I huffed. "And that's what saved me. I could have chosen to revel in my duty. To accept my life for what it was, but I didn't. Jaded as I was at times, I was never truly desensitized. And the thought that I could be bothered or sickened is what kept me going. I was bound to him by my soul, but he was never able to own it."

I paused for a second, feeling myself getting worked up now in a way that I didn't know for sure I could contain. "Do you know what the worst of it was? That every so often he'd make me feel respected. He believed in what he was doing, was so proud of his good intentions. He never saw himself as a villain. Even my service was a means to an end, the cost of my freedom was unfortunate in his eyes, but acceptable as collateral damage. As long as I was respectful, he never went out of his way to harm or humiliate me. But knowing that he could, that was bad enough. But knowing that I could allow myself to forget and that I did on occasion? That was shameful."

"Chalsarda, I—"

"No, please let me finish this now or else I may lose my nerve. It's something that I need to say to you, but out loud so that I can hear it as well. So that it becomes real." Ann looked embarrassed at her interruption but said nothing, so I continued. "When I was forced to do things, I did not agree with or when I was at my lowest points, I always survived on the knowledge that I was a tool. In a way, I was not completely responsible for my actions, for disobeying was something close to impossible. If I were to harm someone, so be it. I was not proud of it, I did not endorse it, even as it was carried out by my hand. So I would put it out of my mind, focus on what I could control, and in this way, I kept my sanity. But I'd never dealt with it, you see? The weight of it all. My actions, how my life was stolen from me, I've yet to confront it. Each and every day I was adding to my pain, and for so long I convinced myself I wasn't in pain. You and Elana and the others are the first people I've allowed myself to call friends in over a hundred years! And now that I am free of Abarta's grasp, I am cursed with the knowledge that for once, I have a choice. Choosing to let you perish would be no choice at all, but I could. And that's the scary bit. Everything I do from today forward, is something that I alone am responsible for. I share your gift and your burden. And I've barely had you for a couple of months, and it has already been exploited. And between the weight of what I've done, the damage I've caused, and what I've yet to do, it's just taking a toll. I'm short tempered. No, I'm angry. But I'm afraid and unsure. I feel something that the day I was freed I told myself I would never feel again. I feel helpless."

"But you're not alone," Ann reassured me. "And I can't tell you that everything will be okay, but at least you're admitting that you're not okay. However, I can help, I will. Elana, Olivia, I'm sure even Wilma; all of us. There are people who will help you through this, the way you've helped Elana and myself."

"No, not the same," I corrected. "My value has been in my capacity for violence. What you're proposing, even just knowing that you will listen, that is something much different, and of far more value."

Ann didn't say anything more on the topic; she didn't have to. The two of us focused on the road for a little while longer.

We'd made it back without further incident. The whole damned thing was a mess. In the span of a day, I'd managed to make enemies of a godling, a harpy, and a magic user who was hiding considerable talent, though to what end I'm unsure. I'd also nearly gotten myself killed on more than one occasion and wounded as I was, I was still no closer to curing Ann. On the plus side, I did manage to disrupt a cult and send a fair number of their members scattering the way one scatters ants by removing the rock they live under. So I guess it wasn't all bad.

I headed straight to the bathroom when we arrived, leaving Ann to her own devices. She'd have to fend for herself for the moment. As I undressed to shower, it became evident to me that the clothes I'd been wearing were beyond salvage. I rinsed in cold water, gently washing away the dried blood and sweat. I gingerly cleaned the area where I'd been gashed open by Birdie. To my delight, I'd found that though the cuts had been long, they had been only skin deep. I'd need to keep the wound properly bandaged, but the muscle was intact.

Having addressed my arm, I gathered what I'd need for the hand. The tincture I'd made wasn't magic, but it sure acted like it was. I dissolved the crushed roots and Epsom salts in ethanol and regarded it briefly. Were I to ingest even a small portion of this, the combination would assuredly mean I'd be extraordinary intoxicated and likely bloated. But that was not to be; I was to soak my hand in it. The pain that flared through my hand and the rest of my body lasted but a moment before I got a handle on it, and it wasn't long before I could see what Birdie's cord was laced with. The slivers steadily extracted themselves from my hand and into the bottom of the bowl. Birdie had certainly spared no expense here. Diamond dust, with the occasional significant sized shard sank to the bottom with a chorus of clinks. Painful as it was, I was fortunate she hasn't thought to use a specific type of metal shaving. If it had been iron, I'd be in a much worse way.

Eventually, the trickles of blood stopped swirling with the concoction and just turned the whole thing a sickly shade of rose, but by then the work had been done. Testing my hand by making a fist was mildly annoying, but it was doable. Numerous as the wounds were, they were the size of pinpricks and would heal up relatively quickly. I was bandaging it for good measure when a small rap on the door caused me to look up.

"Still alive in here?" Ann asked, poking her head into the room.

The answer to that question never came as I saw Ann now with a fresh mind and realized the detail I'd overlooked earlier. The amulet Ann wore to stave off the poison, with its appearance of a sunflower and its six petals acting as a countdown.

The amulet was down to two petals.

17

Ann filled the silence with sarcasm. "A really cool thing that living people do is answer questions about whether or not they're alive."

"I'm sorry, yes, of course, I'm alive. All of that blood must have been quite alarming. I imagine it looked worse than it was." I had a theory, and if I was correct, the last thing I wanted to do was give Ann a reason to become worried.

The door opened the rest of the way as Ann took my reply for an invitation. She took a seat opposite me, sitting on the lip of the bathtub. "You looked wrecked to heck, but I figured if you were dying or something you would have mentioned it to me."

I chuckled softly at that in spite of my concerns. "I'm too young to die."

"Hey, about that," Ann started. "Joking aside, I wanted to ask you something. I mean, people did die today. Two of them at least, right in front of me and that's kind of a first for me. And I don't know if it's just shock or what, but I'm a little freaked out that I'm not more freaked out, you know?"

I nodded in understanding. "There's no way to know how you'll react to seeing death up close until it happens."

The look on Ann's face suggested she understood that but wanted to something more. Her eyes dropped the floor for a moment as she formed the words she needed to say. "The Abbot and that other guy. Did you know them? Had you met them before?"

"I'd known quite a lot about the Abbot," I admitted carefully. "But no, I'd never met him. The other man, I have no idea. I'd never seen him before today. I didn't even know he possessed magical talent until a few moments before he perished."

"If it's all right, I need to ask you about him. Who was he?"

"He was a self-obsessed cult leader who started to buy into his own rhetoric, but that's not what you're really asking, is it?" I let the question sit in the air for a moment before asking one of my own. "Ann, how long do you think I've been visiting this city?"

Ann shifted her posture, looking uncomfortable. "When I first met you, I had assumed for some reason that this was all new to you. I don't know why I thought that. I guess it was just that you were an elf, and I'd never met an elf before, and I had this weird idea of who and what you were before we really hung out. But there's too much evidence to the contrary. You know whoever owns this house well enough that you can just stay here. You took me to see a witch. And you've lived for literally centuries. It's entirely possible you were around before I was born."

I gave a small nod of acknowledgment. "You are correct. And you know that I am not proud of everything I've done."

"You've said as much."

Another pause, this one for my benefit as I decided on what I would say. "I have something that I think you need to

PLAYING DEAD

hear, but I had hoped to never speak of it again. It is not a pleasant topic for me, but no. No, you should hear this. Some years ago, I was instructed by Abarta to follow a girl who was the topic of much discussion. For my employers' part, he considered that she might have fit into his plans. Her life was troubled. Physically abusive father. Not particularly well-liked or understood. I watched her long enough to understand her. I understood that she was a child, and like all children, she had the promise of a future, of blossoming. That future was taken from her. That promise was broken."

"So what did you do?"

"Nothing. It wasn't allowed," The words left with my mouth with unintended venom as the memories crystalized in my mind, the pain every bit as sharp as it had ever been. "She was recruited into the Abbot's home. And even then, I was instructed not to interfere. By then, it wasn't long before Abarta had declared a false alarm and I was to return to him. I'd insisted on rescuing the girl and... and I don't want to think about that. But it must not have been long before the Abbot realized what Abarta had."

Ann sat with the discomfort one obtains when confronted with such raw memories. "What was her name?"

"Wendy Sinclair."

"I think I had a Wendy in my class in the seventh grade," Ann muttered, the words hollow. "I didn't see her in the eighth."

"She would be about your age today," I replied just as flatly.

Uncertainty clung to Ann as I told my story. The fear she felt at knowing how this story would end was apparent. "The Abbot is a monster," I said finally. "Wendy is no longer with us because she wasn't useful to him. The people who follow him, for the most part, they're just like the man who attacked you in the alley. Lifeless. Whatever made them individuals is stripped away, it's stolen. He did something to them, he did something to me, come to think of it, and I wasn't there very long at all. Ann, the Abbot, and his acolyte didn't die because of you, and you need to understand this and know it to be true: It is a good thing that he's dead. He had hurt so many, and he would hurt so many more. And, while I'm confessing, there's something else."

"There's more?" Ann asked incredulously.

"Indeed. I underestimated the Abbot. Everyone did. I charged into his home thinking his power to be of little to no consequence. I was wrong. He'd have killed me if not for you; his power left me limp and lethargic. But it worked both ways, I saw it firsthand. He had the power to heal, unlike anything I'd ever seen before from a human. Instantaneous and complete. And he offered to heal you. But forgive me, I couldn't do it. His cure would come at the cost of your humanity, you'd be alive but only as far as you consider being alive to mean that you weren't dead. But truth be told, that wasn't the reason I'd turned him down."

"You couldn't let Wendy go, couldn't let him get away with it," Ann finished for me. "You couldn't work with someone who'd kill a kid. Am I right?"

"Yes."

"You... you did the right thing." Ann's voice became steadier with each word as if she were checking the math in her head as she spoke. "Yeah. Yeah, screw that guy. The Chalsarda I know isn't cool with, you know, that."

I understood her. I didn't want to say what 'that' was, either. "I'm going to save you, you know. We're going to solve this together."

"I know." Her reply was sincere. She believed in me.

"But we need to talk about your amulet," I continued. "You're down to two petals. I wasn't aware you'd lost so many."

The question was an uncomfortable reminder for her, but there was no sense in dancing around it. "I need you to think about when each one fell off, can you do that for me?"

"Yeah, but downstairs maybe?" she asked. "This bathtub is starting to hurt my butt."

Ann had a point; this wasn't the ideal environment for a conversation. I agreed and cleaned myself up a bit before heading downstairs. She'd already curled up on the couch by the time I joined her.

I sat near her and reiterated my question. Ann's brow wrinkled as she went into thought, trying to remember. "So, the first one fell off when I first passed out, right? You put the necklace on me, and right away we were down one. Then when we were leaving Wilma's shop. I remember I was pissed and stressed about rent, and also mad at myself because I knew that I was being ungrateful, and then ba-zap. Oh, then when I decided I couldn't let you do this alone, I was just about psyched up to go in, and one fell off. Then the last one came when I started hurling potions. So, two left."

I sighed at her response, my fears having been confirmed. "Which would you like to hear first? The good news or the bad news?"

"Good news?"

"The good news is that I know what's accelerating your condition. Your stress levels are playing a major factor in how much time we have. The more excited you get, the quicker the petals fall off."

Ann pursed her lips. "And the bad news?"

"You are a very excitable young human."

I watched Ann sink into the couch as if she were attempting to become one with it. "So what then? This is your way of telling me that I'm on the sidelines?"

"No," I began patiently, careful of my tone. "Quite the contrary. I need you closer than ever because when I find your cure, I'll need to apply it immediately. This is my way of saying you need to work on your breathing exercises. And maybe watch those baby otter videos that you're so fond of."

"They hold hands while they sleep, so they don't drift away from each other! And they wrap themselves in seaweed to stay close to the shore!" Ann's eyes widened in delight as she exclaimed this far too close me for comfort.

"Yes, very good," I reassured her. "Now let's try that with the volume dialed down a bit."

Ann took in a deep calming breath and tried to repeat herself, this time decidedly more monotone. "Otters hold hands while they sleep and they play with stones, and I love them and wish I could have one as a pet, but that would be unfair because they deserve to be free."

I nodded in approval. "Perfect. If we can keep you relaxed, that should almost certainly give me enough time to figure all of this out. Ann, listen to me. I'm not giving up on you, do you understand?"

Her expression didn't change as she answered. "I know."

"Then stay calm and help me pack for our road trip. They have a head start on us, but that doesn't matter. We have our map; we can keep an eye on them. It would be best to go in prepared. Do you agree?"

"Well, we've seen what happens when we go in unprepared, right?" Ann wore a grin as she said it, and her point was well taken. She was heeding my advice and taking this in stride, but more importantly, she was believing in me.

"Too right," I agreed. "I have preparations to make. More to the point, I don't know if your car will survive our journey as it is, so go online and rent a car from whatever spot is closest to us. I believe your car is suited for local travel at least, you can use it to pick up the rental if you'd like. And be sure that we have everything we could need to survive in every potential climate, should the need arise. If they have fled the city as I imagine will be the case, they could potentially wait us out anywhere. And as I am sure you know, outside of the city, there is a lot of nothing where they could hide. Desert, mountains, forests; all exist mere hours away, and they have a decent head start."

This was all busy work for Ann, but the act of performing tasks should keep her mind preoccupied to the point where she won't have time to worry. All the same, she eagerly accepted the assignments, and I was glad for it. In truth, there wasn't much preparation to be done on my end. I'd need to pick out a new bow, rearm myself in general, but then that would be that.

I entered the shed out back where I'd kept my spare archery gear. This home was remarkably useful, and it would be an inconvenience when I would need to leave. The good news, of course, was that I might not live long enough for that to matter.

I stopped moving the instant I had that thought. And then I put a fist through a wall.

Damn you, Alistair. Gods damn you. If you'd only come after me, I'd understand. That would be manageable. But you involved my friends, and I know that I'm not going to be able to let this go, no matter the outcome.

During my service to Abarta, I'd requested permission on numerous occasions to deal with Alistar. I was never granted the privilege, and given my complete lack of a bargaining position, I had nothing but emotion to leverage, which from where I was standing was about as useful as poetry would be to a dog. It wasn't that Abarta held any loyalty to the man; after all, Abarta is a deity, minor as he may be, and Alistair was hired for a job, a task which he was all too happy to see through. It wasn't that. In fact, it wasn't anything. Alistair was smart enough to stay out of the way and did nothing to impede Abarta's plans. Which for Abarta meant that Alistair was beneath him. And for my part of things, I was a useful tool and nothing more. There was no need to risk damaging his tools if he didn't need to and replacing me would have been an inconvenience.

And so for nearly two hundred years, I had to live with the knowledge that the man who took everything from me, humiliated me, was not only walking free but was in all likelihood making the world as worse a place as he could manage, as long as doing so would benefit him. And though I knew there were more dangerous beings than him in the world, people and creatures with more power, more depraved, more of a threat, he was the one who hurt me the most. He was the one whose brand of pain I had felt firsthand, and I had always longed to ensure that he'd never hurt anyone ever again.

And no sooner than I'd been freed had he brought that pain back into my life, hurting someone I'd allowed myself to love, and doing so without a second thought or even a hint of remorse. Ann believed that killing when I had the chance to choose otherwise killed a part of my soul or something along those lines. I didn't believe it to be a matter of being squeamish; she valued life. But if I saved her, and if I had the opportunity to end his life, what was I to do? Was it murder or a moral imperative? Even if he was smart enough to leave me and my friends alone after our business is settled, a man like that does not repent. He wouldn't just see the light and walk a lighter path. He'd hurt someone else, and maybe I could have prevented it.

It wasn't what I should have been thinking about at the moment. Here I'd given Ann busy work to get her mind off the weight of our situation and then I'd been unable to compartmentalize my own feelings. I needed to focus.

The loss of my bow was unfortunate, as replacing it would be an arduous task all on its own, but more than that it was a good bow. All the same, it had not been the bow that I had needed. I'd been relatively lucky in shooting Birdie as I had, and if her full focus had been on me, I don't think I'd have succeeded. That bow had been meant for putting an arrow through plate armor. What I needed was a short bow. Concealable, accurate, and most important of all, quick. The rate of fire would be more important than stopping power.

The thought of shooting at Debbie gave me pause, though. She had a thick skin to rival a rhino when she was at her strongest. I decided on a compromise and selected a low weight recurve instead. It was strong enough that I wouldn't be terribly disappointed in the damage but quick enough that I could get off more than a couple of shots if need be. I took it out to the range for some practice if for no other reason than shooting something would make me feel good.

After getting some shooting in, I went back inside for my attire. There was no need for subtlety anymore. Everyone knew I was coming, and it wasn't like I needed to blend in. I began to strip and selected a more battle appropriate outfit. Well-worn leather pants which would provide a fair bit of protection. Light boots with custom grip pads would ensure I'd keep my footing, but the weight of them wouldn't impair my movement. A tight fitted tank would mean I'd be free to twist and draw as needed without having to worry about snagging an arrow or throwing off my aim at the wrong time. The heavy leather bracers would keep my forearms from being shredded by a bowstring, and while the added weight might throw some off balance, I'd practiced with them long enough that they felt like they were a natural part of me. Finally, I donned a hooded cloak. It was a pale, mossy green that worked as adequate camouflage in a surprising number of environments. It also had enough hidden pockets to carry everything I could want to bring along with me.

Having made ready, I was prepared to leave the shed when I heard Ann jogging towards me, and so I opened the door for her. Her eyes widened a little when she saw me. "Whoa! Awesome!" She exclaimed, gripping the map in her hands.

I smiled in spite of myself. "You like it?"

"Heck yes! You look like a D & D character!"

I offered a small bow of approval. "Well, thank you. Now, what did you need?"

The grin on her face vanished in an instant as she suddenly fumbled with the map in her hands. "Right! Yes! We have a problem!"

I stepped around her to look at the map with her. "Well, what is it?"

I followed her finger to see that the drop of blood we'd used to track Debbie's location was rapidly heading for the edge of the paper. Ann looked up at me through her glasses. "We uh, only used a map of the state."

I ripped the map from Ann's hands and watched uselessly as the droplet of blood inched its way towards the edge of crinkled paper before falling off as if it had found the edge of the world. I watched the blood evaporate before it had the chance it hit the floor.

The map, now just a map and nothing more, collapsed under my clenched fists as I watched our best chance for an expedient resolution fall away without a hope of stopping it. I'd had Debbie, and now she was gone, and all of this could have been avoided. I'd moved on her too quickly at the mall, and when I'd had a second chance, I let my emotions get the best of me, and I'd nearly died for it. Worse still, I'd let Ann down as well, and now? Now there wouldn't be a third chance. I wanted to rage at the injustice of it all, to break something. Or someone. I wanted to do so much.

I let the map fall to the ground.

"That's it," I sighed, walking out of the shed. "I give up. I can't do this."

"That's it?" Ann asked, her voice just above a whisper.

"All of this and you're just going to walk away."

I turned to look at her. "What? No, it's nothing like that, it's just... we need someone else. I knew this was stupid, I knew it was all too big, but I thought if I was smart and if I was quick, then maybe, but no. No more time. We can ask Abarta; I still have ways of contacting him. With your magic you could summon him, I was useful to him once upon a time—"

"I'm not going to let you ask any favors from him."

"Or maybe Freyja? I don't know how to summon her, but surely Elana is in contact with her, though I'd need to find something she would want or at least—"

Ann gripped my shoulders and locked eyes with me, her face a vision of serenity. "No. We're going to do this without gods or wizards or favors or even genies in lamps. Don't lose your focus and don't give up on me."

I took a breath and composed myself. "It's not that I want to, but I don't know what else I can do. I can't do this alone, not anymore."

"That's the whole point of this," Ann repeated. "You're not alone. You have me. And while I might not be the reason you're involved in all of this, I am the reason you haven't given up yet. So, no. I'm not giving up on you either. If you go back to someone like Abarta for my sake, you'll never be free, and I won't be able to live with myself. So, yeah, this is it. This is where you need to find the courage to believe in us and figure this shit out. You in or what?"

I considered her words, and at last, I asked, "Why are you so calm?"

"Because I will literally die if I freak out," Ann deadpanned.

It wasn't funny, but I barked out a laugh all the same. "So this is where we're at? Succeed or die trying?"

"I'd prefer to live trying," she quipped before blinking thoughtfully and adjusting her glasses. "Give me a moment; I can do better. That sounded better in my head."

"Ann, my friend, it's not that I don't appreciate the enthusiasm, we just don't..." I needed a moment to collect my thoughts. I told myself I was done with underestimating her, and it was apparent that she understood the gravity of our situation. And it wasn't that she was just more willing to gamble her life than I was, it was almost like she didn't think our failure was possible. It was a challenge for me to separate that vote of confidence from the answer my mind wanted to insist upon. That she was delusional and desperate.

I took a breath and composed myself. "We are simply out of time, and we don't know where they are. It's not that I don't want to, I do—"

"Good, then we start there," Ann interjected. "Where there's a will there's a way, right? I mean, not my will, I never got around to making one. There's going to be a straight-up fight over my Pilgrim merch. But yeah, sorry, you! You said you want to do it our way?"

I nodded hesitantly which was all Ann needed to continue. "And you can't lie, so we start there. Pretend I'm not here. Pretend that I'm not part of any of this, but you need to follow these people. Where would you start?"

It was something to consider. I usually didn't have the benefit of magic maps in the past. The map, nonmagical as it now was, hadn't moved from the place I had left it. I smoothed it out and studied the edge of the map. The blood of Debbie ran along the 10 Freeway and presumably kept going. I just had to think about what was out there.

"The compound!" I nearly shouted.

"There's a compound?" Ann asked. "Dude, nothing good ever happens on a compound."

"Remember, in the shop? Wilma had mentioned it. I've heard of it; it's supposed to be in the desert somewhere. I had always just assumed that meant someplace like the Mojave or

Death Valley but, well, here. Pull up the maps on your phone!"

"I mean, if you're trying to look at a map, my laptop might be better, but okay." Ann squinted at her phone, and I took her meaning.

A few moments later, we were inside and looking at an aerial view of the entire state. Sure enough, once you crossed the border and traveled beyond the Colorado River and the border town, there had to be hundreds of miles of nothing. Or as close to nothing as you could imagine in a state like Arizona. "That has to be it," I remarked, poking a finger into the screen.

Ann weakly swatted away my finger. "You're going to smudge it."

"Think about it," I continued. "You have a cult. What's a great spot to recruit the young and the confused? Venice Beach would be perfect, obviously. But where do you keep them all once you have them?"

"I'm guessing the middle of nowhere?"

I gave a small nod of approval. "Precisely! With real estate in the city, you can only go so big, but in the desert? You can get away with a lot in the desert."

Ann studied the screen. "Okay, so where though? It's at least a five-hour drive to the border, and we've already had a hell of a day. It's going to be dark when we arrive."

"Then I suppose we'd better get moving."

It was unclear if the car Ann had rented was cleared for out of state travel or not, but the sticker in the corner of the window wasn't from any agency I'd ever heard of, and Ann wasn't protesting the distance, so I thought better of it. She did, however, protest my driving of the car which seemed like an odd time to be concerned with a security deposit. All the same, I had to insist that she at the very least try to sleep on the way there. Getting out of Los Angeles proper was always going to be a grueling task no matter what time we left, and as it stood, the GPS had us getting to the border in about 4 and a half hours without accounting for any time spent stopping for gas. On the best of days, sitting in stop and go traffic is enough to raise anyone's stress levels. The best counter Ann could provide in response was that it would be ridiculous for anyone to drive while wearing a cloak. Ann won the argument. I removed the cloak.

I gathered Ann's favorite pillows and a blanket, and makeshift bedding was created in the back seat with the rest of our gear stored in the trunk. Ann was understandably sore and tired from the day's event, but not exactly sleepy. I provided her with earplugs, chamomile tea, and an assurance that I'd do my best to avoid potholes and bumps. She donned a warm sweater and, doing her best to get comfortable, settled in for a nap.

Truth be told, I could have done with the nap myself, but with my companion asleep, I was left with an unfair amount of time alone with my thoughts. For everything else that I'd been through, much of this was very new to me. I had always wanted a way out, wanted to take responsibility for my own life, and I certainly got my wish. There was a constant, painful awareness in the back of my head that everything that I did next would be my responsibility and mine alone. Alistair had forced my hand to an extent, but Debbie had a good point. I immediately went after her without trying anything else. I was prepared to kill her for Ann's sake. That she was innocent of any crime was irrelevant. The lessons I'd learned from my mother left me ashamed all of a sudden. She was a healer and had raised me to be like her. To help those who need help. Debbie was born to at least one absent parent, raised to hurt those around her and she escaped. By all definition, she needed help.

Finding Debbie was a priority still, but I didn't know what

I was to do when I found her. Killing her felt like the wrong answer, though. The choice to kill her or let Ann die was being forced upon me, but the only one who could ultimately choose any of my actions would be me. No one would ever control me again. Whatever it was I did next, I would have to live with. Or not, depending on the circumstances.

All of that presumed that I could even find Debbie in the first place. I would though. There wasn't another option, and there wasn't time to consider the alternative.

"How'd I do on nap time?" Ann yawned from the backseat.

"Excellent," I remarked. "We're just about to cross the border into Arizona. If you look outside you will be able to see the great Colorado River in a couple of minutes."

"I've seen it," she replied, examining the earwax on her earplugs. "It's not that great."

"Maybe not this stretch of it," I conceded. "But it is the last bit of nature that isn't hot sand and rocks for quite some time, so enjoy it while you can."

The crossing from California to Arizona offered no warm and friendly sign welcoming us or mentioning the Grand Canyon. Maybe that sign existed elsewhere, other roads perhaps or even further up, but not here. Instead, there was an ugly green sign which read 'Arizona State Line Mile 0'. And then there was a combination Wendy's and gas station. A sign indicated they sold something called a Baconator and that this was my last chance to purchase one.

"Would you like a Baconator?" I offered.

Ann's bark of laughter registered with me as somewhere between shock and the funniest thing I've ever said. "Are you trying to tell me that you want a Baconator?"

"I'd prefer never to hear that word again if I have a say in the matter."

"Fine with me, but you're missing out. Not that I want one

right now—I'd rather not risk that being my last meal—but if you can pull over for a second, I'd like to hop in the front seat like an adult."

We were still in time to take advantage of the enormous parking lot and, as Ann opened the door, we were met with a biting cold breeze kicked up by the elements and the highway traffic alike. Buckled up, we again started driving.

"Check it out," Ann said holding her necklace up for inspection. "Still not dead!"

Under the necklace was an ugly bit of necrosis and a couple of familiar looking dead lines. They didn't look as bad as they had earlier though, which I took as a small blessing. "Congratulations, keep it up."

We drove a couple of minutes more in silence. It was getting quite dark now, and the traffic from earlier was beginning to thin out as we headed out into the less populated stretches of the state. Soon there wasn't another car in sight.

"I'm kind of surprised you didn't try to sideline me again." The suddenness of the statement startled me.

I measured my reply under the guise of lowering the heat in the car before I spoke. "Of course not, we're a team now. We're in this together, yes?"

"Yes, but that's not all of it, is it?" she asked.

"No, it's not," I admitted.

"Something I thought about while I was trying to sleep. We need this amulet to stay the way it is for as long as we can, but if you manage to find the cure, you're worried about getting it back to me in time. So you need to keep me close. Am I wrong?"

I gave her shoulder a brief squeeze. "You're not, but that's not all there is to it. Ann, you have shown me friendship in a way that I rarely experience. And I know you're not alone in this, Elana and the rest have all been very kind. But in the past couple of days, you have shown bravery and character in the face of the sort of danger that would send most into a panic. On pure instinct, you came for me instead of playing it safe or hoping for the best. You may not be physically ready for most of the problems we have ahead of us, but I won't make the mistake of underestimating your heart again. You're right. We're in this together."

Ann wrapped her hand around the top of mine and gave it a squeeze of her own. "Thank you. I needed to hear that."

We drove in silence for a while longer after that, until finally, we came upon a speck of dust on the map called Hope, AZ. It was more of an RV park and a tinderbox that had been named The Church of Hope, but the town's sign made for interesting conversation.

"A bit ominous, isn't it?" I said, referring to a hand-painted sign that read 'Your Now Beyond Hope.'

"Not really, it's possessive," Ann replied. "If you're looking for your Now Beyond Hope, maybe this is where you'll find it. Anyway, think we should stop for gas? Try to find hope?"

I shook my head at that. "I didn't see a station, and besides, we're only six miles out from something resembling a real town. We should probably stop there for the night."

Salome was big enough that it wasn't a road sign, but that was about it. Still, in addition to a bar, it also had a motel, and that made it good enough for me. The Sheffler's Motel was right off the highway and was precisely as unremarkable as a motel in the middle of nowhere should be. Apart from their sign, which looked to be at least fifty years old, the building itself was a single-story, plain white structure with a befouled swimming pool that struck me as a health risk even in the dead of night. It must not have been their busy time of year, however, as most of the parking spaces were wide open.

The middle-aged man behind the counter accepted cash with a down payment of a couple of nights' stay and went back to watching his television. That he had customers at all seemed a mild annoyance for him, and he was quick to rush me out of the lobby.

First things first, I made sure that Ann was settled in the room with an insistence on my part that I would unload the car. The walls of the hotel were bare in contrast with the nausea-inducing pattern on the comforters. I wasn't prepared to believe they'd been washed recently, and I used some of the bedding from the backseat on Ann's bed before I got to the rest of it. It was more than cold enough in the room, let alone outside, to make the blankets a necessity, but my cloak would be good enough for the night at least.

I was grabbing my archery gear, the last bit to unpack from the trunk when I heard it. Not far from where I stood, three shots exploded in the night almost simultaneously. The bullet caliber must have been something akin to a cannon and no one up for a little late-night drunken target practice was shooting that fast.

The timing was too coincidental. Those were professional shots taken in the middle of nowhere mere minutes after I'd stopped for the night. I didn't know what I'd find out there if I went looking for it, but my best guess was that it was going to come for me if I didn't find it first, and I didn't need anything to accelerate Ann's heart rate right now. I cursed silently to myself and hooked my quiver to my side and strung up my bow before slamming the trunk and dashing off towards the source and away from Ann.

I sprinted across the street in an instant. After the hotel, there was only one building between me and the vast expanse of the Arizona desert. And it was there, illuminated clearly by a full moon on a cloudless night that I saw him. His back was to me, but he was tall, six and a half feet at least, wearing a well-worn brown leather duster that looked like it had seen hell and survived. And in his hand at his side was a revolver gripped tightly in his fist. But that wasn't all I could see in the moon-light.

At his feet was the broken remains of Birdie's shattered birdcage, and next to it was her corpse.

19

"Caleb?" I asked, my fingers itching to pull an arrow.

"Caleb works just fine," he replied evenly, not turning to face me. "Though I'd also accept Mr. Duquesne. That'd make you Chalsarda."

"It would," I replied just as carefully.

"Seems to me you have something of a harpy problem," he drawled, before correcting himself. "Well, rather you had one, I reckon."

I studied his still form before the body of Birdie that was even now seeping blood into the sand. "So, what now? Are you to shoot me next?"

Caleb holstered his gun slowly, still keeping his back to me. "Well, ain't seen that you've given me cause to. Not yet, anyhow."

The wind was picking up now, billowing both my cloak and his duster, revealing that for his part he carried at least the two guns on his hips. "Splendid news. But just how long do you plan to stand here? I imagine someone else must have heard those shots."

Caleb shrugged his narrow shoulders. "Nearest cops worth a damn would be coming from the La Paz sheriff's station about fifty-five miles away. Doubt anyone else in these parts is paying attention to a couple of shots fired one way or another. Figure we got time."

"Time for what?" I pressed.

"A drink? Maybe talk this thing through? Or we could commence with the fighting if you're so inclined," he opined. "Prefer not to, though."

He turned to face me at that. Aside from his jacket and height, he wasn't particularly remarkable. His brown hair was short, though not well kept. It was dirty and matted as if he hadn't washed the sweat and sand from it in weeks. His stubble also appeared to be less of a fashion choice and just the appearance of someone who hadn't bothered to shave in two or three weeks. Apart from that, he wore heavy denim jeans and a blue button-down shirt. Reputation or not, however, and even if he hadn't just shot down the same harpy that nearly killed me only a few hours prior, I could tell this was someone who could take care of himself from the moment he turned to face me. His voice was calm and reassuring, but his body was a coiled spring. He wasn't certain how I was going to answer, and he was prepared for any eventuality.

"What about her?" I asked.

Caleb glanced at Birdie and then back at me. "Her? Coyotes'll take care of her, less'n you think a monster like that deserves a proper burial. Now, we getting that drink or what?"

My brow creased hearing his words. Birdie was a remorseless killer, of that I had no doubt, but from what I could gather her life was one filled with pain and anger and, on some level, I understood her. It was difficult for me to say with certainty what she deserved, but I didn't feel that becoming carrion was it. It also didn't feel like this was the hill I was ready to die on either. "I can't imagine there will be much there I would care to drink. But I would indeed prefer to avoid more bloodshed if at all possible, so I will accept your offer."

"Glad to hear it. Ever been to Don's?"

"I'm afraid I haven't," I admitted.

"Me neither, but these places are more or less the same. Shall we?"

I looked at my bow and arrows and considered my appearance for a moment. "I'll meet you there if that's quite all right."

Caleb took a careful step toward me. "Wouldn't be tryin' nothin' funny, now would you?"

"On my honor, nothing of the sort," I replied. "I'm just not sure I'm ready to hear a joke about how an elf and a cowboy walk into a bar." Caleb continued to eye me until I sighed and continued. "I'll be right behind you once I am more presentable."

"Then we're in business. See you shortly."

Caleb walked away towards the bar, leaving me alone with Birdie. I decided to spend a moment examining his handiwork. From what I could gather, two shots struck the cage and the rope, before the third pierced her heart. Pierced might not even describe the wound accurately; the round seemed to have a punched a hole in her chest where her heart used to be. Her death came quickly, at least. Judging from the look of surprise etched on Birdie's face I'd wager she never had the time to comprehend how severely she had underestimated her opponent.

Caleb was correct that there was nothing to be done for her now. Instead, I wanted a look at the blades that had ruined my favorite bow earlier. There were eight of them in total, though only three managed to survive intact. Each had the same shape and curve of a cat's claw and had a hair-splitting sharpness that came to a tip that threatened to puncture anything it came into contact with. I couldn't be sure of the metal, but a cautious approach to handling it told me it wasn't iron.

I collected the three working blades and made my way back to the hotel. Our room was facing away from the lobby and the bar, so at the very least I was a bit less likely to be seen coming back. Ann was sitting up in bed, waiting for me expectantly. She breathed an audible sigh of relief when she saw me.

Neither of us spoke immediately as I removed the bowstring from my bow and unhooked my quiver. She was hesitant, but eventually, Ann spoke up. "I heard gunshots. Did you investigate or something?"

"Yes, I did," I said plainly.

"When you didn't come to the room right away, I thought maybe something was going on, but I didn't want to assume and get worked up, and—"

"Ann, I need you to do something for me." My interruption was as direct as I could manage while still speaking to her as an equal.

My friend stared at me expectantly. Pure intentions aside, what I was going to ask felt like it was manipulative and a betrayal. I had hoped she wouldn't see it that way.

"Those shots you heard," I continued. "We were followed. Birdie is dead. And I fear things are about to come to a boiling point, so I need to ask you to trust me when I tell you that I need you to sit out from here. That this isn't me underestimating you, that this is just practical, and it is what we need to do. Can you do that for me?"

"Okay," she said. Just like that, it was okay.

"You're sure?"

"Yeah, I'm sure," she reiterated. "I think this has been hard on both of us, but this feels different. I know that you know what you're doing, and you're going to do your best for us both, so yeah. I'm okay."

I nodded in acknowledgment and stood up to retrieve the remaining potions. "In that case, I need you to do something else." I took out the potion marked 'Slumber' and showed it to her. "A traditional use for this would be to render a room full of people unconscious. If one were to drink this potion, however, it would do something far more. To an outside observer, you may very well appear to be dead. You would be in a sort of stasis, the functions of your body will be slowed to a crawl. Magically. Point of fact, it would take an act of magic to wake you."

"So, Sleeping Beauty rules but without the creepy kiss from a stranger in my sleep?" she asked.

"Precisely, and Wilma will have no issue reviving you, I am certain. And I'll text her to let her know where we are. I do have to warn you that there is a reason we didn't do this in the first place. The effects will be wholly unpleasant, and you're going to feel like death for at least a week after. With your body inoperative, your mind will have difficulty understanding what is happening, and because the magic is concentrated, what you see and hear and feel is totally unknowable. I know this will be hell, but it is your best option. Are you sure you're ready for this?"

"I mean, it's that or dying, right? Let's get it over with."

"Very well," I said, handing her the potion and moving back to my bags. "I shall brew you something to ease into—"

I heard the small sound of the seal of the bottle opening behind me as I lunged in a panic at a startled Ann. "No! Why would you—?"

Ann looked hurt and confused as I snatched the potion away from her with all the speed I could manage. I gave myself the extra second I needed to let the frustration of her impulsive behavior pass. "That was my fault," I said calmly. "I should have explained this better. If you were to drink this straight from the bottle, you would likely fall into a coma. For your purposes, this would be akin to drinking an entire bag of soda syrup without the water and carbonation, and then it leaves you in a coma. As I was saying, I am going to prepare for you a buffer to ease you into this."

"Ah," Ann replied with a hint of understanding. "I like that idea better."

The immediate tension past, I fashioned together a tea of sorts that would slow the effects of the potion enough that her descent into slumber would be more of a gradual slide and less of a clifftop dive into the ocean. It was makeshift, and the taste alone could qualify as an act of aggression, but I was sure it would do the job.

Ann's nose wrinkled at the smell, and she wisely opted to swallow as much as she could rather than endure sipping it. She gagged but did not retch, and after a coughing fit that left me feeling slightly guilty and more than a little sympathetic, she asked, "So how long until I'm, you know?"

"A couple of hours, I would hope. Just try to relax, maybe put on some music. Don't try to fight it. I'll be back, and I'll have you up and fighting monsters with me in no time, okay?"

"Okay," she replied, forcing a smile. I tucked her in and removed my cloak and put on a more sensible jacket for my meeting across the street. I was about to walk out, but thinking better of going out this exposed, I grabbed my beanie on the way out to conceal my head. The desert was cold after all; it would look less conspicuous than my natural ears.

Don's Cactus Bar was opposite the hotel on the other side of Highway 60, and as far as I knew was the only place to get a drink within an hour from here. It was an old adobe building, but aside from that, it was much like the hotel and everything else in this town. It was largely unremarkable. But while the rest of this quaint hamlet sat in deathly silence, the bar was active and lively, the pale fluorescent lights coming from within acting as a beacon. There were two trucks in the parking lot but more than a dozen motorcycles. I had a sense of the sort of crowd that would greet me.

Caleb spotted me the moment I walked in and waved me

to his booth at the edge of the room. The rest of the bar was populated by mostly dirty, tattooed men in leather. Some were shooting pool, most of them merely sat at the bar. All of them focused their attention on me, and I ignored their more salacious remarks as I ordered a wine. My options were either red or white. I opted for red.

Drink in hand, I sat opposite Caleb, who looked disappointed at my glass. "Took you long enough. And I ordered you a whiskey and everything."

There was an extra shot of whiskey next to the glass that Caleb cradled in his hand. "I'm not in a whiskey mood if it's all the same to you, but please be my guest. Unless of course, there is some reason you can't drink both?"

Caleb locked eyes with me at that and swallowed both shots, one after the other. "Hell, woman! I brought you here to talk to you, not poison you! Can we pretend to be civil and just share a damned drink?"

I opened both palms in a show of resignation. "Fair enough, we can talk. What would you like to talk about?"

Caleb gestured to the bartender to bring him another, and her expression was void of tolerance in response. "Not rightly sure. What do colleagues talk about when they're not killing each other?"

Maybe we were colleagues in the loosest sense of the word, but it was still odd for him to refer to us as such. "I suppose you could tell me more about yourself. I've heard stories, but perhaps you would be kind enough to offer your own accounts?"

"Thanks, darlin'," Caleb said as his drink was brought to the table. "Fought a warlock."

"I beg your pardon?" I asked as he sipped his whiskey.

"Yeah, 1910. Fought a warlock. Had a bounty, I aimed to collect, then one thing led to another, and well, that's that."

I studied him for a moment, trying to make sense of the

casual way he brought that up. That wasn't quite what I'd been asking for, I was expecting something a bit more recent. "Well, I for one don't believe that's that, as you say. But why are you telling me this?"

"Well, sure we'd been locked outside of time or some such in a perpetual state of aggression for 'round a hundred years until the dimension or some such shifted and I plugged him and got out. I ain't too good about explaining the magic side of things. But I'm telling you this because I want you to know that you're not the only one who knows what it's like to not be from around here."

"I would argue that our situations are quite different," I countered.

"Sure, different color hides, but it's still a horse." He shrugged. "I'm a relic from another time, and you're from an enchanted forest or wherever it is elves come from. But we're both making do. Thing I don't understand is why you'd want to be wrapped up in something like this."

I sipped my wine and considered how to answer that before deciding on sincerity. "Not by choice, I'm afraid. You're in this for the money, but I've been forced into the job. If I don't succeed, a friend of mine will die."

"Right, you hang around them wizards and the like. One o' them get you mixed up in all this?"

"Quite right."

Caleb adjusted his posture and sighed. "Well, don't think I'm going to walk away over no damn sob story. We all got burdens, but I'll wish you good hunting all the same."

He raised a glass, and I clinked mine to his in response. "Let me ask you," he began thoughtfully. "Rumor has it you're a couple of hundred years old or so. Elf blood or what have you. So, tell me, what is the strangest part of modern day for you?"

"Truly?" I whispered, leaning in a little. "The food."

"I knew it weren't just me!" He laughed, slapping a hand on the table. "None of it tastes right. Not even them grass-fed steers."

"And what passes for fruit and vegetables is astonishing!" I replied.

"I remember when corn was sweet. Never thought folks could ruin corn."

The tension between us eased a bit over the next hour. I got the impression that for everything Caleb was doing to keep up his lone wolf persona, he very well could have just wanted a break to be social with a peer. Men like him don't tend to keep a lot of friends, and for my part, I was willing to accept his ceasefire. I was chuckling in spite of myself now as our conversation continued. "My turn. You experienced something that should never have happened. You now walk in a time that is not your own. Forgive me if this is presumptuous, but that sounds like an incredible opportunity to start over. To be anyone you want. Why would you go right back to this line of work?"

Caleb snorted in response. "Never said I went right back," he protested weakly. Then after a generous sip, he sighed. "Hell, it's not like I had anything to miss and I ain't never done anything different. Fought monsters for money then, might as well fight 'em now. Y'all got cars and smartphones and what not, but mostly things haven't changed. Least of which being the things that go bump in the night. You must know what I mean. I've always been full of fire and you got it in you too."

"But why this job then? Why these people?" I asked. "Debbie's not a monster."

"Battle Born has a name then?" Caleb raised an eyebrow at that. "That's a new one."

"Yes, she does. And while I have no doubts that your skills are impressive, if you know what she is, you have to know that you don't stand a chance of defeating her."

"Don't know about that," Caleb mused. "She's been disconnected long enough that she's damn near mortal. I imagine you wouldn't have taken the job either if that weren't the case."

I would have sworn I didn't so much as blink as he said that, but Caleb's eyes widened in understanding as he looked at me. "You don't know about that, now do you? Well goddamn, girl, look at that! I know something you don't know. You didn't just think you could wound a Battle Born at full strength, now did you?"

My cheeks began to flush at his accusation. In fact, I did think as much. I know how they came to be, but that didn't give me the impression that they were invincible. If Debbie was an example of one that had been weakened, I shuddered to think about what they could do at full strength.

"Don't worry about it none, ain't no one but the almighty that can know everything. You learn something new every day. Speaking of which, I heard about your tussle in Hawthorne. Have a souvenir for you of your handiwork."

Caleb reached into a pocket of his duster and produced a plastic resealable sandwich bag with a bloody bandage inside of it. "A ways back at a rest stop I had a chat with this college-bound kid. Car full of dirty laundry and dreams. And you know what he seen not ten minutes prior? A van full of weirdos and a giant woman. And it just so happened they left this in the trash. You must have really tagged her something good I take it."

He gave the baggie a little toss into the center of the table and stood and stretched his back the way one does at the end of a long day. "You realize what this means, now don't you?" he said, leaning towards me. I kept my eyes locked on his, revealing nothing. Still, he grinned and said, "Then we have an understanding. Now, if you'll excuse me, you see those men that been eyeballing me all night? They call themselves the Howling Pythons. Not so sure they understand all that much about pythons. But what they do understand is running meth through

Arizona, and I've had enough whiskey that I think I can take 'em. See you around, Chalsarda."

As if it were the most casual thing in the world, he walked right up to a potbellied member with a beard that looked to be made of tumbleweed and headbutted him on the bridge of his nose, pretense and banter be damned. Chaos exploded behind me, but I ignored it. It wasn't my fight for one thing, but more importantly, Caleb had left me alone with a remarkable prize.

A bag with Debbie's blood. Fresh blood of a Battle Born.

Of course, I wasn't a fool, and neither was Caleb. It would seem our encounter wasn't quite as happenstance as he'd initially led me to believe. Even this brawl was likely for my benefit, to give me the illusion that I could sneak away undetected. It was something he said earlier, that he knew of my connections in the magical community. He likely figured Ann to be such a person, and he was hoping to follow me to his bounty. He had the components, but not the means to use them, whereas I had the means, but not the components. And since just asking me for my help was likely to be out of the question, Caleb killed the competition and made a show of how much he was an honorable outlaw, only doing what he needed to get by. Clever as he may have thought he'd been he also had no idea that I just gave his idea of a bloodhound a potion to send her into a state of perpetual slumber.

He'd left me with very little choice at the moment in any case. Indeed, I had the most useful means of tracking Debbie in the palm of my hand, perhaps even the only way of doing it in time in a worst case scenario; but if I didn't get to Ann right away, she'd be unable even to make the attempt.

I pocketed the baggie and walked out of the bar, making a note of Caleb along the way. Anyone could tell that he had no issue handling himself. He was quick enough to make the punches of the gang members look outright sloppy, and he immediately disarmed anyone who approached him with a weapon. He always kept his back to a wall, preventing the others from circling on him. But I could also tell that he was dragging it out, peppering with jabs and playing keep away. The reason was apparent: He was waiting for me to leave.

Ann was mere moments away as I dashed across the highway and made it to our room. I entered into a darkened room lit only by the glow of a laptop screen; the music from the playlist was coming from someone called Tame Impala. Or the song had Tame Impala for a title? It wasn't important. For her part, illuminated by the screen, Ann had left her glasses on the nightstand and somehow managed to cocoon herself within what appeared to be the sheets and blankets from both beds. Her head bobbed rhythmically but weakly to the psychedelic tunes, though her body was immobilized.

"Thank the creators, you're still awake," I mumbled to myself as I switched on the lights. "Ann! You've got to wake up!"

Ann squinted in my direction with a jerky attempt to free her arms from the bedding. "Oh shit," she slurred. "Chally, you came back. But why didn't my Dad come with you? He loves me, and you, and Velveeta which is what I was supposed to be named as a baby. I am supposed to be Velveeta Bancroft, it's true. Look it up."

"I need you to focus," I instructed her, doing my best to unravel her enough to make use of her arms and handing the glasses to her. "I need you to scry for me."

"Listen!" she insisted with an urgency usually reserved for telling a stranger where you hid your medication. "So, like, animals are our friends but like, also? All our friends are animals!"

I ignored her and removed the baggie from my jacket pocket. "Ann, listen to me. Time is critical. I don't know how long you'll remain conscious and you're the only one who can help me. I need you to—"

"Fireworks!" she exclaimed, sending harmless crackles of magical energy away from her fingertips and toward the ceiling.

I had to remind myself that while frustrating, this was not Ann's fault and she was, in fact, the victim here. It helped to keep me from shaking her like a new can of paint. "You. Ann. Scry."

I thrust the bag into her, and she studied it for a moment, seeming for a moment like she understood. Then, beaming she said, "Oh, because I'm dying!"

"Yes, and we don't want that. So what do you need?"

"A map?" she asked, poking the bag. "And a pendant. Did you bring mine? Not going to lie though, this probably won't work. I am super high right now, and I think they're waiting for me at my fifth-grade birthday party. I was drinking Hawaiian Punch and talking to a turtle who told me I needed to believe in myself and the cake promised to tell me secrets, but it sounded like if Oscar Isaac was evil so I didn't trust it and then Celeste opened up one of my gifts, and it was—"

While she was babbling, I was doing my best to put together the makeshift conditions for her to scry. There was no paper map in the room and not one in any of the drawers, but I opened up a satellite image in one of the browser tabs on the laptop and zoomed out from our local area just enough to make sure it would cover anything within a reasonable distance of us. And her pendant, the one she'd used before, wasn't in any of the bags, so I ripped a length of fabric from one of the sheets and made a makeshift necklace with an arrowhead I snapped off one of my arrows.

"Okay, try this," I interrupted, abruptly cutting her off.

"Okay!" Ann replied cheerfully, squeezing drops of blood from the bandage over the arrowhead.

If I thought her babbling was terrible before, now she seemed to be chanting a mixture of what sounded like names of soda brands, car companies, and what each of those might sound like in Latin. I watched intently as the arrowhead began to first spin under its own power, then it hung in the air as if attracted to the laptop like a magnet to steel. And as her chanting reached its bubbly crescendo, the arrowhead zipped towards the screen, dinging it lightly before both it and Ann collapsed devoid of energy.

I checked on Ann first, and she was now fast asleep. The energy she must have spent to pull off that scry was all she had left. With my friend secure, I turned my attention to the laptop. There was a dent in the LCD where the tip had struck it, now distorting the colors around it. The location wasn't too far away, maybe thirty miles east there was a town called Aquila and maybe twenty miles due south there was nothing but the mark made by the scry. A direct route was made impossible by a mountain range. It looked like the only way there was to follow the highway into Aquila and then take a service road until I either tested the off-road capabilities of our rental SUV or I went in on foot.

That was the compound. It had to be. Close enough to a populated area that getting supplies wasn't too big of an inconvenience but not close enough that any of the locals might become too curious. It also meant that going in during the day may prove to be impossible without being seen.

But for now, I had time. Ann was safe for the moment. I knew how to find Debbie. I didn't know what to do with her when I did, but I was heading towards a conclusion either way. She didn't deserve to die, and I didn't deserve to make that choice. Just like Ann didn't deserve becoming collateral damage. We don't always get what we deserve, but sometimes if we're brave enough, and strong enough, we can make sure the right people get what they're due.

In more than a couple of ways, I would have an advantage if I left right then and there, stormed the compound in the dead of night and took the whole damned cult by surprise. But I'll never know how that would have turned out for me because for the first time since this all began, I didn't feel like I was sinking. Ann's pulse had slowed to such a rate that she could be mistaken for dead. Birdie had met an ignoble end, but in another way, even she was resting. Caleb couldn't make a move without me. Alistair and Skip and the rest of them could go sit on a cactus for all I cared. And Debbie wasn't going anywhere. And neither should I. I was through with rushing in unprepared, and I was happy to recover and be smart about this.

Some of my time was spent drawing myself a map in case the GPS coordinates weren't wholly accurate. Some more of my time was spent making sure my gear was ready to go when I was. But most of it was spent falling asleep next to my friend. I'd had enough trancing for a little while, and slumber felt like an act of solidarity. It felt good to know who I was fighting for.

I had a dream that night, but that's all it was—just a dream. Sleep is not my default, but I've become fond of it the way one slowly develops a coffee addiction. I tried to limit the amount of sleep I got for the very same reasons one might avoid making four cups before noon a daily habit.

Dreams are unusual for me. When I trance, I can experience perfect recall. Between that and waking life, mine is not a life balanced by the fantastical and the grounded. There was just what there was. Nightmares for that reason are worse for me than they might be for humans since humans are accustomed to them. The thought of facing deep fears that not only could I not comprehend but could not predict or control was one that I did not wish to confront.

But when they're done right, they're beautiful and they make sleeping worth the risk. The other side of living a life so grounded in reality is that you don't know how much you needed the joy of your mind flooding with the images you need to see, the ideas you didn't know you'd forgotten, the worlds that were too amazing to exist—and knowing that all of that beauty came from within you.

This was one of those dreams. I saw my mother, and she was proud of me. She missed me dearly, but she adjusted even if she still thought of me every day. She told me that I had something special inside of me, something I was afraid to share, but it was something that would keep me safe. Always. She was beautiful, and it was beautiful, but it was not real. And all too quickly it had passed, and only the fleeting memory remained, replaced by a poorly insulated motel room and the gentle warmth of my slumbering, dying friend beside me.

I was awake and out the door a few hours after I had shut my eyes. It was still dark outside, but dawn wasn't far off. I didn't leave anything in the hotel room that might have come in handy later, especially considering there was no certainty that I would return. This time, however, I wore the cloak while I drove. Ann wasn't around to tell me it wasn't allowed.

I allowed the dream to linger and keep me company through the first leg of my trip. It wasn't real, but hearing my mother say those words, seeing the pride in her face, I don't know that it mattered. That dream came from me and knowing that my mother loved me was wonderful. And if I could tell her one thing, it wouldn't be that I love her. She knows that. It would be that I miss her too.

With only the occasional gas station open, the town of Aquila was still dead quiet as I passed through, no house lights or passing cars. And by the time I reached the marker on the GPS, the sun was barely beginning to peak over the horizon. Tire tracks leading out into the middle of nowhere confirmed this was the spot. Driving up seemed out of the question, but I couldn't very well leave the car on the side of the road either. The compound was roughly four miles from the road and, assuming I didn't see anything to prevent me doing otherwise, it would be a safe bet to take the car halfway and make the other half on foot.

There would be a few things to consider when I arrived. That woman who had been an apprentice or lieutenant to the Abbot was capable of significant magic, and I got the impression that she hid her potential from everyone, the Abbot included. That concussive blast leveled me and seemed as effortless to her as flicking a crumb from a table. She had also potentially managed to cloak the people of the house from my view. It technically could have been the Abbot or the other man who'd been ready to sacrifice me, but it didn't add up. For one thing, even now I don't believe the Abbot had the power to pull that off. And even if he did, illusionary magic wasn't in his wheelhouse. The Abbot was a one trick pony, but the trick he had learned was devastating. And the other man, he unquestionably had power of his own, but when it transferred into Ann, it had been gone in an instant. There's still much I don't know about what happens when a violent death releases power, but I know enough to spot the level of one by the impact the transference has on another. That man had been a campfire, not a house fire. I couldn't rule out the possibility of a fourth user in the home, but the most straightforward solution pointed towards her.

Then there was the matter of the other cult members. They were no longer under the influence of the Abbot, which worked in my favor only so far as knowing they wouldn't blindly attack without reason. Scarier though was the knowledge that their home, their way of life, their very identity; all of it had been threatened and this compound was their last stand. Leaving and taking back a life in society might have become too frightening for some. If this was all they knew and their backs were against the wall then, well, that's how zealots are made. When the possibility of any other way is gone, people can become more vicious than anyone would like to imagine.

And I had to deal with all of that and finding a way to drag Debbie out of there without killing her. I know how implausible that seems, but Ann was right. Debbie had done nothing worthy of a death penalty, and I wouldn't be her murderer. And now I just had to see how she felt about that proposition and how to turn that into saving Ann's life.

Elana's penchant for improvisation must be a bad influence on me.

As I approached the spot on my map, the reason why I hadn't seen the compound from the road became clear to me. An unsteady-looking rock mound, maybe twenty feet high, created a perfect natural camouflage for whatever was behind it. The tire tracks leading to and away from the compound circled the mound, meaning that while I was on the right track, I also didn't know who could be waiting for me on the other side.

My fingers were stiff from the lingering cold of the desert night, and it took a couple of seconds to warm them up in preparation of what was ahead. I took that moment to pull an arrow and ready it as I hugged the rocks as safely as I could manage and poked my head around the corner.

And I saw the blood.

The compound was surrounded by a wall that covered its perimeter and had two wide doors and a watchtower to control who came and went. Currently, the doors were splayed open to reveal a massacre. Dozens of bodies at the very least were torn asunder. Something nightmarish had happened here, and it was all recent. The cold desert air had kept the blood from drying, giving the air as I approached something of a copper scent.

I kept my bow drawn as I crept inside purely as a cautionary measure, but in my heart, I knew it was pointless. Something inhuman had done this, and it was long gone by now. At a certain point, I stopped counting the bodies or even trying to figure out which limbs belonged to which person. But I made a thorough search, all the same, because I could only think of one person capable of this, and I needed to find her body, because if I didn't, I was afraid of what that would mean.

I never found it. Because Debbie was gone and there was no evidence of another creature or evidence of evocations. There were gashes and tears, but also blood-soaked sharp objects. This was no work of an animal, at least not in the literal sense. But maybe it was in the way that counted.

I was furious. With her, but more with myself. I'd questioned myself, I felt sympathy for her plight, and I hesitated. But no more. No more excuse, no more silver linings, and no more distractions. This was the mass murder of a defenseless people and if that doesn't deserve the harshest of punishments, then what else can bring justice for this senseless depravity?

I wasn't trading Debbie's life for Ann's anymore. I was taking Debbie's life for the ones she stole from those who took her in. Debbie had to die. And I was going to kill her.

21

Taking my time here, however unpleasant, was essential. Debbie had spent time with these people, and it was possible there might be a clue regarding how they planned to take care of her or what their plans were for her. An hour or so passed, and while nothing of that sort came to light, my thorough search did manage to reveal something that was equal parts damning and useful—large, heavy footprints on the north side of the wall leading away from the compound towards Aquila. Someone in the neighborhood of about three hundred pounds walked away from all of this, and Debbie was the only one it could have been. No, not Debbie. After this much carnage, perhaps she didn't deserve a name. The Battle Born did this.

The trail was easy enough to follow for a little while; then, as if I needed any more proof, the tracks led me to the corpse of a coyote with its neck violently snapped, with a multitude of tiny footprints scattering away from the scene. It was possible that they were hungry enough that they believed she would be an easy meal, but that was unlikely. Coyotes prefer carrion, and an attack on a person is rare. The more likely answer was that animals can sense things that people can overlook, and whatever they sensed in her was something they felt they needed to destroy.

It was maybe a mile out when I saw something that added another wrinkle to all of this. Not far off from the trail I was currently following were a second set of prints that had come from the direction of the highway. They led from the road to a rock long and flat enough to nap upon, and then they turned back the way they came.

I'd been followed, but how? I didn't see anyone behind me at any point, and I'd left early enough that I would know, unless...

I took off in a dash back to the car. It was early enough in the morning that the sun wasn't punishing, and my anger fueled me. When I arrived, I immediately began searching the wheel wells above the car tires until I found it. Above the passenger side rear wheel was a magnetic GPS tracker. Caleb didn't need to see me; he was watching my every move from his phone.

Over a hundred years out of time or not, he was adjusting to modern technology just fine, it would seem.

I briefly considered throwing it out in the desert, but common sense won out. He thought he had this all figured out. He knew how to use me to find the Battle Born, he tracked my movements and spied on me as I saw the compound, and he had the same set of footprints I had. But if what I knew about him held true, he wouldn't want to be first to the scene. He would want me out of the way, and what better way of doing that than letting the Battle Born and me tire each other out.

No, I would want him to follow me. But I needed to show him how dangerous I was to follow.

Aguila was, for lack of a better term, a very flat town. It was mostly residential buildings with a handful of businesses, almost none of them higher than a single story, and half of them looked to be abandoned. There couldn't have been more than a couple of hundred people in the town and only a couple of places one could have hidden, but that was going to work in my favor.

I parked at the southern edge of the town and gathered my bow, arrows, and whatever I could pocket and began walking. By leaving the car where I did, he would have no choice but to follow me on foot eventually. And I was making no effort to hide. Anyone who looked out a window would be treated to the sight of an elf ready for battle. The lack of police presence in the area also gave me a level of confidence that it was unlikely anyone but Caleb would have anything to say about it.

The long walk to the northernmost point of town also served another purpose. I was gambling that Caleb wouldn't risk a fight out in the open, especially if he had even a hope that I was leading him to the Battle Born, and that meant he would need to keep his distance if he wished to avoid being seen. So when I reached the derelict packing plant, I had time to pick my spot.

When I was just within sight of the place I dropped into a run around the back, cutting the ruse. I wanted him to know that he'd been had, maybe make him rush in quicker than he might like. Everything was locked and boarded, but the windows were sunbaked and fragile, the paint that had been applied to them heavily faded. Breaking one and getting inside would be easy, but it would also let him know exactly which way I came in.

Which is why I broke three windows.

I climbed in one of the windows and got my first look around. This place had to have been used for some serious food packing at one point, but now it looked to be forgotten. Judging by the thick layers of dust on everything, it had been forgotten for quite some time. That also meant anywhere I planted a foot would make following me a task any child could accomplish.

The lack of a second story made things tricky, but there were still plenty of pillars and shelves to conceal my person from any visitors and leaping into the rafters was the obvious choice.

There were numerous ways into the plant, but any one of them would have made a lot of noise, and I had Caleb at a disadvantage. Come and find me or deal with the Battle Born as is and hope I didn't get to him later. Unfortunately, that pendulum swung both ways, and if I didn't take care of Caleb now, the fight with the Battle Born might leave me weakened enough that I'd be easy prey for him. Still, I was reasonably sure Caleb would come, if for no other reason than I'd hurt his pride.

Sure enough, I didn't have to wait long. A few minutes later and a service door exploded inward after the third time it had been rammed. Sunlight streamed in behind him, adding a touch of illumination to the darkened space. Of all the ways he could have entered, this provided my most challenging shot, and if my arrow didn't put him down right away, he'd be able to hide. I pushed down the urge to pull my bowstring and instead opted for patience.

Caleb took a step inside and addressed the room. "Don't suppose it would do any good to give you the chance to walk out of here?" A moment passed, and he took that as its own answer. "Fair enough, we can do this the hard way, then."

Caleb cautiously entered into the plant, surprising me by not drawing a gun right away. His choice, I suppose, but he had something in his right hand that I couldn't see, and I found that worrisome.

"I ain't got an arrow through my skull yet, so I must assume you ain't looking to kill me," he continued. "That or you ain't got a shot. Gotta be one of the two."

As open as the floorplan was, I couldn't see everything, and as Caleb continued walking away from me, I cursed silently to myself at having to make the split-second decision to follow him or hope that he wandered back into my field of vision.

Devious as he was, I felt following was my best option.

Careful not to make a sound, I leaped over one rafter beam to another. Caleb was still searching, still trying to draw me out. "Never took you for a coward, though, if'n I'm being honest," he drawled, carefully peeking around a corner. "Come to think of it, though, it makes sense, don't it? Word gets around, you're all alone these days, and it seems your solo career is going about as well as a house cat trying to swim upstream. Battle Born about beat you senseless. Then I understand that street preacher fella whammied you. Not to mention the harpy, she damn near killed you as well. Then I took care of her, easy as pie! Stands to reason you'd be worried I got your number as well. Maybe I'll be the one to knock some sense into you finally."

There was some truth to his words, skewed as the information may have been. And he was surprisingly well informed. But I wasn't about to be rattled, even as I made another leap to follow him and find my shot.

"And again, no judgment, no shame or nothing like that. You're just an elf, after all, and that ain't nothing special. Just weird is all. If you think long ears are about to scare me or that your sticks and stones'll break my bones, well darlin', you must not have heard enough about me."

I was mid leap yet again when I realized it all too late. This was the fourth left turn Caleb had made in a row. Something I must have done tipped him off, and he hadn't shown it. I drew an arrow as quickly as I could, but his left hand was already pulling a gun. Disabling shot be damned, I had less than a split second to correct my aim as I released and shot the gun.

The gun spiraled away from him, but not before he managed to get off a shot. His aim was ruined enough that the bullet only grazed my arm rather than pierce my heart, but it burned with the heat of a hot poker all the same. I didn't have the focus to land safely, ignore the pain, and maintain the grip on my bow. One of those had to give, and it was the bow that toppled to the ground.

At the same instant I landed on the beam, I found out what Caleb had been holding in his right hand as a length of chain shot up and wrapped itself around my forearm. My leather bracers protected me somewhat, but not entirely as the exposed flesh the chain touched burned in such a way that I instantly forgot all about the bullet wound. I howled in agony as I felt the burning sensation penetrate parts of me that were beyond physical.

My scream was still echoing out through the plant as Caleb yanked me to the ground. I tried to roll with the motion, to land on the meat of my shoulder to avoid injury, but I was only partially successful. My mind was consumed only with getting the chain away from me. I landed with a sickening thump.

"Cold iron and Fae don't mix, am I right?" Caleb asked smugly. That second cost him as I unwrapped my wrist from the chain and scrambled out of sight. The speed with which I moved seemed to surprise him.

By some miracle of miracles, I had the presence of mind to snatch my bow up with my more functional hand as I got away, though the pain of having been assaulted by that chain was all I could think about for the next precious few seconds. I'd have rather been branded than experience that. The pain of cold iron touches the Fae in our very souls, and humans rarely understood what they were doing when they used it as a weapon.

Two more shots exploded behind me as I made my mad dash away from him, but having to draw his other pistols gave me the small window I needed not to get gunned down right then and there.

I didn't understand how this could happen. I went in with a plan, I had the drop on Caleb, and he still managed to put me on the run. Even now, as I sat behind a rusting conveyor system on the far end of the plant trying to steady my breathing, I had to fight the urge to charge him head on and fill his chest with arrows. Seductive as the idea was, I'd already underestimated him in spite of everything, and there was no doubt in my mind his gun would beat my bow.

My arm was shaking uncontrollably now, and I had to remind myself that it was very temporary to stop myself from screaming. This wasn't the first time I'd been violently struck with cold iron, and it might not be my last. It was unbearable, but it would pass, and if I lost control now I'd only succeed in giving away my location. It was a dangerous but necessary risk. I shut my eyes and focused directly on the pain and its source, accepting it and not flinching from it. The harder I fought this pain the worse it would get. This affliction was pure nature, in that it was something all of my people carried with them from birth to the grave, but at the moment it was difficult not to think of it as evil. I allowed the pain to pass through me, and, thankfully, I hadn't been shot in the meantime.

I just had to think this through. I was stronger, faster, and more experienced than Caleb. Caleb had a chain that could burn me to my core, an indifference towards whether or not I lived or died, and guns. So far it felt like a stalemate. There was a solution here, there always was. I needed to consider what else I had. I dug through the pockets of my cloak and retrieved my items. Three potions, marked Steelskin, Boom Boom, and Ox respectively. The two glamours that I'd yet to use, and a fist full of kinetic beads.

I didn't know for sure if Steelskin would be enough to stop bullets, and with the sort of rounds Caleb was firing, I didn't feel up to the task of field-testing Wilma's work. But if I were lucky, I wouldn't need to. I had a plan just recklessly stupid enough that it would have made Elana proud.

Kinetic beads are precisely what their name implies. To

the casual observer, they would appear to be something not unlike a black pearl. Half the size of your eye, if you need to know. But when thrown, they explode with a pure invisible kinetic energy that has been tightly wound into them, barely contained. One bead might hit you with all the impact of an unprotected strike from a heavyweight boxer. But the trick to them isn't as simple as releasing what has been stored within; the amount of kinetic force released is also proportional to the kinetic energy striking them. So if one bead was a heavyweight's punch, two thrown simultaneously would make each of them strike with the impact of a moderate car accident.

I had six beads.

Six beads and there were a lot of shelves and machinery for Caleb to hide behind. Once I had watched three beads strike an ogre in the chest and send it clear across an entire lake. That lake had to be at least half a mile across, and the ogre never touched the water. It very obviously didn't survive. I didn't know what six beads would do, but this was no time for half measures. I made a silent prayer to the creators, and I flung the handful of mass destruction and ducked back behind the machinery half a second before they struck.

I didn't know what to expect, but it wasn't quite what I got. Every window in the building violently exploded as virtually all of the equipment on that side of the blast soared through the air like a house of cards that went up against a leaf blower. A significant portion of the ceiling even collapsed as a support beam was reduced to twisted metal and gravel. The sound of it wasn't what I expected either. It was incredibly brief and was something not unlike vinyl being torn.

Small borderline ghost town or no, that was bound to bring some unwanted attention.

It was nearly unmanageable trying to breathe with the amount of dust that had been kicked up and even more difficult to see. Charging in and pressing the advantage while the enemy was disoriented would have been ideal, but impossible under the circumstances. Thankfully, his end of the room was worse than mine, so assuming that we weren't overrun with townspeople first, I could wait him out.

I pulled an arrow from my quiver and pulled it to a full draw, ready to unleash it at the slightest movement. I held it constant for a full minute. Then two. Then three. There was no movement, not even a cough, and the dust was already beginning to settle. There was a genuine possibility that I might have killed him, and that thought was unnerving. That wasn't my intent, and even with Caleb bent on putting a bullet in my brain, I didn't think he deserved death. All the same, I wasn't about to shed any tears for him if he met his end here today.

The time for waiting was at an end. I wasn't going to learn anything standing here and time was running out besides. I kept the bow drawn as I tried to make my way through the plant, looking for any sign of Caleb. The mess I'd made didn't make my job any easier. And right when I was ready to give up and get out of there, I saw it—an arm lying limply near a shelving unit. I inched closer to the body only to see the still form of Caleb Duquesne pinned from the waist down, his eyes closed, his body still and without breath. I sighed at the discovery, relaxing my draw on the bow.

And that's when I heard the hammer cock on his gun.

22

My grip tightened on instinct, and I pulled the bow-string so tight I thought it might snap in my hands. Caleb opened his eyes and managed a pained grin. "Well now, looks like you can fight dirty after all. Knew you had it in you."

I locked eyes with Caleb, holding his gaze for a moment before answering. I spent every second of this stare down looking for a way out of this stalemate, but I was coming up short. "So what now?" The question came out of me in a snarl.

"What now?" Caleb asked. "Well I shoot you, that arrow releases into my head. You let go of that arrow and it ain't going to take more than a moth's fart for this gun to go off. That about catch you up to speed?"

"So then it comes down to which of us is more willing to die for our goals, is that it?"

"Well now, there ain't a doubt in my mind that the answer to that question is you. You ain't got an ounce of quit in you," Caleb replied. "So I am willing to begrudgingly be the pragma-tist here and call for a truce and make you a deal."

"Go on."

"The way I see it, the easy way out of all this is we could just kill each other and be done with it. But I think a better option here is that I walk away from all of this in exchange for a promise from you of a favor of my choice. Oh, and while I'm at it, that you lift this damn hunk of junk off of me."

I kept staring at him, waiting for this to make sense. Everything I'd heard about Caleb was that he never gave up on a job once he took it on. It was a matter of principle for him. "Why?"

"Because it's goddamn heavy!"

"Not that," I clarified. "Why would you give up when you're this close?"

"Any number of things, take your pick. Maybe having you owe me one seems like the better prize. Maybe that story you told me about your friend reached my heart, and it just don't seem fair. Or maybe, just maybe, I feel like you beat me fair and square."

"Or maybe I just scare the hell out of you," I offered.

Caleb smirked. "Or maybe that."

"Give me your word, and we have a deal," I said, and as a show of good faith Caleb eased the hammer back down and slid the gun out of reach.

"You have it," he said. "But while I have you, did you really just detonate a bomb for little old me? Far be it from me to argue with results, but that seems like a bit much. And when did you find the time to plant it? I thought I had you every step of the way."

"Shut up," I muttered as I replaced the arrow into my quiver and lifted the ruined shelving off of Caleb to fulfill that condition of my bargain. It was then that I could see the real reason Mr. Duquesne wasn't so eager to take the fight to the Battle Born: His left leg had been broken in the blast severely enough that the bone was sticking out. I couldn't win for losing with this man. "Quite the poker face you have. Do you ever tell the truth?"

"On occasion," he remarked. "Now maybe do the kindly thing here and set my leg?"

I could hear the crowd gathering outside now; few as they were, I imagined this to be the most exciting thing that had happened around there in quite some time. "Unless that is the favor you bargained for, I'm afraid not. Not to worry, I'm sure someone less weird than I will be along shortly with just so many questions. All the best."

To his credit, Caleb didn't protest as I turned and walked out of the plant. There were fewer onlookers than I would have guessed, a dozen at most, and I walked past them without being challenged. I didn't have far to walk in any event. There was only one spot the Battle Born would have realistically gone, and it happened to be next door.

Our Lady of Guadalupe Roman Catholic Mission, the local church. And it was far less grandiose than the name implied. A single-story building that could have just as easily been an office building or a propane company as it could have been a church. Regardless of its size or stature, it was still a place of worship and a place for sanctuary.

I made no effort to hide my presence as I walked in the front door. The building, like most in the town, looked as if it hadn't been updated in at least thirty years. The walls were shades of tan and beige; the interior was poorly lit. Rather than pews, the congregation was expected to sit on folding chairs. Only one chair was being used at the moment, and it was by the Battle Born.

Part of me just wanted to shoot her in the back of the head. I considered all of those bodies at the compound, how my friend was dying in a miserable excuse for a motel, and how all of it would just go away once she was dead. I'd never come back to this town again. Ann could be rid of her poison. All it would take would be one arrow.

But she needed to know who was here to stop her. That what she was and what she became was not natural and why she had to be put down. "On your feet!"

My command got her attention. The Battle Born lifted her head. "So I was right about you," she said softly. "You are just a killer."

"Get on your feet so I can put you in the ground." The coldness of my demand didn't represent the anger building in me.

The Battle Born rose to her feet and faced me at last as I drew an arrow aimed between her eyes. "You're all the same; you know that? If you're not trying to use me, you're trying to kill me. And you're never going to stop until I make you stop."

I released the arrow without another word. It traveled the length of the room in a second and was caught in midair before it could strike its target, but the arrow was only a feint. I dropped the bow the instant I had released the arrow's shaft and dashed forward, reaching into my cloak and flinging the 'Boom Boom' potion at her.

She understood just a moment too late. Her arms were up to take the brunt of the blast, but she couldn't dodge entirely. The potion went off against her forearms with the force of a grenade and propelled her back. The blast scorched her arms, but unfortunately, she didn't lose her footing.

That was something I'd anticipated, but this was all still part of the plan and tied into what I'd picked up from Caleb. She was weakened, somehow, and while I might not have known the mechanics of it, I didn't know that I needed to. That she had been growing weaker was enough to give me confidence in fighting her. And the plan was to keep her defensive and to utilize counter attacks.

She was quick enough to catch an arrow in flight. She nearly killed me at the mall. Trying to overpower her would be a losing proposition. But I could make her think that was my plan. While dashing in I made a show of moving in to strike, but I was waiting and watching for her.

A left hook came, which I ducked under and took a jab at her puncture wound. Then she let a right hook follow that up, and I leaned back, allowing it to sail past wildly as I tapped her twice with jabs to the jaw. Each time she took a shot at me, I was there with a counter, and it was working.

It worked a bit too well. She threw a podium at me. I dodged easily enough, but with the scattering of folding chairs around the room, keeping my balance required more of my attention than I would have liked, and that meant I wasn't in time to create space against her follow up. She came at me with a straight punch, but as I ducked underneath to counterattack, she turned the punch into a grab, pulling me by the neck into a knee strike to my jaw. Before her knee even went down, she had already gripped me with both arms and spun me around and through the front doors like a discus hurl.

"You think that's going to be enough to beat me?" she asked walking out into the street after me. "You might be fast, but you simply don't have the strength to match."

That attack hurt tremendously, and I don't think I even caught anything approaching full power. "Let's make one thing bloody clear," I said through clenched teeth, rolling onto my knees. "I'm not here to beat you. I'm here to kill you."

"Then you came here to die," she said. "I can learn your patterns, and it won't take me more than a couple of direct hits to make sure you don't get up. And, idiot that you are, you're making me do this."

I stayed there until she was within range before tossing the handful of sand I'd managed to grip into her eyes, springing to my feet and kicking out her right knee in the process. As she went down, I put my full strength into turning my body into a kick to the base of her skull with my other foot, sending her down face first and creating separation.

"After what you did last night at the compound, someone has to," I growled.

The Battle Born seemed to shrug off the damage done by my kicks and started to stand. "All I did was leave. I know where I'm not wanted."

She was recovering all too well, so I pulled the remaining potions from my cloak. One of them would make me durable, and the other would greatly amplify my strength. Both had their appeal right now but taking both wasn't an option. Potions are dangerous enough on their own, but there's no telling how they might interact with each other.

She tagged me once, and she'd do it again. I could outlast her; I knew I could. I opted for the Steelskin potion and swallowed it in a single gulp.

The effects were immediate. Head-to-toe I felt smooth and sleek as a rippling tingle flowed through me for an instant before vanishing. I tested my mobility, and I was okay. Better than ever in fact. I felt invincible, and as a bonus, I was even a little shiny.

I pressed my advantage now, sprinting at her as she stood and lifting a running knee to her temple. She certainly hadn't been expecting that, and I didn't give her time to adjust as I sidestepped my way past her and delivered a mule kick to her kidneys. In response, she swung a massive backhanded fist where I'd been, but I was already moving to her blindside, delivering hard shots to her extended rib cage.

She grimaced at the blow, and her expression turned angry as she bore down on me, swinging wildly with both fists. I was able to duck and weave past the first few strikes until I saw what I felt was an opening. I went to parry and counterattack, then I saw my error. Each of those strikes was an attempt to get me to parry, and I fell for it. If I was close enough to parry, I was close enough to grab.

Her grip on my wrist was inescapable, and, had it not been for the potion, my bones would have been jelly. She lifted me off my feet and began to strike me in the face. Reflexively, I tried to get my free hand in up a guard, but without my feet, it was a token effort. Two thunderous blows echoed off my face before I dug a thumb into her eye.

The desperation maneuver worked well enough that she loosened her grip enough for me to kick off her chest and escape. I made a run at her again, but this time I flipped over her and unstrapped my cloak, wrapping it around her head as I came down. Relying more on leverage than strength, I used the cloak to bring her down into the dirt skull first.

"Those people might not have been your friends, but not all of them were looking to use you!" I nearly screamed as I hammered fists into her covered head. "Most of them were sick or being used, themselves. They needed help, and they didn't deserve to be slaughtered!"

A hand shot towards my throat as the Battle Born rolled out from under the cloak. "What the hell are you talking about?" she asked suspiciously.

"About how I'm going to make sure you never kill again!" Her hand wasn't quite in position, and I was able to parry it away from my neck relatively easily. Gripping my cloak, I rolled away from her and removed one of the blades I'd stashed from the birdcage. I held it tightly in both hands and brought it down as hard as I could muster into her calf muscle. I struck bone, and with a howl that rivaled that of any beast I'd ever encountered, she turned on me with blinding speed and caught me flush in the chest with the full force of her might. It put me through two walls and sent my body the length of the entire church.

Had it not been for the potion, there wouldn't have been enough of me to go through the first wall. With the potion, I was afraid of a broken sternum and I had trouble breathing. I used the back wall to prop myself up and catch my breath as the Battle Born gingerly walked towards me, absentmindedly stopping to remove the blade from her calf.

"I hate you," she hissed. "With my whole heart, I hate you! People like you do far more damage to people like me than any Abbot or Gardener ever could. They may look at me and see me as something to be used, but you? You had nearly two centuries to learn about what it's like to be used because of what you were born into. And yet, you've come for me at every step. I told you face to face that I didn't want to fight, that I just wanted to be free, and you're still willing to believe the worst of me, pushing me, oblivious to the possibility of another answer. You didn't learn empathy from surviving your master; you learned cruelty by embracing the life he gave you."

The two of us stood there a moment, the air heavy and loud with our labored breaths. Tears lightly fell down her cheeks and for a moment, her voice quivered. "I didn't kill anyone. I didn't even know they were dead. I just snuck away. With the Abbot dead, there was nothing there for me. But maybe I don't have a choice, do I? Because if it's not you, it will be someone else, and it won't end. So maybe I just go back and do it with a smile and learn to love it, because they were right all along. Or maybe we just kill each other right here, do the rest of the world a favor and remove a couple of monsters from it. So come on, what are you waiting for? Let's get this over with."

She wasn't lying. If she didn't kill those people, I had no idea what did, but that was a concern for another time. I had no way to explain what had happened at the compound, but it wasn't her, and these weren't crocodile tears. For the first time, I saw her for what she was: A child. Her appearance aside, she couldn't have been older than Ann. She could hurt me, but she'd already been hurt so badly. She was scary, but mostly she was just scared. There was a lot to consider, but most of what she had to say was true. My actions were my own, and I was ashamed of them.

I stepped away from the wall and spread my hands in surrender. The fight was gone out of me entirely now, replaced by things far heavier than rage. Guilt. Shame. Sadness. Debbie compared me to Abarta a moment ago and, in my heart, I couldn't blame her. "No, I won't do it. I'm not like him. You're not like them. I believe you. And that's not an excuse for what I've done, but I won't continue this path, and I won't push you to be something you don't want to be."

Debbie sniffed at that, unmoving. "So you don't kill me. That doesn't change anything. They're going to keep coming for me, and soon I won't have the strength to fight back. I barely had the strength for you."

"Then you don't run," I offered.

"I can't stop now," she replied. "I go to them, or they come for me."

"Yes, exactly," I said, locking her gaze. "There's a way out of this, I think. Where we can both get what we want, but you'll have to trust me."

Debbie's laugh was mirthless and sour. "Trust you? You stand to gain from my death, and a minute ago we were ready to kill each other. Why would I trust you?"

I shook my head helplessly at that. "I'm not telling you it will be easy or even that I'd do the same if our situations were reversed. But you said it yourself, they're not going to stop, and whatever comes next is going to be worse. I truly believe I'm the best shot you have. Please, end this with me, and you have my word I'll do everything I can to help you start over. I was wrong."

"I don't want to kill you," Debbie said softly, studying me. "Swear it to me. Swear an oath that you mean what you say."

"I swear to it, Debbie," I said to her solemnly. "I swear by my mother and by my lands and by my honor."

Debbie picked up my bow and walked it to me, thrusting it into my hands. "Don't... don't let me down," she said in a hushed tone. "Everyone else has, but I'm trusting you. This is it for me."

I nodded and took the bow, then fished my phone out of a pocket. I selected the preset number and waited for an answer. "Alistair. I have what you want. Where do we meet?"

That asshole had been right on top of me the entire time. When Alistair gave me the address, I nearly spat. I don't know how he got access to a house in Woodland Hills or if he had to hurt someone to get it, but he had been less than half a mile away from day one. It wasn't even necessary for him to do that, this was merely a power play. A way to let me know he'd been in control the whole time.

I collected Ann from the motel and laid her in the backseat. She was still in her induced state of slumber and thankfully still had both remaining petals around her neck. The plan was working as well as I could have hoped. All the same, I rushed back to Alistair, not willing to waste another second in case things took a turn.

Alistair had made a note to come to the backyard when I arrived, and I found him outside under a rather sizable pergola gazebo, relaxing in a hammock. Between the linen clothes, the bar, and lush surroundings, he almost looked like he was on vacation. Oddly conspicuous amidst all of this was a ring of red tape surrounding his outdoor relaxation center.

Alistair lazily got to his feet as he watched my approach. "Ah, Chalsarda! Good of you to make it. You know, if anyone was going to get this job done, I knew it'd be you. Care for a drink?"

"No, I don't want a drink," I monotoned.

"Suit yourself, though I wouldn't cross that tape if I were you, it's there for your benefit," he remarked, moving to pour himself a drink. "And drop the merchandise, yeah? I imagine that's going to get quite heavy."

He was referring to the fact that I'd been carrying the body of Debbie slumped across my shoulders. I did as he asked and made a gesture for him to inspect her. "No, I don't think I'll be coming out there. You got a knife on you, I expect? Right, well just give her a poke then, make sure she doesn't flinch."

"No more demands," I proclaimed. "We had a deal. How do I cure Ann?"

"Take it easy old girl, you'll get what you want," he replied. "First the poking, then the cure. Just want to be sure I'm getting what I paid for."

My temper was flaring, and it showed, but I still did as he asked. I removed a small dagger from my belt and stuck it deep into her leg and removed it. The body of Debbie remained still, and blood only seeped to the surface rather than pumping out. "Are you satisfied?"

Alistair offered a discerning glance in her direction and gave a nod of approval. "Good enough. How'd you do it?"

"No more questions, you promised—!"

"Yeah, I know what I said, but you can't lie, and that's the best way of me knowing this isn't some sort of trick," he interrupted. "Come on, love; this is fair play."

"Fine," I said hotly. "I tracked her to a small town in Arizona. She'd been weakened somehow, and that gave me an advantage in our fight. It was a long and bloody battle, but in the end, I managed to choke the life from her until she died. Even a

Battle Born has to breathe."

"Yeah. Yeah, that tracks. Heard all about the trail of bodies you left. You two look like shit, by the way, but at least you're walking about." Alistair took a sip of his drink with a mock toast in my direction.

"Enough!" I shouted. "I want—"

"Ann's cure, I know, I heard you the first time. Just take the amulet off of her before she runs out of petals, and well, Bob's your uncle."

I was stunned. I must not have heard him correctly. "But the poison..."

"You know, one of my favorite things about you has always been how gullible you are. Fall for anything, you will." Alistair stared at me a moment longer before sighing in frustration. "The poison was in the amulet, you prat! I gave her an itty-bitty curse, mostly some nausea and gas. You're the one who went and poisoned her."

"So you lied to me," I said aloud to myself.

"Obviously. I've made a career out of it; you just make it look easy."

"And Skip knew about this from the start," I said to myself.

"Course he did, where do you think I got the amulet?"

I was livid. A small part of me had been ready to believe that maybe someone over there had been reasonable and perhaps even felt guilty about what that organization was responsible for. But as it turned out, Skip was just as much of a monster as any of them. Skip had made me a slave hunter and tried to make me feel grateful for it in the process, all the while the whole thing was part of the plan.

"I need to see to Ann. She's outside, but we are not done."

"Well you're absolutely spot on there," Alistair agreed. "Do what you must, I need to arrange a pickup for this... thing... before it attracts ants to my lawn."

I looked down at Debbie, then to Alistair, before dashing to the car outside. I threw open the backdoor and ripped off Ann's amulet. She gasped a deep breath in response and color flooded into her cheeks a second before she retched; the putrid black phlegm mixed with bile exited her mouth in a single hurl. She looked healthier immediately, but she remained asleep. I dropped the remainder of the amulet and crushed it under my heel, furious with both myself and Alistair, not sure who to be more upset with at the moment.

With my heart pumping harder than it had in recent memory, I grabbed my bow and arrows and marched into the backyard, nocking an arrow the second Alistair was in sight; I let it fly. It sunk like a stone the second it passed over the tape.

"Welcome back," Alistair said, leaning down to pick up the arrow. He gave it an underhanded toss to my side of the tape, next to Debbie's body. "Is that out of your system, then? If we're going to have that talk, we ought to do it before my company arrives."

I marched up to the edge of the tape, close enough that I could reach out and grab him. "We are done, do you understand me? You were warned what would happen to you if you stayed."

Alistair wagged a finger at me. "Yeah, I thought about that, and I believe that I'm going to call your bluff. Right scary stuff you proposed, real wrath of the gods, but here's the way I see it. By the time any of that hits my doorstep, I could do unspeakable things to any one of your pets. Any time, any place, and there's not a single one of them that's safe from me. And I don't think you're willing to risk that, which means that you and I are going to maintain a nice, healthy working relationship."

"Unless I kill you right here and now."

"Two problems with that, love," he said gesturing to the tape and walking back to the center of the gazebo. "The first of which being that you're not going to take a step past this line, and would you like to know why?"

"Given that you're a wizard I'd assume you warded the area. Likely you've enough magical traps to kill me, and the tape is for show. For control."

"You are so very close, and yet you are so very off on one important point. You see, the traps I have set to go off won't kill you, I've seen to that. But it will undoubtedly incapacitate you. It will hurt worse than anything has ever hurt you in your life."

"No," I fumed. "It won't."

Alistair paused and gave me a grin. "You're still carrying that around with you? Christ alive, move on. Heaven knows I have."

We were on a timer here before Skip and his crew arrived, so for as much as I wanted to yell and curse, I had to compose myself. "And what is the second thing?"

"The second thing is that you already said it yourself. You're not going to put a hand on me. Remember our deal? You agreed, for such time as we are working together, you will bring no harm to me. You Fae love your deals, and you can't lie. Face it, Chalsarda. I have always been smarter than you, I have always had the control and I always will. I defeated you six different ways before you even saw me and I'm ahead of you right now. You have nothing. No moves I haven't seen coming a mile away. You bore me, but a tool doesn't have to be exciting, now, does it?"

I pulled my knife from my belt and took in a breath. "Actually, Alistair, I believe I have not one, but two surprises for you. You see, you claimed you knew about me. That I'd been set free. But words matter, and when I was set free it was from more than Abarta. I don't even think Elana knew what she was doing; she was just trying to do the right thing. So, you see, you're not the only one who can lie."

"Impossible," Alistair said incredulously. "It's against the rules."

As if on cue, Debbie stood up to the amazement of Alistair, who couldn't hide his disbelief. "Since when have you cared about the rules?" I asked, and then, looking at Debbie, I continued, "I said I'd killed her, didn't I?"

"But she was dead!" Alistair argued. "No pulse!"

"Heart's just a muscle," Debbie added. "I have excellent muscle control."

"Fine then. You can lie, somehow. And your new bestie is the Battle Born. Maybe you're the first elf ever to learn that trick, it doesn't make a difference. Everything I said stands. Unless you somehow don't believe me when I tell you that I can destroy everyone you love, you will do as I say!"

"That's just it, Alistair," I breathed, playing with the knife between my fingers. "I do believe you. And I told you I had two surprises for you."

I wasn't eager for this next bit, and not because it was going to hurt like hell. What I was about to do was my birthright and something I'd managed to keep hidden from everyone, and I did that by so rarely calling upon it. The last time I had, it was when Elana lost control and nearly killed me by encasing me in a wall of permafrost. So call upon it or die. And before that, it had been at least thirty years. But desperate times and all that.

If you've met enough elves and of different varieties, you might eventually learn about an inherent ability or two that they're born with. My mother as an example, with her snow-white hair, pupil-less eyes like perfect amethyst, and skin like pale periwinkles would be a dead giveaway for anyone in the know. But inheriting my father's features allowed me to hide my birthright. Over short distances I could move from one location to another, the way a hummingbird appears to hoover in one location and a split second later is hoovering elsewhere. Blink and you miss it. But what I could do had nothing to do with speed, it wasn't even explainable. It just was.

I saw where I wanted to be, and I stepped between the shadows of the tree leaves and the next moment I was standing beside him, my knife in and out of his femoral artery several times in the blink of an eye.

And I paid for it. Dearly.

I was assaulted with electricity and concussive force and mildew and heat and more than I could make myself aware of. I was right. It hurt, but I'd been prepared for worse. The cacophonous chorus of so much magic exploding around us at once drowned out both of our screams, and as quickly as it began, it was over.

Alistair and I lay together on our sides in the gazebo facing each other; his expression was a portrait of agony that mirrored my own. His breaths were labored, his skin pale and clammy. I had to wonder how much of that was from the blood loss and how much of his own magic he took as blowback.

"You...! You're a..."

"Yeah," I agreed weakly. "And you're never going to tell anyone."

Alistair laughed at that. Or he sobbed. It was difficult to tell, but it didn't matter either way. He would never hurt anyone ever again.

Skip and two of his men entered into the backyard with an air of entitlement that suggested they owned the place, one of them carrying two briefcases. When Skip saw me, his eyes widened in surprise ever-so slightly. "You know, not for nothing, but I'm honestly a little surprised to see you as we wrap this up."

"Yeah, sure, this must be a big day for you," I mocked.

"I'm sure you'll tell all your friends later about how you got to meet the one and only Alistair. Would you like an autograph? Make it out to my biggest fan?"

"No need to be a dick about it, I just meant you technically didn't—"

"Right, right, I know what you meant. You want the bloody corpse or don't you?"

Skip stiffened. "Of course. We'll have to examine the body first."

He made a motion, and one of the men moved to the body of Debbie and felt for a pulse.

"I will say though, great work on that amulet, it did the trick all right," I said, calling his attention back to me. "Kept the elf properly motivated, they never saw it coming."

"Well, you were certainly the... firm negotiator," Skip replied. "Though I suppose it is difficult to argue with results. How is Chalsarda, by the way? And Ann Bancroft, if you've heard anything?"

"Your concern is downright touching," I snarled. "What? You got a crush or something? What's it to you?"

"Come on; there's no need to be like this! It's my job to know, quit busting my balls."

"And what'd you expect from me? A freebie?" I asked with a hint of disdain.

"Maybe a little goddamn professional courtesy, all things considered?" Skip shot back.

"Look, mate, a job's a job." I shrugged. "There is a reason I'm not inviting you lot to stay for tea, and there's a reason you wouldn't accept if I did. Liking each other doesn't have to be part of the deal."

"No, no I guess it doesn't," Skip said glumly. He sat quietly in a lawn chair waiting on his man to finish their examination. "You know, attitude aside, you did good work on this."

"Is that right?" I asked.

"Yeah, I'd call this whole thing one colossal mess, but you? You found a way to keep yourself clean. The Abbot betrayed us, the harpy went on a killing spree, and the gunslinger just downright failed to get the job done. Those maniacs caused more of a mess than they were worth, and between you and me, good riddance. But this right here, these are the kind of results I can work with. Even if you are a prick."

The man doing the examination took several pictures with his phone before he gave the all clear, and Skip stood up and adjusted his blazer. "Good. Send the shots in, let management know it's been handled," he remarked to his man before turning back to me. "Well then, I suppose all that's left is to discuss payment. Have you made a decision on whether you'd like the dagger or the cash?"

I gave the three men surrounding me a careful look, taking into account their relative distance from me, and said, "I was actually thinking it should be both. Call it an incentive for all this new work you're promising."

Skip straightened himself up at that. "Wizard or no, you'd do well not to shake us down here. The whole organization knows where we are. Half a mill is not worth making an enemy that size, believe me."

I put both hands up in surrender. "Fair enough, you win. I had to try, right? Well, let's see the dagger then, I can see why that might prove useful."

The man with the briefcases opened one of them up and presented the contents to Skip. He removed an ornate dagger from the case and gave it to me with both hands. I accepted it, and the illusion of Alistair faded away, revealing myself to them for the first time.

I removed the now worthless, tiny glamour scroll I'd been hiding under my tongue. "Surprise."

Skip, to his credit, didn't show the surprise that was just under the surface for him. "Chalsarda. You idiot. God damn it, you think this is funny? That this is going to work out for you in the long run? Where the hell is Alistair?"

I flicked the dagger into the corpse of Debbie, and immediately the illusion of the dead Battle Born gave way to reveal the blood drained dead body of Alistair.

Skip wasn't able to hide his emotions any longer. In fact, now, he looked sick.

An empty mini liquor bottle, covered in masking tape and marked with the word 'Ox,' fell harmlessly from the hanging tree branches overhead. The three men looked at it in wonder for a moment, unsure of what to make of it. Even if they'd known what it was, it was already too late for them.

That potion is designed to amplify your strength and endurance. 'Strong as an ox' as the old saying goes. They're quite popular with the less physically inclined in the supernatural world. Wizards, occultists, researchers; anyone who has trouble doing a pull-up. But the way it works on a more fundamental level, it takes the strength you already possess and increases it exponentially. Even weakened, I don't know that anyone as strong as Debbie had ever drunk one before. The effect could only be described as overkill.

Debbie crashed into the earth, grabbing the medical examiner by the leg and swinging him into the man with the briefcases. What was left of the two of them would be difficult to describe as people.

For my part, I wasn't prepared for a fight. I was barely standing. But Debbie stood tall and strong. Skip looked to be preparing some kind of spell in a panic. He didn't stand a chance.

"Are you sure you don't need me here for this?" I asked Debbie. I certainly didn't want to be, but it felt polite to ask all the same.

"I'm sure. I know what to do. Go," she said flatly, menacing Skip, who had now fallen onto his back in his panic.

I began to stumble my way out of the yard when Debbie called to me. "Hey! Before you go. I need you to know something."

"Yes?"

Debbie put a foot into Skip's chest to keep him from squirming, but the gentle tone of her voice didn't match her demeanor. "You didn't let me down. We were wrong about each other, but I'm glad I trusted you. Thank you."

I gave her a small wave and turned to leave. "Take care of yourself, Debbie. I'll see you soon."

I wasn't lying.

24

Wilma didn't seem to mind me hanging around her shop, The Gem and The Moon. I'd had to check in a few times over the past couple of months without the looming threat of impending death for myself or others, and it had been quite lovely. Who knows, maybe having a real-life elf in the store was good for sales? Perhaps I should have been charging an appearance fee. I mulled the idea over in my mind while Wilma tended to a customer. Maybe she'd even be amused by the idea.

"Have a blessed day, may the goddess favor you," Wilma said cheerily to her customer as they concluded their business. The young woman in thick goth makeup gave me a sideways glance as she collected her bag and left the shop. Wilma turned her attention to me now that the store was empty. "And you my friend, are right on time as usual. How are you?"

"Better every day, thank you," I replied.

"My medicine never fails, just so long as you keep taking it."

Wilma was referring to the barrage of magical effects

Alistair had blasted me with when I crossed over into his warded area. The trap was designed to weaken me to the point of subservience and had I not killed him in the process, it would have worked. The long-term effects had been more debilitating than I could have anticipated, but Wilma nearly had me fully recovered.

"I know better than to deviate from your directions," I remarked.

"Oh, do you?" she asked. "Is that why you fed an entire slumber potion to Ann?"

"You're never going to let me live that down," I said. "It worked, didn't it?"

"It very nearly didn't," she scoffed. "You should have called me at that point; I could have walked you through a process that… you were lucky. Let's leave it at that."

"Speaking of which, how is her apprenticeship going?" I asked.

"Why? You hoping to have her back all to yourself?"

I shrugged. "That would be nice, but it's not why I asked."

Wilma let out a breath in a huff and leaned across the shop's counter. "It's going well. Frighteningly so, in fact. Between you, me, and the essential oils, she'd scare the shit out of me if she'd been gifted with any noticeable amount of magical output. The kid's a savant! She has the potential to be dangerous as all hell, but she's an ounce of power in a five-gallon jug of instinct, if you get my meaning. From strictly a position of strength, she barely registers. Thankfully, at least for the moment, I'd no sooner worry about her than a mother would need to worry about losing a fight to her newborn."

"Why would a mother ever fight a newborn?" I questioned. "That's absurd and profane. Be better at making analogies."

Wilma waved a hand at me dismissively. "You're missing the point. Her lack of raw strength makes her that more impressive. She understands how magic works as if she is looking at it with an extra dimension. Saying that she's a quick study doesn't begin to cover it. It's taken me decades to understand concepts that she just... knows! In another time, without distractions, she could do so much more than I ever could."

"Her distractions are her choice," I remarked, ending that familiar line of thought. "And frankly, I think she's right to have them. Ann lives in a very dangerous time and in a very dangerous place. Knowing how to defend herself is the right choice for her."

"You don't need to know how to draw an arrow or where to stab someone to protect yourself," Wilma said a bit defensively. "I've been alive eighty-three long years, and do you know how many times I've had to fist fight my way out of a problem? Zero. And I deal with a scarier crowd than you do these days, most of the time at least. I use my words, I gather information, and I make the right deals. That sort of cunning will keep you safer than any weapon."

"No, that will keep *you* safer," I corrected her. "Because you've always been content to stay on the sidelines. And I don't say that to offend you, there's nothing wrong with that, but that is not who Ann is deep down. In her heart, Ann is a fighter."

"Well, maybe she shouldn't be. She's not built for it. She gets winded stocking the shelves, how well do you think she'll fare when someone, or god forbid, some *thing* wants her dead?"

I shook my head at the question. "Nevertheless, you would rather see her prepared than not, wouldn't you?"

"You're right," Wilma conceded. "I think the whole thing is stupid, but you're right. I can't lock her up and that sort of trouble always has a way of finding people like Ann. But hey, between the two of us, she's at least getting one hell of an education, isn't she?"

"I can't think of two people I'd rather have training her," I admitted, but even as I said it, I recognized that there was a nugget of truth in what she was saying. Ann fighting monsters meant that one day she may very well have to deal with an Alistair of her own, and no amount of archery or potion crafting would prepare her for that. She still didn't know all the details of that bloody conclusion, and if I could help it, she never would.

The door chimed just then as more customers arrived, two teenagers with more scarves than should be acceptable in a warm climate. One of them was looking for a deck of tarot cards and was very particular about what sort. I offered a small wave to the teenager who wasn't part of the negotiations and received an awkward wave in return as they found somewhere else to stare.

Eventually satisfied and their purchase completed, the two left the store and Wilma sighed audibly in frustration. "Kids care these days about anything beyond aesthetics," Wilma complained.

"Thankfully you don't have a lawn; they might be tempted to play on it," I teased.

"And 'Get off my boardwalk' just doesn't have the same ring to it."

"I suppose not!" I laughed. Wilma enjoyed the chuckle with me, but after a moment her expression turned a bit more serious.

"You're not just here for a chat today," she said. It wasn't a question. She knew what today was.

"Moving day," I answered. "Is Debbie ready?"

Wilma nodded her agreement. "I don't approve of her cake based, but outside of that, I'd say she's as ready as she'll ever be. I managed to stabilize her strength, recovered a fair bit of it as well. Debbie's no longer as strong as a full-fledged Battle Born, but she's close and she won't have to worry about losing her strength again. And with the Abbott down and his cult disbanded, I've been able to keep a sharper eye on the area. As far as I can tell, Debbie's done a decent job of playing dead; no one's looking for her. And she has that reward money to start over. She's fine. She's better than fine. When I first met her, she was just three hundred pounds of doom and gloom. Now that she realizes that she's done fighting for her life, she acts like a kid."

"She is a kid," I reminded her. "She's barely old enough to drink."

"Physically maybe, but she's seen a few things. Who knows? Maybe she can go have a childhood for once."

"And what about you?" I asked. "Are you ready?"

Wilma made an exasperated sound that bordered on cartoonish. "Please! I am beyond ready to have my space back."

"You are a terrible liar, my friend," I smiled at her and put a comforting hand on her shoulder. "And I don't need one of your little charms to know that you're going to miss her."

Wilma grinned uncomfortably at that. "Maybe I will, but I'll also enjoy having my backroom cleared out."

"I'd like to thank you again for hosting her and healing her. I cannot think of too many places this could have been possible."

Wilma tilted her head. "Well, I'd say that dagger you gave me as payment certainly covered expenses."

"Indeed," I agreed. "Is there anything you'd like to say before we leave?"

"No, Debbie and me said our goodbyes before you arrived. I'd just like to get on with the rest of the day like any other."

I gave her one more squeeze on the shoulder and walked towards the back room. "Very well, we'll see ourselves out, in that case. See you around."

The back of the shop looked dramatically different from what it had been months ago. I guess the number of items hadn't changed, but they were far more compact than they had been. What it lost in its showroom quality it gained in college dorm chic, complete with trash everywhere but the trash can. Debbie sat reading a book on her mattress but dropped it with a broad excited grin when I walked in. "Chalsarda! You're here!" she exclaimed, lifting me off the ground in a hug.

I have never quite come to terms with how terrifying Debbie is when she's happy.

"Of course," I said, happy that my feet were once again on the ground. "You didn't think I'd miss this, did you?"

"Never! I'm just happy to see you," she beamed.

"And I am happy to see you as well," I replied. "Even happier to see that you're fully recovered. Especially your temperament."

"I'm out, and very soon I won't ever have to worry about being hunted ever again. I'd say that is more than enough reason to be happy."

"I would agree," I said with a smile, before realizing what was missing from this scene. "Where are your bags? You're not considering staying, are you?"

"No, nothing like that. It's just that when I said I wanted a fresh start, I meant it. Whatever I need, I'll find it when I get there."

I understood the feeling.

"Okay then, with that out of the way, I need to make sure you know what's going to happen next. I know Wilma has gone over this with you, but humor me, okay?"

"It's not a big deal; I'm ready!" Debbie protested.

"Respect your elders," I scolded. The joke was more for my benefit than hers.

"Fine, but it's not going to change anything."

"Do you still have the glamour Wilma made for you?" I asked.

Debbie messily moved various items off her nightstand

and retrieved the tiny scroll. "Right here."

"Good. Now, the way this will work, you will need to hold the image of what you want to look like in your mind as you swallow the scroll. Be very careful not to lose focus, because this change is permanent. Whatever you decide won't be a disguise, it will become what you are. From this day forward, you will age naturally in that body. And don't worry about being too specific, your subconscious will fill in the blanks."

Debbie nodded impatiently. "Okay, I promise I understand, now can I show what I have in mind? I think you'll like it."

I sighed. "Yes, very well, you're obviously excited."

"Okay, wait right here! I have an outfit, and everything planned!" Debbie then went behind a folding screen that she was more than a head taller than and gulped down the scroll with a swig from a water bottle. She immediately vanished from sight. "Okay, I'm almost done!" she said in a voice that had surprisingly not changed very much. It was perhaps an octave higher, but still recognizable as her. Her voice must not have occurred to her.

A minute later and Debbie reemerged from behind the screen. She was about five foot four, appeared to be maybe twenty years old or so, with thick auburn curly hair kept short. Bright blue eyes, rosy cheeks; I could have sworn I'd seen her before. She wore chinos and a white and stone blue plaid button down shirt. "What do you think?"

"Quite adorable, but more important is that you're happy with the change," I added, not able to get the feeling out of my mind that I'd seen this before. "Tell me, what was the inspiration?"

"You don't get it?" she asked, and then her eyes shot open. "Oh right, hold on!"

Debbie ducked behind the folding wall and put on a straw sun hat.

"No, don't tell me, you…" I let the words trail off in disbelief as I picked up an empty box of something called Unicorn Cakes and looked at the mascot in the corner.

"I did!" she exclaimed.

"You became Little Debbie, are you serious?" I asked.

"No, Little Debbie is a child. I'm the adult version of Little Debbie. I'm Adult Debbie!"

I had considered asking why she didn't just get a tattoo later if she liked those little cakes so much, but then I thought of how many kids with Dire Wolf tattoos would become a Dire Wolf if given the opportunity and decided against it. The change was permanent; there was nothing to gain in making her question the decision now.

"I approve, you look lovely," I said with a smile.

"Hey, look, I didn't do this impulsively," Debbie replied, her smile fading a little. "I can tell you're having thoughts about this, but these snacks, garbage or no, hold a special place with me. Eating them was the first time I'd ever felt joy, even for an instant. I could have been anyone, but I want to be able to look at myself in the mirror and remember that feeling for the first time, every time. Does that make sense you?"

My cheeks heated up in embarrassment at those words. "More than you could know. I'm sorry, you're right. This form was an excellent choice. It's a pleasure to meet you, Adult Debbie."

Debbie's smile returned hearing that. "There you go! So, uh, what's next?"

"Next is the sewers," I said. "Then we get you to your new home."

Leaving through the front of the store wasn't an option. We'd been careful enough up until this point, but if anyone was watching the storefront and noticed Debbie leaving but never entering, she might still be followed. Fortunately for us, some years back Venice Beach had renovated their sewer storm drains, and that was the perfect time for Wilma to very illegally create an exit into the sewers. I navigated the two of us a few blocks away and stopped under a utility hole cover.

"This is it," I told her. "Once you get up to the street, you'll be in an alley with a man who will get you safely to where you need to be. Your new home is in Douglas, Wyoming. It's nothing fancy, but it was cheap, paid in full, and you'll have a considerable savings account remaining. And as a bonus, it's just populated enough that you won't attract attention by moving in, but not so dense that anyone would look for you there. Once you're there, you cannot move for at least a year, and you are to make no significant purchases, and you cannot contact myself or Wilma. I will check in with you when it is safe to do so. I need to hear you say that you understand that part of it."

"I understand," she agreed.

"Good. The man above will also provide all of your new documents—identification, birth certificate; all of it. But as far as he knows, you're just another average, ordinary human looking to get away. He's good, so listen to him." I produced a piece of paper from my hip sack. "This will have all your banking information and how to access your funds. The accounts are numbered only, and the contact listed here will help you transition this into a new account. Anything else that I'm missing?"

"No, but you kind of blew through that like you were avoiding something you'd like to say."

I studied her completely unassuming face for a long second. "You're quite observant, aren't you?"

"I've been trained to be. So what is it?"

"It's you that I'm worried about," I began. "You can punch through a tank, and you have six figures in the bank; you have everything you need to start over and take care of yourself, I'm not worried about any of that, it's just that I've been in a similar place to where you are now. One day I was owned, the next I was free. But I was fortunate because I had people who loved me to be there for me the second I needed them. There was a life for me, and my friends were my safety net. You just started to find people who cared, and I know Wilma, Ann, and myself aren't much, but we're a start. I'm just saying, are you sure you want to leave? It will undeniably harder for you here, but if you want, we will find a way to make it work."

Debbie looked to be at peace as she took a moment to find her words. "Chalsarda, I love you. And I love Wilma. And I love Ann. In the past couple of months, you have helped me to understand that the world isn't as small and bleak as I'd always thought. You gave me the hand that no one else was going to, and that is amazing, and I am forever grateful to you for it. But there are also a lot of ugly memories here as well, and I need to get away from them. Just for a while. I might come back, or I might see what else is out there because just think about it: There is so much that I haven't seen, and even a place like Douglas in the middle of Wyoming is a place that I haven't seen. And the more new places I see and the more new memories I make, the less the old memories will haunt me. That's the hope, anyway. And I'm sure I could tell you the same thing, that you don't have to be here, that you can start over, but we both know that you can't. You have what you need here, and I don't. So thank you so, so much, but I have to leave before I can come back."

I understood all too well what she meant. We all deal with our pasts in different ways, and I could be accused of having not dealt with it at all until recently. She was right, I gave her a hand, but it takes more than the hand being offered. You still have to get back on your feet. You can't hold onto it forever. I don't imagine Debbie will be knocked back down anytime soon.

"You're going to be brilliant out there. The best thing to ever happen to Wyoming," I told her warmly.

"And you have a family here to protect, so don't let them down. I'll miss you."

"I'll miss you too, Debbie."

Somehow, short as she was now, Debbie's hug still lifted me off my feet.

Titles within The Black Pages Series

Book One
Empty Threat

Book Two
Warning Call

Book Three
Playing Dead

Book Four
Storm Chaser

Book Five
Last Shot

ABOUT THE AUTHOR

D anny Bell is a *USA Today* best-selling author and he is so, so tired. He is a Los Angeles native and cannot stress enough that he is very tired. He has won awards and has hobbies and understands, at least academically, that he should take this part of the book seriously but also feels it's important to warn everyone that life is very tiring and that you should nap whenever you can. When he's not creating or napping, you can find him listening to the Mountain Goats, playing *Dungeons and Dragons*, and generally trying to make the world a better place, but now that he's done humanizing himself he would like to end by insisting that he's very tired and would like to go now.

https://www.facebook.com/ElanaRuthBlack/